Publication of this work has been made
possible by a grant from Xerox of Canada
Limited.

Canadian Watercolours and Drawings in the Royal Ontario Museum

1

Mary Allodi

The Royal Ontario Museum, Toronto

Canadian Watercolours and Drawings was designed by John Grant of the Royal Ontario Museum's Information Services. The photography was done by the Museum's Photography Department. The typeface of the text is 10 pt. Palatino, the stock is 70 lb. Colophon, and the book was printed and bound in Canada by The Hunter Rose Company.

Foreword

As media for scenic recording and pictorial expression, drawing and watercolour painting were in the 18th and 19th centuries by all odds the most popular and widespread means of picturing places, people, events, and the environment. Drawing and watercolour painting required neither the paraphernalia and static studio situations of oil painting nor the massive apparatus of early photography. To record his impressions, the artist needed nothing more than pad and pencils or a light and compact kit. Thus the sketch-pad and watercolour box became to English and European travellers the equivalent of the 20th century tourist's camera—used largely as an avocation, with varying degrees of training and skill, and with frequency ranging from highly selective to profligate.

Because they were unique works, treasured by both the original artists and their descendants, a high proportion of these early pictures have survived the passing generations in folios or bound sketchbooks. Since they represent, however, the only existing, wholly original and generally accurate renditions of pre-photography life and times, in this century these drawings and watercolours have gained further recognition as important graphic documents, and have gradually become concentrated in public and large private collections.

Dr. Sigmund Samuel of Toronto began collecting Canadian historical pictures before 1910, at a time when such works were neither well known nor appreciated, and were readily available. His tastes encompassed not only watercolours and drawings, but oils, prints, books, and documents as well—anything graphic relating to early Canada.

In 1914 Sigmund Samuel and his family moved to England, which was then a vast storehouse of Canadian-oriented pictorial material. There he continued his acquisitions until his return, with the full collection, to Toronto in 1939. By this time the collection had far outgrown his own home, and in 1940 he added to the Royal Ontario Museum the first Canadiana Gallery, to house the greater part of his collection.

The Samuel Collection was transferred as a gift to the Royal Ontario Museum between 1940 and 1944, though it hardly became static at that point. Dr. Samuel continued acquiring, constantly expanding his collection, and was active in the Museum until his death.

Following an agreement between Dr. Samuel, the University of Toronto, and the Province of Ontario, construction of the main portion of the present Canadiana Building on Queen's Park Crescent was started in 1948 and completed in 1949, to house both the Samuel Collection and the Ontario Archives. At this time the Samuel Collection became a full-fledged department of the Royal Ontario Museum. In 1958 a new wing was added to the building, enlarging available space for both the Canadiana Department and the Archives.

Dr. Samuel died in 1962 at the age of 95, having endowed the Canadiana Department for the perpetuation of collecting. Welcome gifts have been received as well from numerous individual donors over the last decade. In more recent years, the focus and range of the Department has expanded into the building of a fully national collection of decorative arts in all aspects. Yet collecting of paintings, watercolours, drawings, and prints for the Samuel Collection continues to be one of the most important subject areas for new acquisition. Thus the Sigmund Samuel collection is very much an ongoing proposition in all its phases, and this catalogue of the watercolours and drawings includes holdings as of the end of 1972.

In the Samuel Collection, the best and most numerous representation of early watercolours is a body of detailed and excellent paintings by British military officers stationed at various garrisons in Canada. These men were, by and large, trained and skilled watercolourists, the results of instruction in topographical and cartographical recording at the Royal Military Academy, Woolwich. The officer-graduates of teachers such as Paul Sandby and his successors produced thousands of extremely varied watercolour views of Canada between 1758 and about 1860, from city and garrison life to the eastern Arctic.

The English popular watercolour tradition, from the 1780s on, is also reflected in the work of individual traveller-artists, often the wives or daughters of British military men or civil officials, who made numerous sketches and wash drawings of scenes from their travels, more often than not by canoe, and of far-flung and remote stations and outposts.

It is this combination of popular artistic training and fashion which resulted in the great body of views of English colonial Canada. The same was not true, unfortunately, of the earlier French period, in which very little was ever produced in the way of scenic or topographical illustration, and even less survives. To be sure, a great deal of French documentary illustration exists, but in the nature of engineering drawings and draughtsman's plans of fortifications and buildings. The arts of individual illustration, it appears, were not within the realm of French military training or popular fashion.

Unlike engraved, etched, or lithographed prints, which often included considerable engraver's or printer's licence, the early drawings and watercolours are individual and unique views. Most were sketched on the spot and either completed *in situ*, or finished shortly after. Some were later engraved and published, either singly or as series, generally by English commercial print publishers, and sold in quantity or included as book illustrations. The greater number remained in the portfolios or sketchbooks of their artists, to be carried back to England at the end of a journey or a tour of duty. This is why England was such a rich source of early pictures during Sigmund Samuel's earlier collecting days and, to a diminished extent, still is.

Two major groups in the collections of the Museum are not part of the Samuel Collection. The watercolour and pencil sketches by Paul Kane, from his western travels after 1845, are housed in the Ethnology Department, and were given to the Museum in 1932 by

Raymond A. Willis, the great-grandson of Kane's original patron, the Hon. G. W. Allan. The large group of Coleman watercolours, done on field trips in the early 20th century, are by Dr. A. P. Coleman, the first director of the Royal Ontario Museum of Geology. This collection was left to the Museum on Dr. Coleman's death in 1932, and has recently been transferred from the Geology Department to Canadiana.

This catalogue, compiled by Mrs. Allodi over the past several years, is the first full catalogue of ROM collections to be published, and certainly more such catalogues should be arranged and published in the future. In its 2220 entries, the catalogue includes some 1702 pictures in the Samuel Collection, as well as the Paul Kane sketches and the Coleman watercolours.

In addition to the watercolours and drawings, the Samuel Collection in the Canadiana Department of the Museum now also includes more than 2000 prints, some 150 oil paintings, and some 200 early and rare books, which we intend will be the subjects of future catalogues.

Although such a compilation as *Canadian Watercolours and Drawings in the Royal Ontario Museum* can never be totally up to date to the time of publication, we hope that it should stand for some time to come. It is axiomatic that the further the collection grows, the fewer are the pictures yet needed or, particularly, still available, and the slower becomes the pace of acquisition as the collection becomes more mature.

Though a future catalogue volume may ultimately be necessary to cover more recent additions, the Sigmund Samuel collection as it now stands is among the largest and the finest in the country. Specialized museum collections very often originate as, or grow from, private collections. Thanks particularly to the early start, the foresight and instincts, and ultimately the extreme generosity of one of Canada's earliest and most dedicated individual specialist collectors, the Sigmund Samuel collection of the Museum, utilized in exhibitions, publications, and visual media, will be of continual and permanent benefit to the people of Canada.

Donald Blake Webster
Curator, Canadiana

Introduction

The early painters of the Canadian scene generally had two intentions: to describe the physical contours of a new and developing land, and to enjoy the exercise of painting what they saw in translucent washes of colour. We hope that the arrangement of their works, through illustration and text, biography and index, will provide both information and pleasure to those who use this book.

There is a great deal of latitude in the technical quality of these watercolours and drawings, which have been assembled primarily for their importance as historic records. The artists vary from professional painters to unknown amateurs, from precise military draughtsmen to romantic-minded tourists. Many of the views were painted for personal use and were not originally intended for display beyond the family circle. However, other works were exhibited at the academies or were reproduced as prints by the finest technicians in the field. The watercolours and drawings were usually executed on the spot and gain in immediacy what they may lack in polished studio finish. They are frequently overlaid with colour notes and other written comments by the artists who intended to complete them at home. Sketchbooks abound in detail studies, later to be pieced together into panoramic views. As a whole the collection tells the story of explorations and military campaigns, of immigration and settlement, of the shaping of the landscape and the building of cities, of industry and trade and leisure activities. It is a painted history of Canada.

There are 193 identified and about 80 unidentified artists in the collection, giving a generous sampling of the draughtsmen and watercolourists who worked in Canada from about 1757 through the nineteenth century. Eighteenth century views are in the minority and are usually the work of military men or, less often, of professional painters who accompanied scientific exploring expeditions. During the first half of the nineteenth century the soldier artists still dominate the field, but in each decade there is an increasing number of visiting illustrators and of immigrant painters. By 1850 the professional artists are in the majority in the collection, sharing the field with civil engineers, surveyors, journalists and talented amateurs. It is not until this period that works by native-born artists are represented.

The largest groups of views are of the most populated provinces. Quebec leads off with some 700 scenes, of which over half represent Montreal and Quebec city. Ontario is shown in approximately 600 watercolours and drawings, of which over 100 depict Niagara Falls. The Atlantic provinces are illustrated in about 100 sketches, which include some of the earliest paintings in the collection. Although the Western provinces were the latest to be settled, they are shown in 350 works, due to the large holdings of watercolours by Coleman and Kane. The Arctic, which was painted before it was fully mapped, is represented in some 26 sketches. Portraits and named figure studies account for about 100 items and a handful of ship portraits and genre studies round out the portfolio.

Since Canada was only one of a sequence of military postings for the soldier-painters, and because artists and tourists did not restrict their activities to national boundaries, the collection also contains a sprinkling of views of the West Indies and Europe as well as some 380 views taken in the United States. These subjects are usually combined with Canadian scenes in sketchbooks and portfolios and illustrate the changing itineraries and areas of interest within the scope of the traveller from 1750 to 1900.

It is unfortunate that the liveliest aspect of cataloguing, the process of tracking down authorship, date and place for each watercolour and drawing, cannot be incorporated into the final product. When the work began, little was known about these 'Canadian' artists. No other major collection had published an illustrated catalogue raisonné of their work. Moreover, few watercolours in the collection had any provenance, that is history of ownership, beyond the name of the dealer who sold them. To piece together what information was available, we read through Dr. Samuel's correspondence with the collection's first curator, F. St. George Spendlove, and with auction houses and gallery owners. Visits to other collections were invaluable in rounding out an acquaintanceship with the styles and subject-matters, itineraries and associations of the artists. Gradually a picture began to form which, although it has no place in the individual biographies which follow, does come into focus when they are taken as a whole. It appears, quite naturally, that in any one period many of the artists knew each other, often worked together and frequently exchanged sketches. Thus in the late 1830s James Hope-Wallace and Henry William Barnard used to go fishing together on the Jacques Cartier River, bringing their paint boxes along; Mrs Chaplin, the wife of one of their fellow officers (who also painted) copied their views as well as painting her own compositions. The ramifications and extensions of this "1838 Group" could go on and on. At other times clues came from the watercolours themselves. For instance, examination of a watercolour attributed to Thomas Davies, who died in 1812, showed up an 1814 watermark; this eventually lead to its credit to its rightful author, Charles Ramus Forrest, and to its proper date of 1821-23. At other times subject matter told the story by linking a watercolour with a print. When we recognized that a small sketch of Beauharnois was the preliminary sketch for a published lithograph, it became obvious that a whole group of works which had previously been given to Bartlett were actually by Coke Smyth. And knowing this, it became possible to relate the sketches to Smyth's travels with Lord Durham through the Canadas'. Descendants of the artists have often been of the greatest help in tracing genealogies, or in showing us signed works which helped to substantiate unsigned attributions. Contemporary maps, plans, city guides, printed views, and advice from natives of the area in question helped to pin down the location of many an untitled view.

The publishing of a complete catalogue of the ROM's Canadian drawings and watercolours was initiated by the reorganization of the picture storage area and the re-mounting of all the watercolours in acid-free board. Because works on paper are fragile and especially sensitive to the deteriorating effects of light, the watercolours and drawings are exhibited on a rotating schedule and no more than a small portion of the collection is on view at any one time. For this reason we began to think of and plan a catalogue which would make the whole collection more available to the public without adversely affecting the works themselves. Without the help of many people and the financial support of several institutions such a publication would not have been possible.

In 1965 the University of Toronto provided a grant for brief travels to study unpublished Canadian collections which had similar holdings. In both 1965 and 1968 the Canada Council gave grants for research and photography which produced a 1200-entry catalogue with 320 illustrations, in manuscript form. During the next four years interest in Canadiana grew to such an extent that there was little time to continue with the work on a catalogue; and no publication fund was available. Despite this, the book grew to 2200 entries and 430 illustrations. In 1973 a generous grant from Xerox of Canada Limited finally made printing possible.

The support which the Canadiana Department of the Museum has given this project has been unfailing. I would particularly like to thank Donald B. Webster for his wholehearted backing of the undertaking; Helena R. M. Ignatieff who, through her knowledge of the collection from its formative period and for her interest in the project during all its phases, has been a valued advisor; Janet Holmes, Karen Haslan and Nancy Willson for constructing the subject index and proof-reading the entire manuscript. The Photography Department spared no pains in photographing and printing the illustrations and my special thanks go to Leighton Warren, Margaret Cooke and Allan McColl. Alex MacDonald, Olive Koyama and John Grant of the Information Services Department guided the book to publication.

The directors and staff of many institutions have been helpful and generous with their time and material. They include the Baldwin Room, Toronto Public Library; Château de Ramezay Museum, Montreal; Henry Francis Du Pont Winterthur Museum; Legislative Library of Nova Scotia; Morse Collection, Dalhousie University; Manitoba Provincial Archives; Musée de la Province de Québec; McCord Museum; National and Historic Parks Branch, Department of Indian & Northern Affairs, Ottawa; Ontario Archives; The National Gallery of Canada; The Nova Scotia Museum, Historical Branch; New-York Public Library, Print Room; Provincial Archives of British Columbia; Provincial Archives of Quebec; Public Archives of Canada; Public Archives of Nova Scotia; and in England the British Museum, National Portrait Gallery, National Maritime Museum, Victoria & Albert Museum. I also wish to thank John Bland, Edgar Andrew Collard, J. Russell Harper, Donald C. MacKay, Kenneth R. Macpherson, Charles P. De Volpi, and Peter Winkworth for sharing their knowledge on many occasions. In addition I wish to acknowledge the help of individuals and institutions too numerous to list for their generous cooperation in answering my enquiries over the years.

Mary Allodi
Toronto   June 1974

Notes on Procedure

The main body of the catalogue is arranged by artist in alphabetic order, with biography and works following as sub-headings. Within each artist's works, the views are listed in geographic sequence from east to west, with non-geographic subjects at the end of the group. Exceptions to the east-west arrangement are bound sketchbooks which maintain their original page order, and groups of views from albums or unbound sketchbooks which are kept together as units. Paintings by unidentified artists are listed under geographic and subject headings at the end of the main catalogue.

Each catalogue entry is a brief description of the physical object under *title*; *medium*, such as watercolour (unless otherwise noted all watercolours and drawings are on white paper); *measurement* in inches and (in parentheses) millimetres, with height preceding width; *inscriptions* on the works, printed in italics and maintaining the spelling as found; occasional *explanatory notes* about the subject; and the *accession number*, an inventory number referring to the museum's records on the object.

The index refers to entry numbers and is intended as a finding aid to subjects and locations. The *Geographic Index* is divided by country represented. Within the Canadian section, large groups of views of major cities have been further sub-divided to give an idea of area depicted within the city. Street names indexed are usually those found on city plans contemporary with the date of the view. These sub-headings are not exhaustive because it would not be feasible to list every building in a general view. The *Subject Index* selects topics which, although they may play a minor pictorial role in many of the landscapes, are important as documents of social history. Unless otherwise noted, the subjects listed refer to Canadian views.

ABBREVIATIONS

AAM	Art Association of Montreal
ARCA	Associate, Royal Canadian Academy
ARA	Associate, Royal Academy, London, England
c., ca.	*circa*, about
CdeR	Château de Ramezay, Montreal
CE	Canada East
CESJ	Centennial Exposition, Saint John, N.B., 1883
CW	Canada West
DTS	Dominion Topographical Surveyor
HMS	His Majesty's Ship
IODE	Imperial Order of the Daughters of the Empire
JRR,(C)	John Ross Robertson Collection, Toronto Public Library
KLL	Paul Kane's Landscape Log
KPL	Paul Kane's Portrait Log
LC	Lower Canada
l.c.	lower centre
l.l.	lower left
l.m.	lower margin
l.r.	lower right
MFA	Museum of Fine Arts, Boston
MSA	Montreal Society of Arts
NA	National Academy
NAD	National Academy of Design
NGC	National Gallery of Canada
OA	Ontario Archives, Toronto
OPE	Ontario Provincial Exhibition (1868 Hamilton; 1882 Kingston)
OSA	Ontario Society of Artists
OWCS	Old Water Colour Society, London, England
PAC	Public Archives of Canada, Ottawa
PANS	Public Archives of Nova Scotia
QPEM	Quebec Provincial Exhibition, Montreal
QPEQ	Quebec Provincial Exhibition, Quebec
q.v.	*quod vide*, which see
RA	Royal Academy, London, England
R.A.	Royal Artillery
RCA	Royal Canadian Academy
R.E.	Royal Engineers
recto	right or obverse side of sheet of paper
R.N.	Royal Navy
ROM	Royal Ontario Museum, Toronto
SAAT	Society of Artists and Amateurs of Toronto, 1834
SCA	Society of Canadian Artists, Montreal
(sight)	word affixed to measurement to indicate approximate size only
Stark	Nelda C. and H.J. Lutcher Stark Foundation, Orange, Texas
TCH	Toronto City Hall 1848 Exhibition Catalogue
TIE	Toronto Industrial Exhibition, now Canadian National Exhibition
TPL	Toronto Public Library
UCPE	Upper Canada Provincial Exhibition (1848-67)
UC	Upper Canada
u.c.	upper centre
u.l.	upper left
u.r.	upper right
V & A	Victoria & Albert Museum, London, England
verso	reverse side of sheet of paper
WAA	Washington Art Association
w.c.	water colour
Webster	John Clarence Webster Canadiana Collections, New Brunswick Museum, Saint John, N.B.
/	oblique stroke in quotations to indicate change of line

A M.E.

A.,(active 1814)

Winter Scene with Shepherds *(recto);*
Landscape with an Out-building *(verso)*
w.c. over pencil (recto); pen and ink over
pencil (verso) 11 11/16 x 18 1/2 (294 x 470)
Inscribed: l.r. *M.E.A. 1814*; recto of original
backing *View from Nort as it appeared on the
6th of January 1814*
The word *Nort* has been variously
interpreted as either *York* or *North*; the site
is unidentified. 960.176.6

Ackermann, George

A.(active 1866-76)

Taught drawing at Ontario Institution for
the Deaf and Dumb, Belleville, Ontario,
1871-76. Known for watercolour views of
rural Ontario.

2 View of Tweed, Ontario
w.c., touches of gouache, over pencil.
10 1/8 x 14 9/16 (257 x 370)
Inscribed l.r. *G. Ackermann delt. 1866*
Among the buildings shown is the
Anglican church built between 1860-64.
962.172

2

Ahrens, Carl Henry von
(1863-1936)

Landscape painter. Born Winfield, Ontario. Pupil of G.A. Reid and J.W.L. Forster, Toronto, and William Chase, New York. Associated with Elbert Hubbard crafts movement, East Aurora, N.Y., 1900-c.1906; visited California c. 1907; settled in Toronto c. 1908; painting in United States c. 1919-21; lived near Galt, Ontario after 1921. ARCA 1891. Died in Toronto.

3 Indian and Wigwam
w.c. and gouache over charcoal. 7 x 5 1/4 (178 x 134) (sight)
Inscribed l.l. *Carl Ahrens*
Gift of Sylvia Hahn.   955.11.1

3

Ahrens

Alexander, Sir James Edward
(1803-1885)

Soldier, artist and author. Entered British army 1820; served in Canada 1841-55, first with 14th Regiment of Foot, later as Aide-de-camp to Sir Benjamin D'Urban and Sir William Rowan. Designed monument to General James Wolfe, Plains of Abraham, Quebec. Published several books, including *Transatlantic Sketches* (London 1833), illustrated by his sketches and those of his wife, Lady Eveline Marie Alexander; *L'Acadie* (London 1849); and *Salmon-fishing in Canada* (London 1860).

4 Horseshoe Falls, Niagara
w.c. 11 3/8 x 14 9/16 (289 x 367)
Inscribed l.l. recto of mount *Horse shoe fall–Niagara 1831–J.E.A.*
The figure of Francis Abbott, the 'Hermit of Niagara' is shown hanging in a customary pose from a beam of timber projecting over falls from Terrapin Bridge. Abbott took up residence on Goat Island from June 1829 until his death by drowning on June 10, 1831.   965.125

4

Andrews, George Henry
(1816-1898)

Born at Lambeth, London. Marine
painter, watercolourist and illustrator for
Illustrated London News and *Graphic*.
Accompanied Prince of Wales to Canada
1860. Member OWCS 1840-50; Exhibited
AAM 1868; RA 1850-93; RCA 1880.
Died at Hammersmith, London.

5 Niagara Falls with Terrapin Tower
w.c. over pencil. 15 1/8 x 26 1/16 (384 x
662)
Inscribed l.r. *G.H.A. Niagara, May 1860*
962.111.3

5

Armstrong, William
(1822-1914)

Civil engineer, draughtsman, artist and photographer. Born Dublin, Ireland, son of General Alexander Armstrong. Studied art in Dublin and won prize for architectural drawing. Apprenticed as engineer on English and Irish railways. Emigrated to Toronto 1851. Worked for Canadian railway companies as they expanded to north and west. Partner in firm of Armstrong, Beere & Hime, Photographers & Engineers, *c.* 1858-62. Appointed chief engineer to Wolseley military expedition of 1870-1, sent to subdue North West rebellion. Turned to full time painting in 1880s. Known for watercolour paintings of Canadian landscapes, marines, Indian genre, current events and engineering structures. Taught drawing in Toronto schools; many of his views reproduced in illustrated newspapers. ARCA *c.* 1880. Exhibited AAM 1865; Dublin 1865; OSA 1881-5; Paris 1855; RCA 1880-5; UCPE 1852-62. Died in Toronto.

6 Welcome to Uxbridge

w.c., touches of gouache, pen and ink.
24 1/4 x 28 1/4 (613 x 717) (sight)
Inscribed l.l. *Armstrong 71*; c. on archway, *Welcome to Uxbridge, TN, Success to Narrow Gauge.*
Records celebration, 14 Sept. 1871, of completion of Toronto-Nipissing Railway to Uxbridge. Reproduced in *Canadian Illustrated News*, 7 Oct. 1871, which states that the original picture was painted by Armstrong for John Shedden, president of the railway.   951.117.3

6

**7 Steamer "Chief Justice Robinson"
Landing Passengers on the Ice in
Toronto Bay**
w.c., touches of gouache. 12 1/4 x 16 3/8
(311 x 416)
Inscribed l.l. *Wm Armstrong*; l.r. *Toronto Bay
1852*; verso of mount *Steamer "Chief Justice
Robinson" landing passengers on the ice.*
952.169.6

7

Armstrong

8 Grand Trunk Railway Station, Toronto

w.c. over pencil on sized Whatman board.
10 x 13 (254 x 330) (picture area)
Inscribed incorrectly on old mount *The Don Station of the Grand Trunk Railway, Ontario, 1860.*
The signpost lettered *GRAND TRUNK RAILWAY TRAINS GOING WEST* suggests the station which stood at the foot of Bathurst Street; it opened officially on 14 June 1856. An old photograph shows a version of this painting dated 1857; another version is in the JRR collection, TPL.
960x51

8

Armstrong

9 Skating and Ice-Boating on Toronto Bay
w.c., pastel, touches of gouache, pen and
ink over pencil. 18 1/8 x 18 7/8 (333 x 479)
Inscribed l.l. *Armstrong '88*   952.169.5

10 Toronto Shoreline Pile Drivers
w.c., touches of gouache. 8 15/16 x 12 1/16
(227 x 306)
Inscribed l.l. *Armstrong /83*; lower recto of
mount *After this piling was done a sub-structure
of small pine trees was put under the stonework.
The Trees were brought in scow-loads from the
Humber.*
In November 1882 the government gave a
contract to Messrs Cooke, Jones and Innes
for the construction of harbour
improvements. The work carried out
consisted of a dike separating the harbour
from Ashbridge's Bay, leaving an opening
for the Don River; a deep, navigable
Eastern Channel; improvement of the
Western Channel.   969.272

11 Georgetown Bridge
w.c., pencil and gouache. 16 3/4 x 20 3/4
(425 x 527) oval (sight)
Inscribed l.r. *WA 55* [initials in
monogram]
Watermark: *J. Whatman, Turkey Mill, 185-*
View of the Grand Trunk Railway bridge
over the Credit River at Georgetown,
Ontario.   960.220

Armstrong

12 Niagara Gorge

w.c., touches of gouache, over pencil. 9 3/4
x 13 (248 x 330)
Inscribed l.r. *Armstrong 65*
Shows figures of artist sketching, lady
shading him with umbrella.
Bequest of Miss Edith Mary Maitland
Monro, Toronto.   971.32.1

**13 Tightrope Walker Crossing Niagara
Gorge**

w.c., pencil on prepared ground. 7 5/8 x
11 1/8 (194 x 283)
Inscribed l.l. *Armstrong;* l.r. *Decr. 8/56 [or
59] Send this to Editor of I.L. News.*
Blind-stamp of *Armstrong, Beere & Hime,
Photographers & Engineers, Toronto C. W.* on
lower left.
Farini crossed the gorge at the site
illustrated on 5 Sept. 1860 and 8 Aug. 1864.
Blondin's crossings took place further
downstream on 30 June 1859 and 8 Sept.
1860.   950.61.21.

13

Armstrong

14 View of River from a High Bank
w.c., pen and ink over pencil. 8 7/8 x
12 3/4 (225 x 323)
Inscribed l.r. *Wm Armstrong 98*
Site tentatively identified as Niagara River.
957.254.2

15 First Home in Canada, from Nature, in Palmerston
w.c., touches of gouache, pen and ink.
9 11/16 x 14 3/4 (246 x 374)
Inscribed l.l. *Armstrong*; l.r. *WA* in
monogram; on old label, verso of mount,
title and *No. 16/$15*   955.102.1

15

Armstrong

16 Indian Camp, Owen Sound, Georgian Bay
w.c., touches of gouache, pen and ink on prepared ground. 8 x 11 1/4 (203 x 286) oval   950.224.29

17 Mr and Mrs St. John Running the Rapids, Sturgeon River
w.c., touches of gouache. 21 1/8 x 29 7/8 (536 x 759)
Inscribed l.r. *Armstrong 71*
Reproduced as wood engraving in *Canadian Illustrated News*, 18 Nov. 1871, which describes the scene as—
" . . . a daring adventure on the part of a lady who pluckily accompanied her husband throughout the [Wolseley Red River] expedition, and since her return to Ontario has delivered some interesting discourses on the country, the people, and the scenes which came under her observation during that memorable trip. The lady and gentleman who ran the Island Rapids, on Sturgeon River, are Mr. and Mrs. St. John, the latter being very favourably known in this city as lessee of the Theatre Royal under the maiden name of Kate Ranoe. Mr. St. John, who was formerly an officer in Her Majesty's service, joined the expedition as special correspondent of the Toronto Globe . . ."
957.17.4

17

18 Amethyst Fall, Mackenzie River

w.c., touches of gouache. 11 1/2 x 9 1/4
(295 x 235)
Inscribed l.l. *Armstrong*; l.c. *Mackenzie*
[incomplete]; l.r. of mount *Armstrong* and
title.   957.18.1

**19 Fishing at the Peckaunigum Rapids,
Lake Nipigon**

w.c., pen and ink. 10 x 14 3/8 (254 x 365)
Inscribed l.r. *Armstrong. 73.*; label on old
mount *Nipigon, S. end of Peckaunigum Rapids
/No.13 / $15*   957.18.7

**20 Resting Camp on Lake Superior of Lord
Garnet Wolseley en route to the Riel
Rebellion**

w.c., touches of gouache over pencil. 9 1/4
x 14 1/8 (235 x 358)
Inscribed l.l. *W. Armstrong 04*
Armstrong often repeated his earlier
compositions; this 1904 watercolour
presumably derives from an 1870-71 spot
sketch.   952.169.3

20

21 Indian Camp near Kerrick's Location, Black Bay, Canada
w.c., touches of gouache over pencil.
9 13/16 x 14 9/16 (249 x 370)
Inscribed l.l. *Armstrong 73*; old mount, title.
960x110.10

22 High Island, Thunder Bay
w.c., touches of gouache, on prepared ground. 7 3/8 x 5 5/16 (187 x 135) oval
Inscribed on mount, title.
Traditionally said completed in 1868, although use of prepared ground corresponds to artist's style of 1855-60.
Site either Pie Island or Thunder Cape.
960.176.2

23 High Island, Thunder Bay
w.c. 14 1/4 x 9 (362 x 229)
Inscribed l.l. *Armstrong 75*
A second version of cat. no. 22.
Site either Pie Island or Thunder Cape.
960.176.3

23

Armstrong

24 Near Thunder Cape, Lake Superior

w.c., touches of gouache. 4 3/16 x 8 3/8
(106 x 213)
Inscribed l.r. *Armstrong 81*; title on recto of
mount.   957.18.5

**25 Thunder Cape and Pie Island Looking
West**

w.c. 6 7/16 x 13 1/16 (163 x 331)
Inscribed l.l. *Armstrong 1870*; printed label
on original mount *North Western Silver
Mining Company, Thunder Bay, Canada/for
the Company by Wm. Armstrong, C.I., Toronto*;
title in ink on mount.   960.176.1

26 Thunder Cape, Lake Superior

w.c., gouache. 7 3/4 x 12 1/2 (197 x 317)
(sight)
Inscribed l.r. *W. Armstrong 01*; on mount in
pencil *Finding of Mr. Perry's remains. Mr.
Perry missed the last steamer of the season at St.
Ignace, L. S[uperior] to Thunder Cape . . .*
952.169.2

**27 Surprise Lake, Thunder Bay, Lake
Superior**

w.c., touches of gouache. 8 x 14 1/8 (203 x
359)
Inscribed l.l. *W. Armstrong 09*; verso *Surprise
Lake, Thunder Bay, Lake Superior, McKay's
Mountains, July 22*   957.254.1

**28 Above the Catholic Mission,
Kamanistiquia River**

w.c., touches of gouache, pen and ink.
9 x 14 (228 x 355)
Inscribed l.l. *Armstrong 73*; label on old
mount *No. 38 Above Catholic Mission,
Kamanistiquaa R. near Fort William,
L. Superior. $10*   957.18.4

29 On Kaministiquia River

w.c. 4 1/4 x 8 3/8 (108 x 212)
Inscribed l.l. *Armstrong 81*; on mount *On
Kaministiquia R. McKay's Mountain*
957.18.6

30 Indians and Beached Canoe

w.c., gouache. 16 3/4 x 12 1/8 (425 x 308)
Inscribed l.l. *Armstrong 72*; verso of mount
Rough Original, No. 45, $10 in ink on old
label.   957.18.8

**31 Northern Ontario Landscape with
River and Woods**

w.c., touches of gouache. 9 3/4 x 12 7/8
(248 x 327)
Inscribed l.r. *Armstrong*
Bequest of Miss Edith Mary Maitland
Monro, Toronto.   971.32.2

32 Indian Camp, Great Lakes

w.c., touches of gouache, over pencil.
10 9/16 x 16 11/16 (268 x 429)
Inscribed incorrectly on verso *Great Slave
Lake, Canada*   950.224.24

**33 Buffalo Hunters Camp, White Horse
Plains, Manitoba**

w.c., pen and ink, touches of gouache on
toned ground. 5 3/8 x 7 3/8 (137 x 187)
Inscribed on mount, l.r. *Armstrong*; l.l.
*Buffalo Hunters Camp. White Horse Plains/
no.13*; verso *Buffalo skin wigwams
White Horse Plains House was the
Hudson's Bay Company post near
Headingly, Manitoba.*   950.61.1

34 Fort Macleod, Alberta

w.c., pen and ink. 8 1/8 x 10 7/8 (206 x
276)
Inscribed l.r. *W. Armstrong 1902*; verso of
old mount *Macleod, N.W.*
A similar view is in the JRRC, TPL.
961x110.6

**35 Blackfoot Indian Encampment,
Foothills of the Rocky Mountains**

w.c., touches of gouache. 24 x 30 (609 x
762)
Inscribed l.r. *W. Armstrong*   952.169.1

Armstrong

36 Rocky Mountain Gorge

w.c., touches of gouache. 28 1/2 x 23 (724 x 584) (sight)

Inscribed l.r. *W. Armstrong 1852*; verso *Hind of the Myatt Valley, Rocky Mtns., from sketch by Captn. Palliser.*

John Palliser (1817-87) hunted on the American prairies 1847-8 and surveyed the Canadian west for the British government 1857-61.   961x110.2

37 Yosemite Valley from Mariposa Trail

w.c., pen and ink, touches of gouache. 19 1/2 x 28 (495 x 711)

Inscribed l.r. *Armstrong*; l.l. title.   962.170

The Armstrong-Rowan Portfolio

The following 14 watercolours and 4 views by Frederick J. Rowan (q.v.) were painted about 1855 and remained together in the collection of the Rowan family. They are the gift of the C.W. Jefferys Chapter of the Imperial Order of the Daughters of the Empire, Toronto.

38 Toronto Ice Boat

w.c., touches of gouache and pencil, on prepared ground. 5 1/8 x 8 1/16 (131 x 207) oval

Recto of mount: l.l. *Toronto*; l.c. *Ice Boat*; l.r. *WA*   965.138.14

39 Niagara Falls by Moonlight

w.c., touches of gouache, scraping, on prepared ground. 6 3/4 x 8 7/8 (172 x 226) oval

Recto of mount: l.l. *Niagara*; l.r. *Armstrong* 965.138.1

40 Frozen Railway Water Tank at Niagara

w.c. over pencil, scraping, on prepared ground. 7 3/4 x 11 (197 x 208) oval

Recto of mount: l.l. *Niagara*; l.c. *Frozen Tank*; l.r. *1855*   965.138.2

40

Armstrong

41 Niagara from the American Side

w.c., touches of gouache, over pencil on prepared ground. 5 1/8 x 8 1/16 (131 x 207) oval

Recto of mount: l.l. *From S. side of American Falls*; l.c. *Niagara*; l.l. *Armstrong*   965.138.5

42 Icicle at Niagara

w.c., touches of gouache over pencil on prepared ground. 8 1/16 x 5 1/8 (207 x 131) oval.

Recto of mount: l.l. *Icicle. Niagara.*; l.c. *Winter of 55-56*; l.r. *Armstrong*   965.138.8

43 St. Joseph Island, Lake Huron

w.c., touches of gouache over pencil, scraping, on prepared ground. 5 3/16 x 8 1/16 (132 x 207) oval

Recto of mount: l.l. *St. Josephs Id*; l.r. *Armstrong*   965.138.6

44 Manitowaning Bay, Lake Huron

w.c., touches of gouache, scraping, on prepared ground. 5 1/8 x 8 (131 x 203) oval

Recto of mount: l.c. *Manatawawning Bay*; l.r. *Armstrong*   965.138.7

45 Entrance to Manitowaning Bay

w.c., touches of gouache over pencil, scraping, on prepared ground. 5 1/8 x 8 1/16 (131 x 207) oval

Recto of mount: l.l. *Entrance to Manatawawning Bay*; l.r. *Armstrong*   965.138.9

46 Sault Ste Marie

w.c., touches of gouache over pencil, scraping, on prepared ground. 5 1/8 x 8 (131 x 203) oval

Recto of mount: l.c. *Sault St Marie*; l.r. *Armstrong*   965.138.4

47 Sault Ste Marie

w.c., touches of gouache, scraping on prepared ground. 5 1/8 x 8 (131 x 203) oval

Recto of mount: l.c. *Sault St Marie*; l.l. *Armstrong*   965.138.10

48 Sault Ste Marie Lugger

w.c., touches of gouache over pencil, scraping, on prepared ground. 5 1/8 x 8 1/16 (131 x 207) oval

Recto of mount: l.l. *Sault St Marie Lugger*; l.r. *Armstrong*   965.138.11

49 Lakeshore Encampment, Ontario

w.c., touches of gouache and pencil, on prepared ground. 5 1/8 x 8 (131 x 203) oval   965.138.13

50 Upper Fort Garry, Winnipeg

w.c. over pencil on prepared ground. 5 1/8 x 8 1/16 (131 x 207) oval

Recto of mount: l.l. *Stone Fort*; l.c. *Red River*; l.r. *Armstrong*   965.138.3

51 Indian Settlement on a Plain

w.c. over pencil on prepared ground. 6 3/4 x 8 13/16 (173 x 224) oval   965.138.12

50

B B.T.
..,(active 1857)

Middle initial could also be read as *J.* or *I.*

52 Quebec from the St. Lawrence in Winter
w.c. 6 1/2 x 10 1/16 (165 x 255)
Inscribed recto of mount, l.r. *Quebec/57, B.T.B.*; verso *From Crowes Wrexham, August 1926 R.L.H.*; mount *From the Harmsworth Collection*   953.163.5

53 Quebec from the St. Lawrence in Winter
w.c., touches of gouache, over pencil.
6 5/16 x 9 1/2 (106 x 241)   960x276.116

B M.L.
..,(active 1866)

Middle initial could also be read as *F.* or *S.*

54 Lake St. Charles Near Quebec, C.E.
w.c., over pencil. 6 9/16 x 10 1/8 (154 x 257)
Inscribed l.r. *M.L.B., Jany. 13th 1866*; verso of mount *Lake St. Charles near Quebec, C.E., Auntie Fan from Maggie. January 1866*
955.190.9

B ack, Admiral Sir George
(1796-1878)

Naval officer, artist and author. Entered Royal Navy as midshipman 1808; rose to full admiral 1867. Accompanied Sir John Franklin on arctic expeditions of 1817, 1819-22, 1824-27. Led overland expedition in search of Sir John Ross 1833-35; explored Great Fish River, renamed Back River. Explored arctic coast in 1836. Knighted 1839. Recorded his journeys in pencil and watercolour; wrote two books about his arctic explorations, illustrated with engravings after his watercolour views. Died in London.

55 Mountain Fall, Coppermine River and Canoes of the Franklin Overland Expedition
w.c. over pencil. 8 1/4 x 12 (210 x 305)
Inscribed verso in ink *A View of Part of the Mountain Fall, Slave River, and the Canoes of the Expedition in the distance, July 1820. Geo. Back. For W.E. Cook Esquire* [the Coppermine River flows from Great Slave Lake]; verso of mount *Presented to Miss Adelaide E.C. Moon by her Aunt, Mrs. R. Candle nee Cook, who was first cousin to Sir George Back the painter of this picture. The Expedition was that carried out by Sir John Franklin in 1820. 1891*   969.145

Back

Baigent, Richard
(active 1860-1890)

Painter. Drawing master, Upper Canada College, Toronto, c. 1869-89. Known for watercolours and drawings of still life and historical or genre subjects; a few early oil paintings. ARCA 1880; OSA 1872. Exhibited UCPE 1864-6 (prize 1866).

56 The Block House and Bloor's Brewery, Toronto
w.c., pen and ink. 10 1/2 x 14 3/8 (267 x 365)
Inscribed verso of mount *Bloor's Brewery from a sketch in 1865*
Watermark: *J. Whatman*
Bloor's Brewery was established in Rosedale Ravine in 1830, operated until 1864, and the building torn down in 1875. A Baigent w.c. of the same subject is in the JRR coll., TPL. For Paul Kane's similar rendering of the subject, see cat. no. 1110.
968x341.15

Bainbrigge, Philip James
(1817-1881)

Educated at Royal Military Academy, Woolwich. Commissioned as 2nd Lieutenant, Royal Engineers, 1833. Posted to Canada 1836-42. Completed numerous watercolour views of the Maritimes, Quebec and Ontario. Promoted to Major-General and retired in 1863.

57 Expedition on the St. Lawrence River in Winter
w.c., touches of gouache, over pencil. 8 1/8 x 13 3/4 (206 x 354)
Inscribed verso *Expedition on the St. Lawrence River, Quebec. P. Bainbrigge*   960x276.10

57

58 Quebec from the Citadel
w.c., over pencil. 10 7/8 x 30 1/4 (276 x
768) (on 2 sheets joined)
Inscribed l.r. *P.J. Bainbrigge 1836*; verso
*Quebec from the Citadel, P.J. Bainbrigge, Royal
Engineers, 1836* 960x276.12

copies after Bainbrigge

59 Chatham Barracks
w.c. over pencil. 6 1/8 x 8 3/4 (156 x 223)
Inscribed l.r. *H.M.* [faint pencil]; verso
*Chatham Barracks, U.C., from a sketch by
Bainbrigge, R.E. Jan. 1841*
An original Bainbrigge w.c., identical
excepting one figure, is in coll. PAC. This
copy is most probably by Hampden
Moody (q.v.). 955.145.3

58

Baines, Henry Egerton
(1840-1866)

Born in Shrewsbury, England, son of Dr. Egerton Baines and Mary Rice. Lieutenant in Royal Artillery; served in Canada from *c.* 1863. Published account of 1863 yachting holiday on Lake Ontario with fellow officers stationed at Cobourg titled *Cruise of the Breeze* (n.d., n.p.). Died at Quebec from injuries received fighting fire of 14 October 1866.

60 Island of Orleans by Moonlight

w.c., touches of gouache. 7 x 10 5/8 (178 x 270)

Inscribed l.l., *I. of ORLEANS, C.E./H.E.B./23.8.66*   964.196.1

61 Quebec from Orleans, with Bathers

w.c., touches of gouache, over pencil. 6 3/4 x 9 3/4 (172 x 248)

Inscribed l.l. *H.E.B.*; old label *View of Quebec and the basin from the Island of Orleans* 964.196.2

61

Baines

Balfour, H.L.
(active 1852)
Topographical artist; probably Henry
Lowther Balfour, lieutenant, Royal
Artillery, 1849-52.

62 Halifax, Nova Scotia
w.c., touches of gouache, over pencil. 7 1/2
x 10 5/8 (191 x 270)
Inscribed l.r. *HLB/Oct./52*; u.l. *Halifax
NS/24th Octr 1852*; recto of mount, l.l. *H.L.
Balfour delt.*   955.102.5

62

Barnard, Lieutenant General
B Sir Henry William (1799-1857)
Born at Wedbury, England, son of
Reverend William Henry Barnard, also a
topographical artist. Educated at
Westminster School and Sandhurst.
Commissioned in Grenadier Guards 1814.
Posted to Canada 1838-42. Died while
serving in Bengal, India. For his portrait,
see cat. no. 1431.

63 Bridge at Ste Anne de Beaupré
w.c., touches of gouache on grey paper.
14 1/4 x 21 1/8 (362 x 536)
Faint pencil sketch of figures and working
drawing for St. Anne's bridge on verso.
963.39.4

64 Quebec from Ste Anne's Road
w.c. and soft pencil. 8 3/8 x 14 1/4 (213 x
362)
Inscribed recto of mount: *Distant view of
Quebec from St. Anne's Road–& Isle of
Orleans.*
Faint pencil sketches and same title on
verso.   949.41.39

**65 Hills of Ste Anne's and Isle of Orleans
from Quebec**
w.c. over pencil. 6 5/8 x 9 3/4 (168 x 247)
Inscribed verso *Hills of St. Anne's and Isle of
Orleans from Quebec, Aug. 1838*
Two small pencil sketches of house and
trees, and an account of expenses for
lodging, tailor, etc., on verso.   949.41.2

66 Waterfall in the Woods of Ste Anne's
w.c. over pencil. 5 7/8 x 9 (150 x 239)
Inscribed verso *St. Annes Lower Canada/too
low too narrow/but something like*   949.41.23

**67 View from the Backyard of the Jesuit
Barracks, Quebec**
w.c., touches of gouache, over pencil.
9 9/16 x 14 3/8 (243 x 365)
Inscribed l.c. of mount *Part of the Jesuit
Barracks/Quebec, these occupied by the 2nd
battn. Grenadr. Guard 1838*; verso *View from
the back yard of the Jesuit college, Quebec–now
used as a Barrack.*   949.41.34

67

68 Grenadier Guards at Quebec
w.c., touches of gouache, over pencil.
10 1/16 x 14 1/8 (257 x 362)
Inscribed l.c. of mount *Montmorenci–Hills of
St. Anne's–Isle of Orleans–View of Quebec
from the outside of the Porte St. Louis. 2nd Battn.
Grenadr. Guards marching out 1838*; verso
*Porte St. Louis–Isle of Orleans in the
distance–Quebec*   949.41.17

68

Barnard

69 Protestant Cathedral, Quebec

w.c. over pencil. 9 13/16 x 14 3/8 (250 x 365)

Inscribed verso and on mount, title.

View taken from the Place d'Armes looking toward the Protestant Cathedral, and Ste Anne Street, with the spire of the Catholic Cathedral in the background.

949.41.14

69

Barnard

70 House of Assembly from the Grand Battery, Quebec

w.c. over pencil. 10 5/16 x 14 7/16 (262 x 366)

Inscribed verso, title.

The first House of Assembly of Lower Canada met in the chapel of the former Bishop's Palace from 1792 until 1831. The chapel was demolished and replaced by a new parliament house between 1831 and 1833; the Legislative Assembly met in this building (shown in view) until it burned in 1854. A second parliament building was erected on the site in 1859 and housed Quebec's Legislative Assembly until it burned in 1883. The area is now Montmorency Park.

949.41.11

70

Barnard

71 Citadel of Quebec from Wolfe's Cove
w.c. over pencil. 9 3/4 x 13 3/4 (248 x 349)
Inscribed l.c. of mount *Citadel of Quebec–looking down the St. Lawrence*; verso *Quebec from Wolfe's Cove*   949.41.41

72 Des Carrières Street and Part of Quebec Seen from the Citadel
w.c. and soft pencil. 14 x 12 13/16 (355 x 325)   949.41.35

73 Interior of the Citadel (recto)
From the Citadel Looking Towards the Island of Orleans (verso)
w.c., touches of gouache, over pencil. 14 1/4 x 20 15/16 (362 x 532)
Inscribed u.l. (recto) *from the interior of Citadel, Quebec*; l. to r. (verso) *Isle of Orleans/St. Lawrence looking up the river/Montmorenci/Part of Citadel, Quebec*
962.87

74 Military Works
w.c. over pencil. 10 x 14 (254 x 355)
949.41.28

75 View from the Garden of Government House, Quebec
w.c., touches of gouache, over pencil. 9 3/4 x 13 1/2 (248 x 343)
Title inscribed on verso.   949.41.36

76 View from the Racecourse on the Plains of Abraham
w.c., touches of gouache, over pencil. 6 3/4 x 10 1/16 (172 x 255)
Inscribed lower recto of mount *Race Course on the plains of Abraham. Citadel of Quebec in the distance 1838*   949.41.31

77 Road from Wolfe's Cove to the Height of Abraham, Quebec
w.c., touches of gouache, over pencil. 6 5/8 x 9 3/4 (170 x 249)
Title inscribed on verso.   949.41.4

78 St. Lawrence River and Wolfe's Cove from the Heights of Abraham, Quebec
w.c., over pencil. 9 9/16 x 13 7/16 (243 x 341)
Inscribed verso *St. Lawrence River from the heights of Abraham near Quebec.* Unfinished landscape in w.c. on verso.   949.41.32

79 Quebec from My Window
w.c. 14 x 13 1/16 (355 x 332)
Title inscribed on verso. Composition shows Des Carrières Street, the Public Gardens and Monument of Wolfe and Montcalm.   949.41.45

80 Wolfe and Montcalm Monument, Public Gardens, Des Carrières Street, Quebec
w.c. over pencil. 10 1/8 x 14 1/8 (257 x 358)
Inscribed l.r. recto of mount *Wolfe's and Montcalm monument/Quebec/. Citadel in distance*; l.l. recto of mount *X Window from*

which the 'long view' was taken (corresponds to X on house. For 'long view' see cat. no. 79)   949.41.12

81 View from the Montcalm and Wolfe Monument, Towards Lévis
w.c. over pencil. 7 5/16 x 10 1/8 (186 x 257)
Inscribed verso, *Wolfe monument Quebec*
949.41.7

82 Wigwam at Pointe Lévis Near Quebec
w.c., touches of gouache, over pencil. 7 3/4 x 12 (197 x 305)
Inscribed recto of mount, *Indian Wigwams. Squaw making baskets. taken from Point Levi opposite Quebec. Spt.1838;* verso *A Wigwam on Pt. Levi near Quebec*
Small, unfinished w.c. sketch of figures and buildings in landscape on verso.
949.41.29

83 Quebec from Pointe Lévis
w.c., touches of gouache, over pencil. 9 5/8 x 16 1/4 (245 x 412)
Inscribed verso *Citadel of Quebec from Point Levi–Indians and Wigwams*   949.41.43

Detail of 75

83

84 Quebec from St. Charles River
w.c. over pencil. 10 3/16 x 14 3/8 (259 x 365)   963.39.3

85 An Inland View Near Lake St. Charles
w.c. 10 11/16 x 14 11/16 (272 x 373)
Inscribed verso *An inland view, near Lake Charles Canada*   949.41.13

86 Upper End of Lake St. Charles, Quebec
w.c. over pencil. 6 11/16 x 9 3/8 (170 x 238)
Inscribed lower recto of mount *Upper End of Lake Charles. Lower Canada 1839*; verso *Upper End of Lake Charles near Quebec* 949.41.3

87 Near Lake St. Charles in Autumn
w.c. over pencil. 10 3/16 x 14 3/16 (259 x 360)
Inscribed lower recto of mount *Autumn in Canada. View of my red pencil case near Lake Charles*   949.41.42

88 Chaudière Falls, Quebec, At Sunset
w.c. over pencil. 8 3/4 x 12 1/2 (222 x 317)
Inscribed verso *Sunset from Nature at Chaudiere, Canada*; lower recto of mount *Part of the Chaudiere fall from above, looking up the river, Canada*   949.41.15

89 Fall of the Etchemin River Near Quebec, with Fisherman
w.c. over pencil. 6 9/16 x 9 3/4 (167 x 247)
Unfinished w.c. sketch of tree on verso. 949.41.30

90 Squaws at the Indian Village of Lorette Near Quebec
w.c. over pencil. 9 7/8 x 12 1/2 (251 x 317)
Inscribed lower recto of mount *1838* and above title.   949.41.37

Barnard

91 Jacques Cartier River with Bridge

w.c. over pencil. 9 1/2 x 13 3/8 (241 x 340)
Inscribed verso and lower recto of mount
Jacques Cartier, Canada, 1839   949.41.40

92 River Jacques Cartier

w.c., touches of gouache. 9 3/4 x 13 5/8
(247 x 346)
Inscribed verso *River 'Jacques
Cartier'/Canada/Hope fishing.* Most
probably refers to James Hope-Wallace,
q.v.   949.41.33

93 Waterfall on the Jacques Cartier River

w.c. over pencil. 6 1/2 x 9 3/4 (165 x 247)
Inscribed, verso *Jacques Cartier River, Lower
Canada*   949.41.9

94 Landing Place at Sorel

w.c. over pencil. 7 1/4 x 11 1/4 (184 x 286)
Inscribed verso *Landing Place at Sorell–Sir J.
Colborne's in the distance.*
Sir John Colborne was
Commander-in-Chief of the Forces in
British North America from 1835, and
Governor-in-Chief 1839-40. Near the
landing place at Sorel was a lodge serving
as residence for the Governor in summer,
which may be the indistinct building in this
view referred to as 'Sir J. Colborne's.'
949.41.6

94

95 Road Between Drummondville and St. Antoine

w.c. over pencil. 6 7/8 x 10 1/2 (175 x 267)
Inscribed verso *Road between Drummondville & St. Antoine, October 30th 1838. H.B.*
949.41.10

96 Breaking up of the Ice on the St. Lawrence Opposite Montreal

w.c. over pencil. 7 15/16 x 10 11/16 (202 x 271)
Inscribed verso *Sketch of Montreal from Point St. Charles, 15th January 1840/From the collection of immense Masses of Ice in the St. Lawrence in front of the City/the water rose 25 feet above its usual level, and flooded the Cellars of the Merchants Stores on the wharves/also the lower parts of the City and suburbs.; lower recto of mount Canada 1840* and title.
949.41.20

96

97 Notre Dame Street, Montreal
w.c., touches of gouache, over pencil. 8 x
12 1/4 (203 x 311)
Inscribed lower recto of mount *Notre Dame
Street, Montreal, Canada 1840.*
Same view copied by M.M. Chaplin in
1841; see cat. no. 258.   949.41.1

97

Barnard

98 Wigwam Near Montreal
w.c. over soft pencil. 6 1/2 x 9 3/4 (165 x 247)
Copy of w.c. by James Duncan, cat. no. 725.
949.41.8

99 Fort Lennox, Ile aux Noix, Richelieu River
w.c. over pencil. 7 3/8 x 10 3/4 (187 x 273)
Inscribed l.l. *Illinois, Lake Champlain* (in black ink over original pencil inscription, which has been mis-read). Unfinished landscape in pencil on verso.   964.69.3

100 Rouses Point, Lake Champlain
w.c. over pencil. 7 3/8 x 10 5/8 (187 x 270)
Inscribed l.l. *Fort Rouse or Rouse's Point Lake Champlain.* Pen and ink sketches of figures, architectural details and a house on verso.
964.69.4

101 Little Falls, New York
w.c. over pencil. 8 x 11 7/16 (203 x 290)
Inscribed verso *Little Falls, Valley of Mowhawk, N.Y.*   964.69.6

102 Trenton Falls, N.Y.
w.c. over pencil. 12 x 16 1/8 (305 x 409)
Inscribed verso *Trenton Falls.*   964.69.5

103 Trenton Falls, N.Y.
w.c. over pencil. 11 3/4 x 16 3/8 (298 x 415)
964.69.8

104 Weedsport on the Erie Canal
Pencil and w.c. 7 1/4 x 11 1/8 (184 x 283)
Inscribed l.l. *Weedsport on Erie Canal–extra Exclusive, Sept. 13th 1838*   949.41.21

104

Barnard

105 Erie Canal and Montezuma Marshes
w.c. over pencil. 7 1/2 x 12 5/8 (191 x 321)
Inscribed verso *The Erie Canal as it crosses
the Montzema Marshes. It is said 11,000 men
died during the cutting the canal thru these
marshes.* 949.41.24

106 Passenger Boat on the Erie Canal
w.c. over pencil. 8 1/2 x 12 1/4 (216 x 311)
Inscribed, lower recto of mount *Passenger
Boat on the Erie Canal/HWB* 949.41.16

107 Rochester on the Genesee River
w.c. over pencil. 11 7/16 x 16 1/2 (290 x
420)
Inscribed lower recto of mount *Falls of the
Gennessee in Rochester, United States. X Sam
Patch's last leap/who is said to have lept into the
falls of Niagara from the rocks near the Terrapin
Tower.* 964.69.9

108 Falls of the Genesee Below Rochester
w.c. over pencil. 8 x 11 7/16 (203 x 291)
Inscribed verso, title. 964.69.2

109 Distant View of the Falls of Niagara
w.c., touches of gouache, over pencil.
10 1/2 x 20 1/2 (267 x 520) 949.41.18

110 Niagara Falls
w.c. 10 1/4 x 15 1/8 (260 x 384) 964.69.1

111 American Falls, Niagara
w.c., touches of gouache, on blue-grey
paper. 6 7/8 x 10 1/16 (174 x 255)
Inscribed verso *American Falls, Niagara, July
1840* 964.69.7

112 Moss Island, Niagara
w.c. over pencil. 12 1/4 x 17 (311 x 432)
949.41.44

113 Terrapin Tower from Goat Island
w.c. over pencil. 12 5/8 x 20 1/4 (321 x 514)
Pencil sketch of houses on verso.
949.41.27

114 Terrapin Tower, Niagara
w.c. over pencil. 13 3/4 x 18 1/2 (349 x 470)
Inscribed verso *Terrapin Tower & Fall*
949.41.19

115 Niagara from Goat Island
w.c. over pencil. 7 3/8 x 11 (187 x 279)
Inscribed recto of mount *Niagara from Goat
Island, 1838* 949.41.5

**116 Niagara from the Bridge to Goat
Island**
w.c. over pencil. 7 5/16 x 10 5/8 (186 x 270)
Inscribed lower recto of mount *from the
Bridge halfway across the rapids between the
American shore and Goat Island/Niagara 1838*
949.41.25

117 Clifton House Hotel, Niagara
w.c. over pencil. 13 1/16 x 18 1/2 (331 x
470)
Inscribed verso *Hotel on the English
Side/Canada*; lower recto of mount *Hotel at
Niagara/ on the English side/looking onto the
America fall* 949.41.26

117

118 Clifton House seen from Goat Island
w.c. over pencil. 16 7/8 x 13 (428 x 330)
Inscribed verso *Biddell's Tower, American
shores & Clifton Hotel*; lower recto of mount
*English Hotel, Niagara from the foot of Biddell's
Tower, Goat Island*   949.41.38

119 Landscape with Lake
w.c., touches of gouache, over pencil. 5 x 7
(127 x 178)   949.41.22

Bartlett, William Henry
(1809-1854)
Born in Kentish Town, London.
Apprenticed to architect John Britton,
1821-28; spent most of this period
sketching English countryside. Associated
with publishing firm of George Virtue from
1831. In 1832 began illustrating Dr.
William Beattie's travel books with views
of England and the Continent. Visited
United States and Canada in 1836 and 1838
to paint illustrations for Nathaniel Parker
Willis' travel books. His 117 Canadian
views, sketched during the summer of
1838, were published as steel engravings in
Willis' two-volume *Canadian Scenery*, 1840.
From 1844 he both wrote and illustrated
travel books on Europe, America and the
Near East. Edited *Sharpe's London Magazine*
1849-52. Died at sea between Malta and
Marseilles.
Bartlett's picturesque views of both the
United States and Canada were much
copied from the time of their publication as
steel engravings.

Attributed to Bartlett

120 Cap Santé, River St. Lawrence
Pencil and w.c. on grey paper. 8 3/4 x
12 15/16 (222 x 328)
Inscribed u.r. *Cap Sante, R. St. Lawrence*
Variant of engraving of same title, Willis I,
121.   955.208.2

**121 Lake Memphramagog, Eastern
Townships, P.Q.**
Pencil and brown wash on blue-grey paper.
8 3/8 x 12 1/2 (213 x 317)
Unfinished pencil sketch of landscape and
listing of sites in England and Ireland on
verso.
Variant of engraving *A Settler's Hut at the
Frontier*, Willis II, 19.   955.208.3

121

122 Indian Scene on the St. Lawrence
Pencil, sepia wash, touches of gouache, on blue-grey paper. 9 3/16 x 13 1/16 (233 x 331)
Inscribed u.r. *W . . . in place . . . Thousand Islands*
Variant of engraving of same title, Willis II, 91.   955.208.1

Copies after Bartlett

123 Quebec from the Citadel
w.c. over pencil. 11 3/16 x 15 9/16 (284 x 395)
Copy after engraving, Willis I, 125. 951.67.8

124 Wolfe's Cove
black wash. 4 11/16 x 7 1/16 (119 x 179)
Inscribed recto of mount with above title.
Copy of engraving, Willis I, 127, by same artist as cat. nos. 126, 131-3.   951.81.3

125 Wolfe's Cove, Quebec
w.c., touches of gouache, over pencil. 9 3/8 x 13 1/2 (238 x 343)
Watermark: *J. Whatman 1848*
Variant copy of engraving, Willis I, 127, with two figures added to foreground.
Bequest of Estate of Mary Adelaide Lindsay, Port Perry, Ontario.   970.50.7

126 Lake Beneath the Owl's Head Mountain, Eastern Townships
black wash. 4 13/16 x 7 3/16 (122 x 182)
Inscribed recto of mount with title.
Copy of engraving, Willis II, 27, by same artist as cat. nos. 124, 131-3.   951.81.4

127 Nelson's Pillar, Montreal
w.c., pen and ink over pencil. 16 3/4 x 12 7/16 (425 x 315) (sight)
Inscribed l.l. *Nelson's Monument, Montreal;* l.r. *W.H. Bartlett 1838*
Copy of engraving, Willis I, 113.   951.40.1

128 Rapids on the Approach to the Village of Cedars
w.c., touches of gouache, over pencil. 9 1/8 x 13 3/4 (232 x 349)
Copy of engraving, Willis I, 111, by same artist as cat. no. 129.   960.250.22

129 Village of Cedars, River St. Lawrence
w.c. over pencil. 9 3/8 x 14 (238 x 355)
Copy of engraving, Willis I, 112, by same artist as cat. no. 128.   960.250.21

130 Canoe Building at Papper's Island, Ottawa River
w.c., touches of gouache, over pencil. 5 3/8 x 7 5/16 (137 x 185)
Copy of engraving, Willis I, 11. Papper's Island is one of the Chaudière Islands.
951.187

131 Mill on the Rideau River near Bytown
black wash. 4 7/8 x 7 1/8 (124 x 181)
Inscribed recto of mount with title.
Copy of engraving, Willis II, 8, by same artist as cat. nos. 124, 126, 132-3. The mill, situated at the confluence of Rideau Falls with the Ottawa River, was built in 1830 by Jean-Baptiste St. Louis.   951.81.1

132 The Squaw's Grave, Ottawa River
black wash. 4 3/4 x 7 1/8 (121 x 181)
Inscribed recto of mount with title.
Copy of engraving, Willis I, 36, by same artist as cat. nos. 124, 126, 131, 133.
951.81.5

132

133 Lac des Allumettes près de la rivière d'Ottawa

black wash. 4 11/16 x 7 3/16 (119 x 182)
Inscribed, lower recto of mount, with title, by same artist as cat. nos. 124, 126, 131-2.
951.81.2

134 Toronto

sepia wash over soft pencil. 17 x 23 (432 x 584)
Copy of engraving, Willis I, 87, by same artist as cat. no. 135.   960.58.1

135 Fish Market, Toronto

sepia wash over black crayon. 15 3/4 x 11 5/8 (400 x 574)
Copy of engraving, Willis I, 88, by same artist as cat. no. 134.   960.58.2

136 View on the Hudson near Weehawken

w.c. 12 1/2 x 19 7/8 (317 x 505)
Inscribed, l.c. *View on the Hudson in 1836*
Copy of engraving in *American Scenery*, published 1840.   968x341.16

Note: see cat. nos. 245 and 637 for signed copies of Bartlett views.

Basire, James
(1730-1802)
English draughtsman and engraver of architectural views and reproductions of drawings. Taught engraving to artist William Blake. Not known to have visited Canada.

137 View of the Banks of the River St. Lawrence

Black and grey wash over pencil, with black wash borders. 5 15/16 x 8 5/16 (151 x 211)
Inscribed lower l. to r. *J. Basire/Basire F. Vue des bords du fleuve St. Laurent juin 1783*
Watermark: Lily.   968.252.2

137

Beaufort, Rear Admiral Sir Francis (1774-1857)

Naval hydrographer. Born in England, son of Daniel Augustus Beaufort. Lieutenant 1796; commander 1800. Surveyed entrance to Rio de la Plata, 1807. Retired from service 1846.

138 The City of Quebec from the Anchorage

grey and black wash over pencil. 7 x 29 1/2 (178 x 749)

Inscribed, u.c. with title; lower margin, l. to r. *Telegraph* [below Citadel Hill], *Governor's house* [below Chateau Saint Louis], *Landg Place* [below docks], *Frans. Beaufort 1809*.

Watermark: *J. Whatman 1804*   967.16

138

Belfield, W.
(active 1851)

Probably William Belfield, paymaster with 88th Regiment, stationed at Halifax from 31 May 1850 until 18 June 1851.

139 View of Halifax from the Micmac Encampment at Dartmouth

w.c., touches of gouache, over pencil. 9 1/8 x 14 7/8 (232 x 378)

Inscribed l.r. *W.B./13/3/51*

This particular composition of foreground figures, beached canoe and tents was employed from the late 18th century onwards. Belfield's view repeats in every detail (with addition of sailboat and seagulls, right middle distance) the w.c. attributed to William Eager (q.v.), PANS collection. The same Micmac encampment with varying background landscapes, can be found in: 1. w.c. dated 1785, Sotheby (Toronto) cat. 29 May 68, lot 233; 2. Sotheby (Toronto) cat. 28 Oct. 69, lot 329; 3. w.c. by J.G. Toler dated 1808, PAC coll; 4. w.c. by James Cockburn dated 1827, this cat. no. 388; 5. w.c., Webster coll. cat. no. 5961.   949.213.8

139

Berczy, William
(1744-1813)

Born Johann Albrecht Ulrich Moll in Wallerstein, Germany, son of diplomat. Studied at Academy of the Arts, Vienna, *c.* 1762, and at University of Jena *c.* 1766. Changed his name to Berczy in 1770s and travelled in Central Europe. Married Charlotte Allamand in Switzerland, 1785; spent next five years in Italy. Appointed drawing master to household of Marquis of Bath, London, 1790. Sailed for America, 1792, with group of German immigrants, as land agent for Marquis of Bath. When plans to settle in New York State fell through, he brought group to Markham Township, Upper Canada, 1794. Travelled to London in 1799 in attempt to settle dispute over land title. Returned Canada 1801, and earning living as a painter in Montreal by 1804. Best known for portraits in oil, w.c., gouache, pastel and ink; also designed buildings and painted historical and religious subjects in oil. Died while on visit to New York.

Berczy rarely signed his paintings. Of the following portraits, cat. nos. 140-3 were acquired from descendants of the artist; cat. nos. 144-5 from descendants of the subjects. See also cat. no. 2061 (a copy after Berczy).

140 William Berczy, Self-Portrait
gouache. 4 7/8 x 4 (124 x 102)
Earliest of three known self-portraits, probably painted in Vienna *c.* 1762.
968.298.1

141 William Berczy, Self-Portrait
w.c. and gouache. 10 5/8 x 8 1/2 (270 x 216)
Painted *c.* 1790; unfinished and retouched around hands, coat.   968.298.2

141

142 Portrait of Charlotte Berczy
Pencil, faint brown wash, on prepared
ground. 5 5/8 x 4 1/2 (143 x 114)
Portrait of the artist's wife, Charlotte
Allamand Berczy (1760-*c*.1833).   968.298.4

142

Berczy

143 The McTavish Family
grey wash. 8 x 11 3/4 (203 x 298)
Thought to be sketch of Marguerite
Chaboillez McTavish and her four
children, taken shortly after death of her
husband, fur trader Simon McTavish
(1750-1804) of Montreal.   968.298.5

143

Berczy

144 Portrait of Alexander McDonell
w.c., gouache, over pencil. 11 1/8 x 9 7/8
(282 x 251)
Original paper matt, painted with black
wash, is held in place with narrow strips of
manuscript, one of which bears part of
artist's signature.
Alexander McDonnell (1762-1842) was
representative in Legislative Assembly of
Upper Canada, speaker of the Assembly
and Sheriff of Home District. He served in
War of 1812; became member of Legislative
Council 1831.   970.85.1

144

Berczy

145 Portrait of Robert Isaac Dey Gray
w.c., gouache, over pencil. 11 x 9 3/4 (279 x 247)
Original paper matt painted with black wash over yellow w.c.
Robert Isaac Dey Gray (1772?-1804), Solicitor-General of Upper Canada 1794, elected to represent Stormont in Legislative Assembly 1796. Drowned in loss of vessel *Speedy* on Lake Ontario, October 1804.
970.85.2

145

Berczy

Bessau, Oscar
(active 1850-57)

Born in France. Studied under Isabey and Ciceri. In Canada by 1850, working as w.c. landscape artist. Exhibited St. Lawrence River views at NAD, N.Y., 1855. Collaborated with Charles Lanman on illustrations for *Adventures in the Wilds of the United States and British North American Provinces*, Philadelphia 1856. Moved to Washington, D.C. about 1855. Exhibited, NAD 1855; WAA, 1857.

146 Kingston, Canada West
w.c. over pencil. 6 15/16 x 10 (176 x 254)
Inscribed verso *Kingston, C.W., Nov. 5th 185 . . .* ; lower recto of mount *Bessau, Canada, 1850/Kingston, Canada West, 1850*
968x341.13

Best, W.R.
(active 1851-60)

English architect and illustrator. Author of a set of views of public buildings in St. John's, Newfoundland, published as lithographs in 1851 and 1858.

147 A View Combining Signal Hill, The Narrows, Cochrane Street and South Side of St. John's, Newfoundland
w.c., touches of gouache, over pencil.
12 3/16 x 19 3/16 (310 x 487)
Inscribed lower recto of mount with title. Similar in composition to the 1851 lithograph by W. Spreat after Best *St. Thomas' Church, The Narrows, &c. from Government House,* but taken from a slightly different angle.   950.224.17

147

Best

Bouchette, Joseph
(1798-1879) *copy after*

Topographical artist. Eldest son of Colonel Joseph Bouchette (1774-1841) whom he succeeded as Surveyor-General of Lower Canada.

148 Montreal from the Mountain
w.c., black pencil. 9 9/16 x 15 1/16 (243 x 382)

Inscribed l.c. *April 1835/View of the City of Montreal taken from the Mountain/A.T.* Copy of lithograph by L. Haghe after drawing by Joseph Bouchette Jr., published in Colonel Joseph Bouchette: *British Dominions in North America*, London 1832. 955.225.2

Bouchette, Robert Shore Milnes
(1805-1879)

Fourth and youngest son of Colonel Joseph Bouchette (1774-1841), Surveyor-General of Lower Canada. Trained as topographical draughtsman by his father. Called to the bar of Lower Canada, 1826. Implicated in Rebellion of 1837, imprisoned and banished to Bermuda. On return to Canada, became law clerk in Quebec Attorney General's office and Commissioner of Customs for Canada, 1851-75. Painted w.c. landscapes, some of which were published as lithographs.

149 American Fort at Rouses Point
pen and black ink, grey wash. 9 x 12 5/8 (228 x 320)

Inscribed u.c. in pencil *This sketch is rough and improperly executed but may be sufficient to convey an idea of the Fort J Btte*; l.c. in ink *Sketch of the American Fort at Rouses Point, on the River Richelieu about 20 chains South of the Old Line found erroneous, and is considerably within the New established Line, or Parallel 45° North Latitude; it can mount 64 pieces of Cannon and is Bomb proof with respect to its commanding position (see Plan of the Boundary Line). This Sketch was taken by Colonel Bouchette on board the Steam Boat in May 1818–and Copied by/Robert Bouchette Junr.* Fort Montgomery was begun in 1817 but construction was halted the next year when the Americans discovered that it was on the Canadian side of the border. The boundary dispute lasted until 1842, when the Webster-Ashburton Treaty established a new line north of the site of the fortress, which had meanwhile become known as "Fort Blunder". 951.40.5

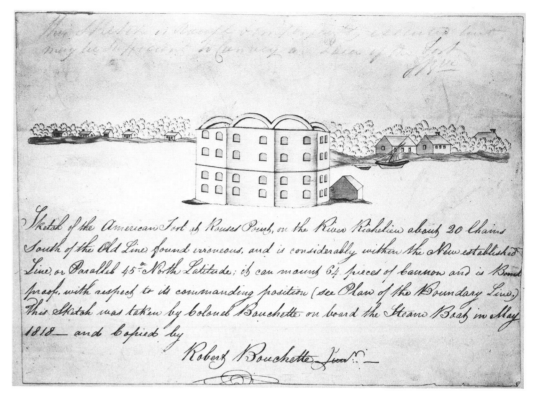

149

150 American Forts at Rouses Point
pen and ink. 6 1/4 x 11 1/4 (159 x 286)
Inscribed l.c. *Rough Sketch of the two American
Forts. JB/by Robert Bouchette Junr*; u.l. *Small
American Fort*; l.r. *Large American Fort* (in
pencil); l.l. *New Line, 45° N. Latde*; l.r. *Old
Line* (in ink).   951.40.6

Note: see cat. no. 1472 for Roebuck copy
after a w.c. by Colonel J. Bouchette.

Brenton, Edward Pelham
(1774-1839)
Born in Rhode Island, son of Rear-Admiral
Jahleel Brenton and brother of Sir Jahleel
Brenton. Entered Royal Navy 1788;
promoted to Lieutenant 1795 and stationed
in Newfoundland about this date.
Appointed commander of frigate *Spartan*
1810; served on North American station
1811-13. Painted topographical views of
places visited throughout his service.
Retired in 1815 to write on naval subjects.

**151 Pointe Lévis from the Castle Windows
at Quebec**
w.c. over pencil. 14 7/8 x 21 3/4 (378 x 552)
Inscribed verso with title; verso of mount
E.P. Brenton   955.225.1

151

Bunnett, Henry Richard S.
(active 1881-1889)

Painter. Born in England. Allegedly former army officer living under assumed name. In Montreal during 1880s painting landscapes and recording historic buildings in oil and w.c. Many views commissioned by David Ross McCord. Left Montreal 1889; illustrated book on British army uniforms by Walter Richards, published London, 1890s. Exhibited AAM 1885-9; QPEQ 1887; RCA 1888.

Many of Bunnett's views are copies of earlier prints. The inscriptions, not necessarily made by the artist, are often in error as to location, name and date of origin of the buildings.

152 Rigolet, Labrador
w.c., touches of gouache, over pencil. 3 1/4 x 4 7/8 (83 x 124)
Inscribed l.r. *H Bunnett*; verso *Rigolette, 1810. Painted 1888.*
Copy of engraving from *Harper's New Monthly Magazine*, April 1861. 957.265.9

153 L'Islet, Quebec
w.c. over black crayon. 2 7/16 x 5 3/8 (62 x 136)
Inscribed l.r. *HB* in monogram (see detail); verso *1820, L'Islet.*
Copy of engraving after John J. Bigsby in his book *The Shoe and Canoe*, London 1850. 957.265.65

154 Mill, Baie St. Paul
w.c. 5 1/16 x 4 (129 x 101)
Attributed to Bunnett but possibly by Ross (q.v.). 957.265.18

155 Farm House, Berthier en Haut
w.c. 5 3/16 x 4 5/8 (132 x 117)
Inscribed l.l. *H Bunnett*; verso *Manor House, Berthier 1780.*
Same building painted in oil by Bunnett in 1886, McCord Museum coll., is identified as 'Cuthbert's storehouse, Berthier en haut'. 957.265.27

156 Twin-spired Church, Quebec Province
w.c. over pencil. 6 3/8 x 8 9/16 (162 x 217)
Inscribed l.r. *H Bunnett*; verso *St. Jean Baptiste de Berthier 1812.*
Twin-spired building similar in style to church of Ste Geneviève at Berthier en Haut. 957.265.52

157 Twin-spired Church with Portico, Quebec Province
w.c. 9 1/8 x 7 (232 x 178)
Inscribed l.l. *H Bunnett*; verso *Parish Church, De Lanaudiere, 1720, Bunnett, 1893* 957.265.20

157

158 L'Ange Gardien Below Quebec, 1889
w.c., touches of gouache, over pencil.
4 3/16 x 4 7/8 (106 x 124)
Inscribed l.r. *HB*; verso, title.
Distant view of town and church, habitant on snowshoes in foreground.   957.265.48

159 Chicoutimi Ferry
w.c., pen and ink, over pencil. 3 3/8 x 4 7/8
(86 x 124)
Inscribed verso *Chicoutimi*   957.265.50

160 Ruins of Château Bigot, Charlesbourg 1851
w.c. 3 1/16 x 4 3/8 (77 x 111)
Inscribed l.r. *H Bunnett*; verso, title.
957.265.30

161 General Hospital, Quebec
w.c. 3 x 6 5/16 (76 x 160)
Inscribed l.r. *H Bunnett*; verso *1693 General Hospital, Quebec, St. Roche*   957.265.23

162 Hope Gate, Quebec
w.c. over pencil. 5 9/16 x 5 9/16 (141 x 141)
Inscribed l.r. *H Bunnett*; verso *Hope Gate, Quebec City, 1756-1871*   957.265.25

163 St. John's Gate, Quebec City
w.c. 4 5/8 x 7 5/16 (118 x 193)
Composition probably derived from the Sarony & Major lithograph, published N.Y.
c. 1850.   957.265.29

164 St. Louis Gate, Quebec City
w.c. over pencil. 5 11/16 x 4 11/16 (144 x 119)
Inscribed l.l. *H Bunnett*; verso *St. John's Gate* (in error).
Copy of engraving after W.O. Carlisle in *Recollections of Canada*, London 1873.
957.265.47

165 Château Haldimand, Quebec
w.c. 3 7/8 x 8 1/2 (98 x 216)
Inscribed l.r. *H Bunnett*; verso *Chateau Haldimand/Quebec City/1885*
Two 1880 oil views of Chateau Haldimand by Bunnett are in McCord Museum. The building was erected 1784-87 and destroyed by fire 1838.   957.265.34

166 Parliament House and Château St. Louis, Quebec
w.c., pen and ink. 3 1/2 x 9 (89 x 229)
Inscribed verso *Chateau St Louis Quebec 1650 Residence of Governor.*
Copy of engraving by J. Smillie Jr. in *The Picture of Quebec*, Quebec 1829.   957.265.49

167 Top Floor, Martello Tower, Plains of Abraham, Quebec
w.c., pen and ink. 4 3/4 x 6 1/8 (121 x 155)
Inscribed l.l. *H Bunnett*; verso, stamped with three crests bearing reversed inscriptions.
957.265.5

168 Top Floor, East Martello Tower, Plains of Abraham, Quebec
w.c. 3 3/8 x 6 3/16 (86 x 157)
Inscribed l.r. *H Bunnett*; verso, title.
957.265.57

169 Martello Tower, Quebec
w.c., grey-brown wash, over pencil. 7 x
8 5/8 (178 x 219)

Inscribed l.l. *H Bunnett*; verso *Dr. Bounmi . . .* and stamped with crest.   957.265.2

170 Crypt under Martello Tower, Quebec
w.c. over pencil. 3 1/2 x 5 7/16 (89 x 149)
Inscribed l.l. *H Bunnett*; verso, title.
957.265.44

171 Church of St. Joseph, Deschambault
w.c., gouache. 3 7/8 x 4 1/2 (98 x 114)
Inscribed l.r. *H Bunnett*; verso, title and
1774   957.265.51

172 Lake St. John
w.c. over pencil. 5 1/16 x 3 15/16 (128 x 100)
Inscribed verso, title.   957.265.10

173 Seminary at Nicolet
w.c., touches of gouache, over pencil. 4 3/4 x 6 1/2 (121 x 165)
Inscribed l.r. *H Bunnett*; verso *Nicolet College, 1893*   957.265.21

174 Wayside Cross, St. Denis on Richelieu River
w.c. 4 3/16 x 1 5/16 (106 x 59)
Inscribed l.r. *HB*; verso *Cross at St. Denis–On Richelieu*   957.265.31

175 Wayside Cross at St. Marc on the Richelieu
w.c., pen and ink over pencil. 4 13/16 x
2 5/16 (122 x 59)
Inscribed l.r. *HB*: verso, title.   957.265.32

176 Old House at St. Marc, Richelieu River
w.c. over pencil. 4 13/16 x 7 11/16 (122 x 195)
Inscribed l.r. *H Bunnett*; verso *1885–Old House at St. Marc. Shattered during Rebellion 1837*   957.265.58

177 Manor House, Boucherville
w.c., touches of gouache, over pencil.
5 3/16 x 10 (132 x 254)
Inscribed l.r. *H Bunnett*; verso, title.
957.265.40

178 Church of St. Francis Xavier, Longue Pointe
w.c., pen and ink. 6 7/16 x 2 15/16
(163 x 75)
Inscribed l.l. *H Bunnett*; verso *St. Fr. Xavier, Longue Pointe, 1770–On Richelieu*   957.265.35

179 Longue Pointe Church Keystone 1726
black and blue-grey wash. 2 x 2 3/8 (51 x 60) (sight)
Inscribed on keystone *St. FS 1726*; verso, title.   957.265.38

177

180 Fort St. John, Barony of Longueuil
w.c. over pencil. 3 1/8 x 9 7/8 (80 x 251)
Inscribed l.l. *H Bunnett 1888;* verso, title.
An 1885 Bunnett oil in McCord Museum
shows the fort from the inland side.
957.265.36

181 Fort St. John, Barony of Longueuil
w.c. 3 15/16 x 9 15/16 (100 x 252)
Inscribed l.r. *H Bunnett;* verso, title.
Copy of a 1776 view of the fort, engraved
1789 and published as illustration in
Thomas Anburey: *Travels Through the
Interior Parts of America,* London 1791.
957.265.55

182 Manor House, Terrebonne
w.c., touches of gouache, over pencil; cut in
outline and laid down on black paper.
4 1/4 x 6 7/8 (108 x 175)
Inscribed l.r. *H Bunnett;* verso *Manor House,
Terrebonne, Joseph Masson*   957.265.22

183 Intendant's Palace, Montreal
w.c., pen and ink. 3 5/16 x 7 1/16 (84 x 179)
Inscribed verso *Palace of the Royal Indendant,
1698-1793, painted in 1886*
An undocumented reconstruction of the
building current in the late 19th century.
957.265.64

184 Old Jail, Montreal
w.c., pen and ink. 4 5/8 x 9 1/4 (118 x 235)
Inscribed l.l. *H Bunnett;* verso, *College
of L'Islet, 1780*   957.265.33

**185 Residence of William Molson,
Notre Dame Street, Montreal**
w.c., pen and ink, over pencil. 4 3/16 x
5 5/8 (106 x 143)
Inscribed l.r. *H Bunnett;* verso *Residence,
Wm. Molson*   957.265.1

186 Park House, Panet Street, Montreal
w.c. 4 1/16 x 5 11/16 (103 x 145)
Inscribed l.r. *H Bunnett, 1888*; verso *Park House–Built by Judge Panet–afterwards res. of Chief Justice Reid*   957.265.3

187 First Methodist Church, Montreal
w.c., pen and ink, over pencil. 4 1/8 x 7 1/4 (105 x 184)
Inscribed l.l. *H Bunnett*; verso *First Methodist Chapel, St. James St.*   957.265.4

188 Governor's Residence, St. Paul Street, Montreal
w.c., pen and ink. 4 x 6 3/16 (102 x 157)
Inscribed verso with title and *1650-1850*
An undocumented reconstruction of the Maisonneuve residence current in the late 19th century.   957.265.6

189 East Tower, Fort de la Montagne, Montreal
w.c., pen and ink. 7 1/4 x 5 1/16 (184 x 128)
Inscribed l.r. *H Bunnett*; verso *Priest's Farm, E. Tower*   957.265.8

190 Stairs to East Tower Crypt, Fort de la Montagne, Montreal
blue and brown wash. 4 5/8 x 3 3/4 (117 x 95)
Inscribed l.l. *H Bunnett*   957.265.16

191 Chapel Under Eastern Tower, Grand Seminary, Montreal
w.c., pen and ink. 5 5/16 x 3 1/2 (135 x 89)
Inscribed l.r. *H Bunnett*; verso, title; mount *Chapel under eastern tower, Fort de la Montagne* 957.265.41

192 Grey Nuns Courtyard, Youville Square, Montreal
w.c., pen and ink. 5 x 5 (127 x 127)

Inscribed l.r. *H Bunnett*; verso *Grey Nuns courtyard, Youville St., painted 1887, built 1710* 957.265.14

193 Bachelors Hall, Montreal
w.c., pen and ink. 3 5/16 x 3 1/2 (84 x 89)
Inscribed l.r. *H Bunnett*; verso *Batchelors Hall, St. Antoine near Windsor St., Hon. John Young, Robert Anderson, John Dougall.* 957.265.15

194 Court House, Montreal
w.c., pen and ink. 4 7/16 x 7 7/16 (113 x 189)
Inscribed l.r. *H Bunnett*; verso *French Army H. Q. Quebec, 1700–painted in 1884*
Copy of engraving after James Duncan published in *Hochelaga Depicta*, Montreal 1839.   957.265.17

195 St. Thomas Church, Notre Dame Street, Montreal
w.c. 6 5/16 x 6 3/16 (160 x 157)
Inscribed l.r. *H Bunnett*; verso, title and *1887*
The first St. Thomas Church was built in 1840 at the expense of Thomas Molson and stood at the corner of St. Mary Street (later Notre Dame Street East) and Voltigeurs Street. This view shows the second church on the site, built after the fire of 1852 and demolished in 1929.   957.265.26

196 Customs House, Montreal
w.c. 5 3/16 x 4 5/8 (132 x 117)
Inscribed l.l. *H Bunnett*; verso *Customs House, Montreal. Customs House Square–1830*
Copy of line engraving after view by James Duncan published in *Hochelaga Depicta*, Montreal 1839.   957.265.28

197 American Presbyterian Church, St. James Street, Montreal
w.c. 4 5/16 x 6 5/8 (101 x 168)

Inscribed l.l. . . . *Bunnett*; verso *Original St. Gabriel's Church, Montreal.*
Inscription confuses this church with an earlier Presbyterian church which stood on St. Gabriel Street.   957.265.24

198 Original Pulpit, American Presbyterian Church, Montreal
w.c., pen and ink, over pencil. 5 9/16 x 4 1/2 (141 x 114)
Inscribed l.l. *H Bunnett*; verso *Original Pulpit/St. Gabriel Church/Montreal* (in error; see cat. no. 197).
Although no views of the interior of either Presbyterian church have been found for comparison, Mr Edgar Andrew Collard draws our attention to the description of the American Presbyterian Church interior from an 1831 letter by William Lyon MacKenzie:
'The pulpit is of the most costly mahogany, with crimson cushion, very splendid.'
An 1886 grey wash view of the same subject by Bunnett is in the McCord Museum.   957.265.45

199 Nelson's Monument, Montreal
w.c. over pencil. 6 7/8 x 4 1/4 (175 x 108)
Inscribed l.l. *H Bunnett*; verso, title and *1806*
Possibly copied from the engraving after W.H. Bartlett, in *Canadian Scenery* I, 113. 957.265.46

200 Château de Vaudreuil, St. Paul Street, Montreal
w.c., pen and ink. 3 11/16 x 5 3/8 (94 x 136)
Inscribed verso, title and *1723-1803*
An undocumented reconstruction of the building current in the late 19th century. 957.265.53

201 Hôtel Dieu Chapel, St. Paul Street, Montreal
w.c. 3 13/16 x 4 5/16 (97 x 125)
Inscribed verso *Chapel of the Black nuns/St. Paul Street/Montreal 1771*
Copy of engraving after James Duncan, *Hochelaga Depicta*, Montreal 1839. 957.265.54

202 Maison Beaubien, St. Gabriel Street, Montreal
w.c. over pencil. 3 15/16 x 4 1/2 (100 x 114)
Inscribed l.l. *H Bunnett*; on mount, title and *1793*   957.265.56

203 Côte des Neiges Tannery, Montreal
w.c. over pencil. 5 x 5 3/16 (127 x 132)
Inscribed l.r. *H Bunnett*; old mount, title and *1795*   957.265.59

204 St. James Street, Montreal
w.c., touches of gouache, over pencil. 4 15/16 x 8 (125 x 203)
Inscribed l.l. *H Bunnett*; on mount, title and *1800*
A variant of the line engraving after John Murray published by Adolphus Bourne, Montreal 1850.   957.265.61

205 Corpus Christi Procession, Montreal
w.c. 6 7/16 x 4 1/8 (164 x 105)
Inscribed verso, title and *1806.*
Date too early, as costumes indicate 1880 period.
957.265.42

206 Corpus Christi Procession Outside the Shrine
w.c. 4 x 4 1/8 (102 x 105)
Inscribed verso *Corpus Christi, outside Shrine, 1806*   957.265.39

207 Old Well, Lachine 1884
w.c. over pencil. 4 1/4 x 5 7/16 (108 x 138)
Inscribed l.r. *H Bunnett;* verso, title.
957.265.11

208 "Anson Northup", First Steamer on Red River
w.c., gouache, over pencil. 3 7/16 x 5 7/16 (87 x 138)
Inscribed l.r. *H Bunnett;* verso, title.
The *Anson Northup,* first stern-wheeler in western Canada, sailed from 1859 to 1862.
957.265.63

208

209 Fort Ellice, N.W.T.
w.c. over pencil. 3 1/2 x 5 1/16 (89 x 128)
Inscribed l.r. *H Bunnett*; l.l. *Fort Ellice*
957.265.7

210 Log Cabin
w.c. over pencil. 5 3/8 x 4 7/16 (136 x 103)
957.265.12

211 Residence de Lausanne
w.c., touches of gouache. 5 3/16 x 6 3/8
(132 x 162)
Inscribed l.l. *H Bunnett*; verso
*Boucherville/house of Godfried de Lauzanne
1690.*   957.265.19

212 Quebec Merchant, 1800
w.c. 4 9/16 x 2 1/2 (116 x 63)
Inscribed verso, title.
Copy of aquatint illustration in John
Lambert: *Travels Through Lower Canada*,
London 1810, I, 310.   957.265.37

213 Quebec Gentleman, 1800
w.c. 4 1/2 x 2 (114 x 51)
Inscribed verso, title.   957.265.38

214 Jesuit Priest, 1720
w.c. 3 3/16 x 1 3/4 (81 x 44) (sight)
Inscribed verso, title.   957.265.38

215 Black Nun, 1720
w.c. 3 1/8 x 1 1/4 (79 x 32) (sight)
Inscribed verso, title.   957.265.38

216 An Old Stone Sink
black and blue-grey wash. 2 x 3 3/4 (51 x
95)
Inscribed on sink *721+MƆNC*; verso, title.
Sink from the Ferme St. Gabriel at Pointe
St. Charles, belonging to the religious of
the Congrégation de Notre Dame.
957.265.38

217 Open Air Clay Oven
w.c., touches of gouache. 3 3/4 x 5 1/4 (95
x 133)
Inscribed l.r. *H Bun . . .* (incomplete); on
mount, title.   957.265.60

218 Log Cabin and Outdoor Oven
w.c., touches of gouache, over pencil.
4 1/16 x 4 11/16 (103 x 119)
Inscribed on mount, *Indian dwelling.*
957.265.62

Burrows, John
(1789-1848)
Civil engineer. Born Plymouth, England.
Commissioned in Prince of Wales
Regiment. First settler on present site of
Ottawa. Appointed by Colonel John By
(q.v.) as clerk of the works on Rideau
Canal; remained as superintendent on its
completion. Died in Ottawa.

**219 View of Ottawa River with Bridge
Over Chaudière Falls**
w.c., pen and ink. 13 7/8 x 25 9/16 (352 x
649)
Inscribed verso *Hull, Lower Canada/about
1828*
The wood truss bridge was built in 1828
and replaced with a suspension bridge in
1843. Several Burrows drawings of works
on Rideau canal are in PAC collection. See
also cat. no. 220.   955.222

219

By, John
(1781-1836)

Topographical artist and military engineer. Educated at Royal Military College, Woolwich, England. Commissioned in Royal Artillery 1799; transferred to Royal Engineers same year. First posted to Canada 1802-11, working on Quebec fortifications and building of canal at the Cascade Rapids, St. Lawrence River. Rose to rank of lieutenant-colonel 1824. In charge of construction of Rideau Canal from Ottawa to Kingston on second posting to Canada, 1826-32. His headquarters at junction of Ottawa and Rideau rivers became known as Bytown, later Ottawa. Returned to England in 1832. Died in Sussex, England.

220 Plan and Section of First Eight Locks of Rideau Canal

w.c., pen and ink. 27 5/16 x 95 7/8 (694 x 2435) joined at centre.

Inscribed l.r. in ink, in Colonel By's hand *John By/Lt. Colonel Royl. Engrs/Comg. Rideau Canal/Upper Canada/20 November 1827;* l.l. [in script] PLAN *and* SECTION/*of the First Eight Locks of the Rideau Canal/Canal Bay and Valley/Ottawa River/Lt. Coln. J. By Commanding Royal Engineers.*

Buildings indicated on the plan are the Barracks and Guard House on Citadel Hill, the two Government Storehouses beside the canal, the store, Smiths Shop and Carpenters Shop in the Engineers Yard near the bridge. The section view shows Colonel By's house on Nepean Point. (See detail illustration.) Although this plan is signed by Colonel By, it was not necessarily drafted by him. See cat. no. 219 for a view painted by one of his engineers.
960.47

220

Detail of 220

Byron, G.R.
(active 1858-1865)

Topographical artist, known for views of Ontario, Quebec and Nova Scotia.

221 Harbour Scene by Moonlight
w.c., touches of gouache. 7 5/8 x 13 3/4
(193 x 349)   970.143

Caddy, John Herbert
(1801-1883)

Born at Quebec, son of Colonel John Caddy, R.A. Studied at Royal Military Academy, Woolwich, England, 1815-16. Commissioned in Royal Artillery as second lieutenant 1825, lieutenant 1827, captain 1840. Served in West Indies 1828-41; in Canada 1842-4 when he retired on half-pay. First city engineer in London, Ontario, 1841-51, and engineer for Great Western Railway, Hamilton, 1851-6. Devoted himself entirely to painting from 1856; had studio in Hamilton and taught at Wesleyan Female College. Exhibited UCPE 1858-68. Died in Hamilton.

222 Grenadier Island, Thousand Islands
w.c. over soft black pencil. 6 7/8 x 12 7/8
(175 x 327)
Inscribed, verso of mount *Grenadier Island/Lake of Thousand Islands*   962.166.2

223 Near Gananoque, Thousand Islands
w.c. over soft black pencil. 7 15/16 x 15 3/8
(202 x 390)
Inscribed, verso of mount *From near Gananoque/looking up the Lake of Thousand Islands*   952.166.3

224 Ontario Town on Lakeshore
w.c., pen and ink. 6 7/8 x 21 (175 x 533).
954.176.2

224

225 Dundas Marsh from Burlington Height Near Hamilton
w.c. over pencil, touches of gouache.
11 7/16 x 15 7/8 (291 x 403)
Inscribed verso, title and *Cootes Paradise near Hamilton*   957.64.8

226 Dundurn, the Residence of Sir Allan MacNab, Hamilton
w.c. over soft black pencil. 11 1/2 x 16 (292 x 406)
Inscribed verso *Dundurn, the Residence of the late Sir A.N. Macnab, Bt., Head of Burlington Bay*
Sir Allan MacNab died in 1862.   957.64.9

226

Caddy

227 Burlington Bay, Hamilton
w.c. over pencil. 9 1/2 x 12 3/4 (241 x 324)
957.64.1

228 Burlington Bay, Hamilton, C.W.
w.c. over pencil. 5 5/16 x 12 3/4 (135 x 324)
Inscribed, verso, title.   957.64.2

229 Burlington Bay, Hamilton, C.W.
w.c. over pencil. 5 3/8 x 12 3/4 (136 x 324)
Inscribed verso, title.   957.64.3

230 Burlington Bay, Hamilton, C.W.
w.c. over pencil. 5 3/8 x 12 3/4 (136 x 324)
Inscribed verso, title.   957.64.4

231 Burlington Bay, Hamilton, C.W.
w.c. over pencil. 5 5/16 x 12 3/4 (135 x 324)
Inscribed verso, title.   957.64.5

232 American Falls, Niagara, from Road to Ferry
w.c. over pencil. 10 x 13 7/16 (154 x 341)
Inscribed verso, title.   957.64.6

233 Canadian Fall from Road to Ferry
w.c. over pencil. 10 x 13 1/2 (254 x 343)
Inscribed verso, title.
Watermark: *J. Whatman 1839*
957.64.7

234 Horseshoe Falls, Niagara
w.c. over pencil. 9 5/8 x 13 7/16 (244 x 341)
Watermark: *J. Whatman 1844*
956.112

235 Lake and Hills
w.c. over soft pencil. 10 15/16 x 18 3/8 (278 x 467)
Inscribed verso *Mr. Hilton-W.E.W. . . . Niagara River, Caddy*   957.259.1

236 Falls of Niagara
w.c. over pencil. 9 9/16 x 13 3/8 (243 x 339)
Watermark on mount: *J. Whatman 1834*
The Terrapin tower, built in 1833 and torn down 1876, is omitted from this view.
956.26.6

237 Shebahwahning, Manitoulin Islands, Lake Huron
w.c. over pencil. 11 7/16 x 13 5/8 (290 x 346)
Inscribed verso *Shebahwahning, Manitoulin Islands, Lake Huron, Canada, July 1854.*
Watermark: *J. Whatman, Turkey Mill*
The site is now named Killarney.   960.272

237

238 From Little Current, Manitoulin Island
w.c. 8 1/2 x 12 1/8 (216 x 308)
Gift of Mrs A.V. Stupart, Toronto.
965.249.1

239 Sault Ste Marie from Canadian Side
w.c. 11 1/2 x 20 3/4 (292 x 527)
Gift of Mrs A.V. Stupart, Toronto.
965.249.3

240 Sault Ste Marie from the Canal
w.c. over soft black pencil. 8 x 14 (203 x 356)
Inscribed verso of mount *Sault Ste Marie from Canal JHC* [in monogram].   952.166.1

241 Rapids in the Woods
w.c. 13 1/8 x 20 5/8 (333 x 524)
Gift of Mrs A.V. Stupart, Toronto.
965.249.4

242 Potterdale, Cumberland, England
w.c. 12 1/4 x 18 1/4 (311 x 464)
Gift of Mrs A.V. Stupart, Toronto.
965.249.2

Caldwell, Lieutenant

Possibly William Bletterman Caldwell (active 1814-57); commissioned as ensign, 60th Regiment of Royal Americans, 1814; promoted to lieutenant 1814, while stationed at Quebec City; captain 1831, major 1846. In 1840 took corps of pensioners to Red River; Governor of Assiniboia 1848-55, when he returned to England and retired.

243 Falls of Montmorency Near Quebec
brown wash on grey paper. 6 9/16 x 10 3/16 (167 x 259)
Inscribed verso, title (ink) and *Lt. Caldwell* (pencil).   951.41.10

Camillieri, Nicholas
(active 1800-1827)
Marine painter. Active in Amsterdam 1800-21. Known for watercolour paintings of American Mediterranean fleet off Malta in 1820s.

244 Brig of War "Fair American"
w.c., pen and black ink, touches of gouache, over pencil; black wash borders cover an earlier title. 16 1/4 x 20 3/4 (413 x 527)
Inscribed l.r. *Cammillieri of Malta*; verso *A G. Brigant of War/Fair America/Command Decartour* (pencil)
Ship shown flying American flag with 13 stars, used 1777-94. A brig of this name was in service of South Carolina State navy in 1770s. 'Decartour' may refer to Commander Stephen Decatur (1751-1808) who commanded several privateers during American Revolutionary War.   960x276.206

244

Campbell, M.L.

245 Quebec from the Opposite Shore of the St. Lawrence
black and grey wash on Reynolds Bristolboard. 13 x 18 (330 x 457)
Inscribed l.r. *M.L. Campbell*; l.c. title.
An amateur's copy of the engraving after W.H. Bartlett, published in *Canadian Scenery* 1842.   955.102.3

Carpenter, W.
(active 1861)
An accomplished watercolourist who painted views of Quebec province, New Hampshire and New York States.

246 Glen Ellis Fall, White Mountains, New Hampshire
w.c., touches of gouache, over pencil.
13 7/8 x 9 7/8 (352 x 251)
Inscribed l.l. *Glen Ellis Fall/White Mountains/New Hampshire, U.S./W. Carpenter 1861*   955.190.6

247 Trenton Falls Near Utica, New York
w.c., touches of gouache, over pencil on grey paper. 10 1/2 x 14 13/16 (267 x 376)
Inscribed l.l. *Trenton Falls/near Utica New York/W Carpenter 1861*   955.190.7

248 Falls of St. Anthony, Mississippi River
w.c. over pencil. 9 7/8 x 13 7/8 (251 x 352)
Inscribed l.c. *Falls of St Anthony/Mississippi River/W Carpenter/1861*   955.190.5

Chandler, Kenelm
(active 1784-1804)
Officer in 60th Regiment of Foot (Royal American); Barrack Master at Quebec from *c.* 1784-1804.

249 South East View of Port Talbot
w.c. over pencil on laid paper. 12 x 19 (305 x 482)
Inscribed verso *South East View of Port Talbot Septr. 1803. Dunwich–Middlesex*
Watermark: *J. Whatman*
Possibly the earliest view of the Talbot settlement; the first tree was cut in May 1803 and this w.c. shows Thomas Talbot's house on the hill.   959.121

249

Chandler

Chaplin, Millicent Mary
(active 1838-44)

Wife of Lieutenant-Colonel Thomas Chaplin of Coldstream Guards, stationed in Canada 1838-40. Painted watercolour landscapes of Ottawa area, Quebec, Maritimes and genre figure groups. Frequently copied works of fellow artists such as James Hope-Wallace (q.v.) and Henry William Barnard (q.v.).

250 Landing Place, Pictou
w.c. over pencil. 7 13/16 x 6 1/2 (198 x 165)
Inscribed l.l. *MMC 1841*; verso, title.
955.109.1

251 Pictou from the North East
w.c. 7 1/8 x 11 13/16 (181 x 300)
Inscribed l.l. *MMC/1841*; verso *Norway Point/Pictou from North East*; recto of old mount, title. 955.109.3

251

252 Pictou from the North West
w.c. over pencil. 8 1/4 x 11 3/4 (210 x 298)
Inscribed l.l. *MMC/1841*; verso *Pictou/N.
Scotia/from the North West* 955.109.4

253 Halifax from Unicorn Steamer
w.c. 5 x 11 1/2 (127 x 292)
Inscribed l.r. *MMC*; verso *Halifax/N.
Scotia/from Unicorn Steamer* 955.109.2

254 Saint John, New Brunswick
w.c. over pencil. 7 9/16 x 11 1/2 (192 x 292)
Inscribed verso *St. John's New
Brunswick–1842* 957.106.14

255 Fredericton
w.c. over pencil. 7 5/16 x 11 3/4 (186 x 298)
Inscribed l.l. *MMC/1842*; verso, title.
957.106.13

**256 Fishing Village in Gaspé Bay, St.
George's Cove**
w.c. over pencil. 7 9/16 x 11 3/4 (192 x 298)
Inscribed recto of mount, title.
The site is probably St. George, N.B.
955.109.5

257 Tadoussac
w.c. over pencil. 11 7/16 x 14 7/8 (290 x
378)
Inscribed l.l. *MMC/1841*; verso
*Tadousac–at the Mouth of the River
Saguenay/First Station of the Hudson's Bay
Company./July 24th* 955.109.6

257

Chaplin

258 Notre Dame Street, Montreal

w.c. over pencil. 7 5/8 x 11 7/8 (194 x 302)
Inscribed l.r. *MMC/1841*; verso, title.
Copy of an 1840 w.c. by H.W. Barnard; see
cat. no. 97.   957.106.15

259 Quebec Town on a River Bank

w.c. over pencil. 7 5/8 x 11 3/4 (194 x 298)
957.106.16

attributed to Millicent Mary Chaplin

260 Micmac Indian Figure Studies

w.c. over pencil. 10 1/2 x 16 3/4 (267 x 425)
Inscribed l.r. *Micmac Indians*
Similar figure studies by Mrs Chaplin are
in the PAC collection.
Gift of Mrs F. St. George Spendlove,
Toronto.   969.299.5

260

261 Indian Figure Studies
w.c. over pencil. 6 x 6 1/2 (152 x 165)
The construction of figures here more
stylized than those seen in signed Chaplin
watercolours. Possibly the original
composition by an unidentified artist
which Chaplin copied in an identical w.c.
(with added landscape) signed and dated
1839, in the PAC collection.
Gift of Mrs F. St. George Spendlove,
Toronto. 969.299.4

Churchill, Miss L.
(active 1873)

262 McKay's Mountain from Fort William
w.c. over pencil. 9 x 11 3/8 (229 x 289)
Inscribed l.l. *L. Churchill*; l.r. *McKays
Mountain from Fort William, 21 July 1873*
Gift of the Estate of Dr Clara C. Benson of
Port Hope through Mr V.B. Blake,
Executor. 965.41.1

Clementi, Reverend Vincent
(1812-1899)
Born in London, England, son of musician
Muzio Clementi. Attended Cambridge
University; ordained minister of Church of
England. Emigrated to Peterborough,
Ontario in 1853. Lived in Lakefield and
Peterborough. Exhibited sketches of
Canadian wild flowers at UCPE 1858;
drawing of natural history specimen
reproduced in *Canadian Illustrated News*,
16 Apr. 1881.

263 A Lumber Raft on a River
w.c. over pencil. 7 9/16 x 10 3/16 (192 x
259)
Inscribed l.r. *Rev: Vincent Clementi / Delt. 1866*
959.39.9

263

Cleveley, John, II
(1747-1786)

Born in Deptford, England, son of shipwright and marine painter John Cleveley. Studied under Paul Sandby (q.v.). Draughtsman with Sir Joseph Banks expedition to Orkneys, Hebrides and Iceland, 1772; and with Captain Constantine John Phipps expedition of 1773 in search of a northern route to India, but which only reached area north of Spitzbergen.

Engravings of the following views illustrate Captain Phipps' book *A Voyage Towards the North Pole Undertaken by His Majesty's Command 1773* (London 1774).

264 H.M.Ships "Racehorse" and "Carcass" at Anchor in an Ice Field and the Ships' Company Playing on the Ice on 31 July 1773

w.c., pen and ink. 14 1/2 x 18 3/8 (368 x 467)

Inscribed l.l. *Jno Cleveley Jun' Delin*
Watermark: *IV*, on laid paper.
A variant of this composition, signed and dated 1784, is in the V&A collection; another version, with figure changes, is in the Baldwin Collection, TPL.   962.65.5

265 H.M.Ships "Racehorse" and "Carcass" Lodged in the Ice and the Ships' Company Hauling Launches on 7 August 1773

w.c., pen and ink. 14 3/8 x 13 1/4 (365 x 463)

Inscribed l.l. *Jno Cleveley Jun Delin*.
Watermark: Crown and Lily over V̂ ⊃ L on laid paper.
A signed Cleveley w.c. of the same composition, with figure variations, is in the Baldwin Collection, TPL.   962.65.4

266 H.M.Ships "Racehorse" and "Carcass" Under Full Sail, Forcing Through the Ice on 10 August 1773

w.c., pen and ink. 14 7/16 x 18 3/16 (367 x 462)

Inscribed l.l. *Jno Cleveley Jun' Delin*
Watermark: Shield bearing Lily surmounted by Crown over finial V ⊃ on laid paper.   962.65.3

264

Clinton, Lieutenant-Colonel

A British officer who is said to have served in Canada in the 1830s.

267 Falls of Montmorency
w.c. 20 x 13 3/4 (254 x 349)
Inscribed, verso *Quebec from Montmorency*; and in a later hand *View of the Falls of Montmorenci by Lt. Col. Clinton of Ashley Clinton, Hants.* 968.251

Cochrane, T.?F.?
(active 1813)
Possibly Sir Alexander Forrester Inglis Cochrane (1758-1832), younger son of Thomas Cochrane, 8th Earl of Dundonald. Served in Royal Navy from early age; present at capture of Guadeloupe, January 1810, and appointed Governor of the island until 1814. In 1814 appointed to command of the North American station, especially in unsuccessful attempt against Baltimore and New Orleans. Returned to England at end of 1814; Commander-in-Chief at Plymouth, 1821. Died in Paris, 1822. This artist might also have been Sir Thomas John Cochrane (1789-1872), commander of frigate *Surprise* on coast of North America 1811-14 and 1820-24. He had served in West Indies until 1809.

268 Passaic Falls, New Jersey
w.c. 14 5/16 x 19 (363 x 482)
Inscribed verso of old mount *Vue de la Grande Chute de la riviere Passaic dans le New-Jersey, Etats Unis de l'Amerique. Dess. par T.F.*[initials unclear] *Cochrane, Avril 18, 1812, Gua . . .* [cut off]/*Guadeloupe 1813*
952.18.2

268

Cochrane, Vollie
(active 1875)
An unidentified copyist after Cornelius
Krieghoff (q.v.).

269 Habitant Farm in Winter
w.c., gouache, pencil, pen and ink.
20 15/16 x 27 (531 x 686)
Inscribed l.l. *Vollie Cochrane, 1875*
Copy of an 1853 oil painting by Cornelius
Krieghoff.   961.110.9

269

Cochrane

Cockburn, James Pattison
(1779-1847)

Said to have been born in New York.
Studied at Royal Military Academy,
Woolwich, England 1793-5. Posted to
Canada as Lieutenant-Colonel, 60th
Regiment, 1826-32. Director of Royal
Laboratory, Woolwich, 1838. Reached rank
of Major-General.

Known for his European and Canadian
topographical watercolour paintings.
Exhibited with the Norwich Society of
Artists, 1809. Wrote and illustrated books
on European travels which were published
in 1810, 1811, 1820, 1822 and 1823. His
description of Quebec scenery, *Quebec and
its environs* was published in Quebec in
1831, illustrated with eight etchings after
his watercolours. Twelve of his Canadian
views were published as aquatint
engravings in London, 1833. Exhibited
NAD 1836.

Note: The term *counter-impression* in the
following entries refers to faint outline
compositions often found on the old
mounts to which Cockburn's watercolours
were or are affixed. These faint imprints
are reverse impressions of the pen-and-ink
portions of Cockburn views, caused by
pressure of the original drawings against
the sheets of backing paper, resulting in the
printing of a 'ghost image'.

**270 Rapids on the Ste Anne's River,
Quebec**
brown wash. 15 1/2 x 22 3/8 (393 x 568)
Cockburn's pencil sketch of same site (Ste
Anne du Nord River) is in PAC coll.
950.224.7

270

271 View from Ste Anne's Mountain

w.c. over pencil. 12 3/8 x 19 1/8 (314 x 485)
Inscribed l.r. *Quebec from St. Ann Mountain,
1829 J C*; verso *View from St. Ann's Mountain
1829–J.C. Quebec*   942.48.99

272 House at Ste Anne de Beaupré

w.c. over pencil. 5 1/4 x 8 1/4 (133 x 210)
Inscribed verso *St. Ann–below Quebec–Jas.
Cockburn* (ink); *House at St. Ann–below
Quebec 1827* (pencil).   942.48.37

**273 Ruins of the Franciscan Monastery at
Château Richer**

w.c. over pencil. 3 3/8 x 4 3/4 (86 x 121)
Inscribed verso *Chateau Richer*   942.48.33

**274 Between L'Ange Gardien and Ste
Anne's**

w.c., pen and ink. 11 11/16 x 14 7/8 (297 x
377)
Inscribed recto of mount, title; verso *Sept,
1829*
Unfinished landscape in soft black pencil
on verso.   942.48.36

**275 Looking Down from the Bridge at the
Top of the Fall of Montmorency**

w.c., pen and ink. 11 x 18 7/8 (279 x 479)
Inscribed verso *Looking from the bridge to the
top of the Fall of Montmorency J.C. 1829*
942.48.41

276 The Bridge of Montmorency

w.c., pen and ink. 10 5/8 x 17 (270 x 432)
Inscribed verso *Bridge of Montmorency–
11 July 1829. J.C.*
Counter-impression on verso of mount.
942.48.42

**277 A Morning View of the Falls of
Montmorency**

w.c. 17 5/8 x 26 1/2 (448 x 673)
Inscribed l.l. *J. Cockburn*; verso *The Falls of
Montmorency at Quebec, Canada.
Morning–This Painting was executed expressly
for Wm. Beadon Esqr.–Barrister at Law, by Jas.
Cockburn, Colonel Royl. Arty–January 19th
1843. Time of day Morning.* Painted eleven
years after the artist's return to England.
959.159.1

**278 Bridge of Montmorency when it was
Broken**

w.c., pen and ink, over pencil. 11 1/8 x
18 5/8 (282 x 473)
Inscribed verso *Bridge of Montmorency when
it was broken 1829–J.C.*   942.48.40

279 The Winter Cone of Montmorency

w.c. over soft black pencil, scraping. 14 7/8
x 22 1/8 (377 x 561)
Inscribed verso of mount *The Winter Cone of
Montmorency of 1827–J.C.*   960.274

280 The Cone at Montmorency

w.c. over pencil. 14 5/8 x 18 5/8 (371 x 473)
Inscribed verso *The Cone at Montmorenci
1829 J Cockburn*   952.69.3

281 The Cone at Montmorency

w.c. over soft black pencil, scraping. 15 1/8
x 11 1/4 (384 x 565)
Inscribed verso *The Cone at Montmorenci
1829 J Cockburn–*   952.69.4

279

282 The Falls of Montmorency

w.c. over pencil. 11 11/16 x 19 15/16 (297 x 506)   949.39.6

283 Picnic at Montmorency

w.c. over pencil. 17 x 15 7/8 (432 x 657)
Inscribed verso *Falls of Montmorency-Quebec in the distance-J.C.*
A variant of the aquatint after Cockburn published by Ackermann & Co., London 1833.   940.27.2

284 Wayside Cross Near Beauport

w.c. over pencil. 3 3/8 x 4 9.16 (86 x 116)
Inscribed verso *near Beauport/Oct 18, 1829*
942.48.43

285 Village of Charlesbourg

w.c., pen and ink over pencil. 10 1/2 x 14 1/2 (267 x 368)
Inscribed verso *Village of Charlesbourg near Quebec/15 June 1830/J.C.*   942.48.38

286 Village of Charlesbourg

w.c., pen and ink. 9 3/4 x 13 1/2 (248 x 343)
Inscribed verso *Village of Charlebourgh/15th June 1830/J.C.*
Counter-impression on verso of mount.
942.48.39

286

287 Cape Diamond from Lauzon
w.c. over pencil. 16 3/16 x 25 1/4 (411 x
641)   953.131.4

287

Cockburn

288 From the Seigniory of Lauzon Looking Towards the River

w.c., pen and ink, over pencil. 12 7/16 x 19 1/4 (316 x 389)
Inscribed l.r. *from Sir John Caldwell's, Quebec*
The Seigniory of Lauzon was the estate of Sir John Caldwell (1775-1842) at this period. 942.48.98

289 The Artist Sketching Quebec from Pointe Lévis

w.c., touches of gouache, over pencil. 16 x 25 3/16 (406 x 640)
Preparatory painting for an aquatint engraving published by Ackermann & Co., London 1833. 953.131.2

289

Cockburn

290 Quebec from Pointe Lévis

w.c. over pencil. 12 7/8 x 19 1/2 (327 x 495)

Inscribed l.c. *Quebec*; u.r. skyline *St. Charles River*; u.l. skyline *Citadel* 942.48.50

291 Cape Diamond from Pointe Lévis Side

w.c. over pencil. 12 13/16 x 19 1/2 (325 x 495)

Inscribed l.c. *Quebec from Point Levy side* 942.48.55

292 Quebec from Mr Davidson's at Pointe Lévis

w.c. over pencil. 11 1/8 x 19 5/16 (282 x 490)

Inscribed l.r. *Quebec from J. Davidson's, Point Levy*; verso *Quebec from Mr. Davidson's at Point Levy–1829. J.C*

Cockburn described the view from Mr. Davidson's villa in the booklet *Quebec and its environs*, Quebec 1831. 942.48.51

293 Quebec from the Top of the Hill on the Lévis Side

w.c., pen and ink over pencil. 10 1/8 x 17 7/8 (257 x 454)

Inscribed verso *Quebec from the top of the Hill opposite on the Po*[int Lévis Side] *Oct. 8th 1829. J.C* 942.48.54

294 Micmac Indians at Pointe Lévis

w.c. over pencil. 10 x 14 (254 x 355)

Inscribed verso *Micmac Indians at Point Levi, 1829. J. Cockburn* 942.48.52

295 Pointe Lévis

w.c. over pencil. 10 1/2 x 18 11/16 (267 x 474)

Inscribed on tavern sign *F COTE TAVARN HOUSE* 942.48.53

296 Quebec from the road above the St. Charles River Basin

w.c. over pencil. 6 1/8 x 9 1/2 -155 x 241)

Inscribed verso *Quebec from above Bay realle. Sept. 20th 1830 Jas. Cockburn* 942.48.58

297 River St. Charles from Dorchester Bridge

w.c. 5 1/4 x 8 1/4 (133 x 209)

Inscribed verso *River St. Charles from Dorchester Bridge Quebec–June 8th. 1830/Jas. Cockburn* 942.48.31

298 Quebec from Dorchester Bridge

w.c. over pencil. 14 1/2 x 20 3/8 (368 x 517)

Inscribed verso *Quebec from Dorchester Bridge–J. Cockburn*

Watermark: Shield bearing Lily surmounted by Crown, on laid paper. 952.69.1

299 Quebec Seen from the East Bank of the St. Charles River

w.c., touches of gouache, over pencil. 17 7/16 x 26 3/8 (443 x 670) 953.131.6

300 The Citadel from the Ice Bridge of 1830

w.c. 12 x 16 11/16 (305 x 424)

Inscribed verso *Citadel of Quebec from the Pont formed in the year 1830–J. Cockburn R.A.* 949.39.10

301 Quebec from the Ice Bridge of 1830

w.c. over pencil. 12 x 17 (305 x 432)

Inscribed on shanty sign *TAVARN KEEPER*: verso *Quebec from the Pont of 1830 J. Cockburn* 952.69.2

302 Village of Jeune Lorette, a Huron Settlement Near Quebec

w.c. over pencil. 17 1/4 x 26 1/8 (438 x 663) 953.131.5

302

303 Village of Indian Lorette

w.c. over pencil. 11 13/16 x 19 1/4 (300 x 489)

Inscribed l.r. *Indian Lorette J.C.*; verso *Village of Indian Lorette. 1829. J.C.*   942.48.30

304 Marchmont from the Plains of Abraham

w.c. over pencil. 6 5/8 x 9 3/4 (168 x 247)

Inscribed verso *Marchmont from the Plains of Abraham Quebec J Cockburn*

The house named Marchmont was built for Sir John Harvey (1778-1852), probably *c.*1812.   942.48.64

305 Looking Towards the Citadel from the Plains of Abraham

w.c., pen and ink over pencil. 13 5/16 x 15 1/8 (338 x 384)

Inscribed l.l. *From the Plains d'Abraham*; verso *Looking towards the Citadel from the Pla[ins of Abraham] & a road going down to Campbells ship ya[rd].*   942.48.63

306 View from One of Percival's Falling Inclines

w.c. over pencil. 13 1/8 x 19 (333 x 482)

Inscribed l.l. *From Percival's Incline. Wolfes Cove*; u.l. to r. *Heights of Abraham Citadel St. Lawrence*; verso *From one of Percival's falling–Quebec–1828. J.C.*

View taken from the Spencer Wood property, owned by the Hon. Michael Henry Percival from 1815 until 1835.
942.48.48

307 Cape Diamond and Wolfe's Cove from Pointe à Pizeau

w.c. over pencil. 17 1/2 x 16 3/8 (444 x 670)

A variant of this w.c. (with added figures) was engraved in aquatint and published by Ackermann & Co., London 1833.
940x27.1

308 Wolfe's Cove Near Quebec

w.c. over pencil. 3 3/8 x 4 5/8 (86 x 117)
942.48.47

309 Wolfe's Cove

w.c. over pencil. 5 7/16 x 9 1/2 (138 x 241)

Inscribed verso *Wolfe's Cove, 18th Sept. 1834. Jas. Cockburn* [in ink]; *Wolfe's Cove, 18th Sept. 1830* [in pencil].   942.48.49

310 Wolfe's Cove

w.c. over pencil. 6 x 9 1/2 (152 x 241)

Inscribed verso *A Cove, Quebec. Jas. Cockburn*
942.48.46

311 Emily Montague's House at Sillery Cove

w.c., pen and ink. 9 x 13 1/8 (228 x 333)

Inscribed verso *Emily Montague's House at Sillery Cove–Oct 29th 1829. J.C.*

Emily Montague was the nom-de-plume of Frances Moore Brooke (1724-89), author of *The History of Emily Montague*, London, 1769. Her husband was garrison chaplain in Quebec 1760-68, living at Quebec and Sillery.   942.48.34

312 The Cove, Quebec

w.c. over pencil. 6 x 9 7/16 (152 x 239)

Inscribed verso *Cove, Quebec–Jas. Cockburn*
951.82.2

313 Country Road Near Quebec *(recto)*
View from 8 Miles' Point, Quebec *(verso)*

w.c. over pencil (recto); pencil and brown wash (verso). 4 3/8 x 6 1/16 (111 x 154)

Inscribed verso *from 8 miles' point*; recto of mount *Scene near Quebec*   942.48.45

314 Entrance to the Road on the Ice at Carouge

w.c. over pencil. 6 x 9 3/8 (152 x 238)

Inscribed verso *Entrance to the road on the Ice at Carouge–March 4th. 1830. J.C./John Cockburn in his Great Coat–a ship wrecked in the distance.*

The figure referred to is the artist's son, John Henry Cockburn, who was stationed in Canada at this time. See also cat. no. 354.
942.48.101

315 Ruins of the Church at St. Augustin de Quebec

w.c. over pencil. 5 1/4 x 8 1/4 (133 x 209)

Inscribed verso *Ruins of St. Augustin Church near Quebec–1827*   942.48.44

316 Champlain Street, Lower Town, Quebec

w.c. over pencil. 6 x 9 3/8 (152 x 238)

Inscribed verso *Part of the lower Town under the Citadel–near this spot Genl. Montgomery the American General, was killed–J.C*   942.48.92

317 Lower Town Wharves

w.c. over pencil. 6 x 9 3/8 (152 x 238)

Inscribed on sign on building *J SIMSON*; verso *Lower Town–Quebec/Jas. Cockburn*
942.48.91

Detail of 317

Cockburn

317

Cockburn

318 Lower Town Wharf and Shipyards
w.c. over pencil. 6 x 9 7/16 (152 x 239)
Inscribed on sign on building *SHIP
BUILDING*; verso *Lower Town-Quebec/Jas.
Cockburn* 951.82.3

318

319 Champlain Street, Looking Toward the Stairs to Upper Town

w.c. over pencil. 6 x 9 3/8 (152 x 238)
Inscribed verso *Cul de Sac, Quebec/Jas. Cockburn/8th Oct 1830*   942.48.94

320 Cul-de-Sac

w.c., pen and ink. 10 1/2 x 14 5/8 (266 x 371)
Inscribed on sign on building *LONDON COFFEE HOUSE*; on fence, handbill dated *August 9th 1830*; verso *Cul de Sac Quebec March 20th 1830. J.C. The snow fell from the Kings . . .* [illegible word] *when drawing.*
Counter-impression on verso of mount.
The London Coffee House is the Chevalier House, now restored.   942.48.93

321 Winter Scene from King's Wharf

w.c. over pencil. 10 1/4 x 14 5/8 (260 x 371)
Inscribed verso *Winter Scene, Quebec, from King's Wharf. J.C. Feby 16th. 1830*
942.48.62

322 The Citadel from King's Quay

w.c. over pencil. 6 x 9 3/8 (152 x 238)
Inscribed verso *Citadel of Quebec from King's Quay J. Cockburn*   953.163.3

323 Hope Gate

w.c., pencil, pen and ink. 3 3/4 x 5 5/8 (95 x 143)
Inscribed verso *Hope Gate, Quebec*   942.48.77

324 Hope Gate

w.c. over pencil. 6 x 9 3/8 (152 x 238)
Inscribed verso *Hope Gate, Quebec–J. Cockburn*   953.183.2

325 Prescott Gate

w.c. over pencil. 6 x 9 3/8 (152 x 238)
Inscribed verso *Prescott Gate Que*[bec]/
J Cockb[urn]   953.183.3

325

Cockburn

326 St. John's Gate
w.c. over pencil. 6 x 9 3/8 (152 x 238)
Inscribed verso *St. Johns Gate Quebec*
J Cockburn   953.183.1

326

Cockburn

327 The Esplanade from the Ramparts
w.c. over pencil. 4 1/2 x 7 1/2 (114 x 191)
Inscribed verso *The Esplanade from the Ramparts J Cockburn*
Congrégation church included in view.
942.48.66

327

Cockburn

328 National School from the Ramparts

w.c., pen and ink, over pencil. 12 1/8 x 18 13/16 (308 x 478)

Inscribed on school sign *NATIONAL SCHOOL/REPOSITORY of BIBLES and other BOOKS and TRACTS of/the SOCIETY for promoting CHRISTIAN KNOWLEDGE;* verso *The National School from the Ramparts-Quebec June 12th-1819-J.C.* Counter-impression on verso of mount. Congrégation church included in view. 942.48.71

329 The Esplanade from the Engineer's Office

w.c., pen and ink. 11 1/8 x 18 15/16 (282 x 481)

Inscribed verso *The Esplanade of Quebec from the Engineer's Office-June 18th 1829. J.C.* Watermark: Plumed Crown over I&M and cut date. Counter-impression on verso of mount.   942.48.65

330 The Esplanade from the Ursuline Bastion

w.c., pen and ink. 10 3/8 x 18 1/2 (263 x 470)

Inscribed verso *The Esplanade from Ursuline Bastion-1829. J.C.*   942.48.69

331 The Esplanade from the Ursuline Bastion

w.c., pen and ink over pencil. 10 x 18 1/2 (254 x 470)

Inscribed verso *The Esplanade from the Ursuline Bastion-June 13th, 1829. J.C* Counter-impression on verso of mount. Cricket game included in view.   942.48.68

332 From the Pump on the Esplanade

w.c., pen and ink, over pencil. 10 9/16 x 18 3/4 (268 x 476)

Inscribed verso *From the Pump on the Esplanade-Quebec, June 13th-1829. J.C.* Counter-impression on verso of mount. 942.48.70

333 Parliament and Château from the Grand Battery

w.c., pen and ink, over pencil. 10 5/8 x 19 (270 x 482)

Inscribed verso *The Parliament and Chateau from the Grand Battery-13 July-1829. J.C.* Watermark: Plumed Crown.   942.48.74

333

334 The Château St. Louis Looking West Towards the Citadel
w.c., pen and ink. 11 x 18 3/4 (279 x 476)
Inscribed verso *Chateau St. Louis–26th. June 1829. J.C. Quebec*
Counter-impression on verso of mount.
942.48.87

334

Cockburn

335 The Château St. Louis Looking East Towards the St. Charles River

w.c., pen and ink. 11 7/8 x 18 7/16 (301 x 468)
Inscribed verso *Chateau St. Louis–Quebec 26 June 1829. J.C.*
Counter-impression on verso of mount. 942.48.86

336 The Montcalm and Wolfe Monument

w.c., pen and ink. 9 5/8 x 14 3/8 (244 x 365)

Inscribed verso *Wolf Monument–Quebec–July 1829 J.C*
Counter-impression on verso of mount. 942.48.76

337 Place d'Armes, Quebec

w.c., pen and ink. 11 7/8 x 18 13/16 (301 x 478)
Inscribed verso *Quebec–Place darmes. 1829. J.C.*; on handbill on pillar *WATERLOO . . . STEAM BOAT . . . GARRISON AMATEURS . . . POOR CONTLUMOR . . . MILLER and his MEN* [a performance by the garrison's theatrical group]. 942.48.73

338 St. Louis Street from the Gate

w.c., pen and ink. 9 7/8 x 18 7/8 (251 x 479)
Inscribed verso *St. Louis Street from the Gate–Quebec–18 June 1829. J.C.*
Counter-impression on mount.   942.48.84

339 Chief Justice Sewell's House and the St. Louis Gate

w.c., pen and ink. 13 x 18 5/8 (330 x 473)
Inscribed verso *Justice Sewell's house and St. Louis Gate–19th June. Quebec–1829. J.C.*
Shows house at 87 St. Louis Street, built 1803-4 for Jonathan Sewell (1766-1839), Attorney General and Chief Justice of Lower Canada 1808-38.
Counter-impression on verso of mount. 942.48.85

339

340 St. Louis Street

w.c. over pencil. 11 3/16 x 16 9/16 (284 x 421)

Inscribed verso *St. Louis St. July 1st. 1830 J C*   942.48.83

341 St. Louis Street

w.c., pen and ink, over pencil. 10 x 14 1/2 (254 x 368)

Inscribed on two signs over doorways *A.B. ROBERTS* and *DUBBINS*; verso *St. Louis Street, May 28th. 1830 J.C.*   942.48.82

342 Quebec from St. Louis Road

w.c. over pencil. 11 3/16 x 17 1/4 (284 x 438)

Inscribed verso *Quebec from St. Louis' Road/July 1st, 1830 J.C.*   942.48.56

343 Hollands' Burial Ground, Ste Foy

w.c. over pencil. 3 7/16 x 4 9/16 (87 x 116)

Inscribed verso *Hollands' Burial Ground/St Foy/18 Oct 1829*   942.48.61

344 The Seminary, Quebec

w.c. over pencil. 6 x 9 1/2 (152 x 241)

Inscribed verso *Seminary at Quebec. Jas. Cockburn*   942.48.79

344

Cockburn

345 Jesuit Barrack and Quebec Market Place

w.c., pen and ink over pencil. 13 1/8 x
18 5/8 (333 x 473)
Inscribed verso *Jesuit Barrack and Quebec Market Place 1829 J.C.* (Area now occupied by the Hotel de Ville.)
Counter-impression on verso of mount.
942.48.72

345

Cockburn

346 Fabrique Street
w.c., pen and ink. 10 3/8 x 14 1/2 (263 x 368)
Inscribed verso *Fabrique Street, Quebec April 21st. 1830 J. Cockburn*
Counter-impression on verso of mount. 942.48.90

346

Cockburn

347 Ste Anne Street
w.c., pen and ink. 9 3/4 x 14 3/8 (248 x 365)
Presbyterian church included in view.
Counter-impression on verso of mount.
942.48.88

348 Ste Anne Street
w.c., pen and ink. 10 1/4 x 13 1/2 (260 x 343)
Presbyterian church included in view.
Counter-impression on verso of mount.
942.48.89

349 Ste Hélène Street, now McMahon Street
w.c., pen and ink. 10 3/8 x 14 3/8 (263 x 365)
Inscribed verso *Quebec, 3d April 1830*; recto of mount, *Near Palace Street.*
Counter-impression on verso of mount.
942.48.95

350 St. Stanislas Street
w.c., pen and ink. 10 1/2 x 14 1/2 (267 x 368)
Inscribed verso *Quebec, 3rd April 1830*
Trinity Anglican Chapel included in view.
Counter-impression on verso of mount.
942.48.97

350

Cockburn

351 Ste Anne Street Near the English Church

w.c. over pencil. 8 3/8 x 6 (217 x 152)
Inscribed verso *Near the Church. Quebec Jas. Cockburn* 942.48.78

352 Artillery Barracks

w.c. over pencil. 6 x 9 3/8 (152 x 238)
Inscribed verso *The building on the left is the dauphine Barracks where the officers of artillery live on left–The front is the Comd. officers quarters & their adjutant. The Men's continue further to the right. The distance is the country thro' which the St. Charles river flows–and Artillery Barracks, Quebec. Augt. 1831 J.C. John & his son in the Garden.* This refers to the artist's son, John Henry Cockburn, who was serving in Quebec at this time, and to his grandson.
See also cat. no. 314. 960x276.18

353 Entrance to the Artillery Barrack

w.c., pen and ink over pencil. 10 7/16 x 14 1/2 (265 x 368)
Inscribed verso *Entrance into the Artillery Barrack yard at Quebec–5th. April–1830 J.C* Counter-impression on verso of mount. 942.48.67

354 Artillery Barracks from St. John's Bastion

w.c., pen and ink. 10 7/16 x 14 1/2 (265 x 368)
Inscribed verso *Artillery Barracks Quebec from St. John's Bastion–J.C.–May 10th. 1830* Counter-impression on verso of mount. 942.48.100

354

355 Quebec from St. John's Bastion
w.c., pen and ink. 4 5/8 x 7 5/8 (117 x 193)
Preliminary sketch for cat. no. 375.
942.48.96

356 The Suburb of St. John
w.c. over pencil. 11 1/2 x 18 3/4 (292 x 476)
Inscribed on house sign *GOOD GINGER
BEER . . . T.G.M.*; verso *Suburb of St. John,
Quebec, July 1830*   942.48.60

**357 Montcalm's House Opposite the
Ramparts**
w.c., pen and ink. 10 1/8 x 17 5/8 (257 x
448)
Inscribed verso *Montcalm's House–
Quebec–1829–J.C.*
Shows houses, 45-49 des Remparts, where
the French commander lived in 1758.
Counter-impression on verso of mount.
942.48.81

358 Montcalm's House from the Battery
w.c., pen and ink, over pencil. 10 1/8 x
14 5/8 (257 x 371)
Inscribed verso *Montcalms House from the
Battery March 5th 1830 J.C.* (see cat. no. 357).
Counter-impression on verso of mount.
942.48.80

359 Hôtel Dieu from the Battery
w.c., pen and ink. 10 3/8 x 14 1/2 (263 x
368)
Inscribed verso *Hotel Dieu from the Battery
opposite Montcalm's House March 5th 1830
J.C. Quebec*
Counter-impression on verso of mount.
942.48.75

360 The Manor House in St. Roch Suburb
w.c., pen and ink. 11 13/16 x 17 3/4 (300 x
451)
Inscribed verso *The Manor house in St.
Roche's Suburb, Quebec July 15th 1829. J.C.*;
l.r. *Manor House all burnt down*   942.48.59

361 General Hospital from Lind's Lane
w.c., pen and ink over pencil. 12 1/4 x
18 5/8 (311 x 473)
Inscribed lower recto & verso *General
Hospital from Linds Lane, 1829. J.C.*
942.48.57

362 Iron Foundry at St. Maurice
w.c. over pencil. 6 1/8 x 9 5/8 (155 x 244)
Inscribed verso *Iron Foundry at St.
Maurice/J.P. Cockburn*   942.48.35

363 Old French Fort at Chambly
w.c. over pencil. 5 1/4 x 8 5/16 (133 x 211)
Inscribed verso *Old French Fort at
Chambly/Canada/Jas. Cockburn*   954.173.1

364 St. Helen's Island
w.c., pen and ink over pencil. 11 3/8 x
18 15/16 (289 x 481)   942.48.29

365 Longueuil from St. Helen's Island
w.c., pen and ink over pencil. 12 5/8 x
18 1/16 (320 x 459)
Inscribed verso *Longueuil from St. Helen*
942.48.28

366 Montreal Waterfront with Lumber Rafts
w.c. over pencil. 10 7/16 x 18 5/8 (265 x 473)
942.48.27

367 Woodland Scene in Winter with Sleigh
w.c., pen and ink over pencil. 9 5/8 x 12 7/8
(244 x 327)
Inscribed verso *Wood Scene near . . .* [cut off]
942.48.32

QUEBEC CITY ALBUM I

Ten watercolour views of Quebec City
mounted and bound into an album titled
CANADA. COCKBURN DRAWINGS.

**368 Looking Up Mountain Street Towards
Prescott Gate**
w.c., pen and ink, over pencil. 10 1/8 x
14 3/8 (257 x 365) (sight)
Inscribed verso *Looking up Mountain Street
Quebec March 5th 1830. J.C*
Counter-impression of cat. no. 368 on verso
of mount.   951x205.1

**369 Neptune Inn from the Foot of Mountain
Street**
w.c., pen and ink, over pencil. 10 x 14 1/2
(254 x 368) (sight)
Inscribed verso *Neptune Inn from the foot of
Mountain Street–Feby. 23d. 1830 J.C.*; on shop
signs & poster in view, l. to r. *. . . YSE* & CO.
*/HIPSON/[NE]PTUNE INN . . .
STRICKLAND/GARRISON THEATRE . . .
CHARLES XII . . . MY LANDLADYS . . .*
Counter-impression of variant view of
Neptune Inn on verso of mount.   951x205.2

**370 Lower Market with Notre Dame des
Victoires Church**
w.c., pen and ink, over pencil. 10 1/4 x
13 1/8 (260 x 333) (sight)
Inscribed on mount *Lower Market, Winter 1830*
Counter-impression of cat. no. 382 on verso
of mount.   951x205.3

371 Hôtel Dieu from St. John Street

w.c., pen and ink over pencil. 10 x 14 1/2
(254 x 362) (sight)
Inscribed on mount, title.
Counter-impression of cat. no. 372 on verso
of mount.   951x205.4

372 Artist Sketching above the Artillery Barracks

w.c., pen and ink over pencil. 13 1/2 x
19 1/8 (343 x 485) (sight)
Inscribed verso *The Artillery barrack and Mess Room-7 July 1829-J.C.*
Counter-impression of variant artillery
barrack view on verso of mount.   951x205.5

373 Gun Drill, Artillery Barrack Yard

w.c., pen and ink over pencil. 11 x 15 1/8
(279 x 384) (sight)
Inscribed on mount *Artillery Barrack Yard 1829.*
Counter-impression of barrack gate
on verso of mount.   951x205.6

374 Inside Barracks Yard

w.c., pen and ink over pencil. 13 3/4 x
18 1/2 (349 x 470) (sight)
Inscribed on mount, title.
Counter-impression of cat. no. 375 on verso of
mount.   951x205.7

375 View from St. John's Bastion

w.c., pen and ink, over pencil. 12 1/2 x
19 1/8 (317 x 485) (sight)
Inscribed on mount *From St. Johns' Bastion 13
June 1829*
Counter-impression of cat. no. 376 on verso
of mount. See cat. no. 355 for preliminary
sketch of this view.   951x205.8

376 Street in Suburb of St. Roch

w.c., pen and ink, over pencil. 10 1/2 x
14 1/2 (267 x 368) (sight)
Inscribed on mount, title and *Quebec, 10 June
1830*
Counter-impression of cat. no. 377 on verso
of mount.   951x205.9

377 Suburb of St. John

w.c., pen and ink over pencil. 10 1/4 x
14 5/8 (260 x 371) (sight)
Inscribed on shop sign, l.c. *MINERAL
WATER*; on mount, title.   952x205.10

QUEBEC CITY ALBUM II

Ten watercolour views of Quebec City
mounted and bound into an album titled
CANADA. COCKBURN DRAWINGS

**378 From Buade Street Looking Toward
Grand Battery, July 1830**

w.c., pen and ink over pencil. 10 x 13 (254 x
330) (sight)
Inscribed verso and on mount, title.
Counter-impression of cat. no. 371 on verso
of mount.   951x205.11

379 St. John Street, Quebec 1829

w.c., pen and ink over pencil. 12 x 18 (305 x
457) (sight)
Inscribed on mount, title.
Counter-impression of figures on verso of
mount.   951x205.12

**380 View of the Esplanade, Congrégation
Church and National School from the
Ursuline Bastion, Quebec**

w.c., pen and ink, over pencil. 12 1/2 x
19 1/4 (317 x 489) (sight)
Inscribed verso *From the Ursuline Bastion
Quebec 1829 J.C.*
Counter-impression of street scene on verso
of mount.   951x205.13

381 St. Peter Street

w.c., pen and ink over pencil. 13 1/2 x
18 1/2 (343 x 470) (sight)
Inscribed l.c. *St. Peter Street/Quebec/1829*
Counter-impression of cat. no. 379 on verso
of mount.   951x205.14

381

382 Cul-de-Sac, Looking Toward the Château

w.c., pen and ink. 14 1/4 x 10 1/4 (362 x 260) (sight)

Inscribed on shop signs, l. to r. *[ANT]HONY BISSON/CHANDLER/GROCERY STORE/WINE VAULTS*; verso *Cul-de-Sac, looking toward the Chateau, March 29, 1830, J.C.* Counter-impression of street scene looking towards stairs to Upper Town on verso of mount.   951x205.15

382

Cockburn

383 Looking to the French Cathedral and Jesuit Barrack

w.c., pen and ink. 10 1/2 x 14 1/2 (267 x 368) (sight)

Inscribed verso, title and *Quebec. May 11th 1830. J.C.*; mount *Buade Street*

Counter-impression of variant of cat. no. 384 on verso of mount. 951x205.16

384 St. John Street from the Corner of Palace Street

w.c., pen and ink over pencil. 10 1/4 x 14 1/2 (260 x 368) (sight)

Inscribed verso, title and *Quebec. May 1830. J.C.*; shop signs in view, l. to r. *H.M. DEFOY Notaire Public/MARCOUX FURRIER/ THOS. HOBBS/JAS. WOLF/VAL . . . INN*

Counter-impression of street scene on verso of mount. 951x205.17

384

385 Ste Famille Street with a Funeral Procession

w.c., pen and ink. 10 5/8 x 14 1/4 (270 x 362) (sight)
Inscribed on mount *Hope Street*.
Counter-impression of soldiers outside building on verso of mount. 951x205.18

385

Cockburn

386 The English Church from the Ursuline Convent

w.c., pen and ink over pencil. 10 1/8 x 13 3/4 (257 x 349) (sight)
Inscribed verso *The English Church from the Ursuline Convent, March 30th 1830. J.C.;* mount *Rue du Parloir. English Cathedral.* Counter-impression of street scene on verso of mount.   951x205.19

387 Monument to Wolfe and Montcalm

w.c., pen and ink over pencil. 9 1/2 x 14 1/4 (241 x 362) (sight)
Inscribed verso *Monument to Wolf and Montcalm. 1829. J.C.* Counter-impression of two Quebec gates on verso of mount.   951x205.20

QUEBEC ALBUM III

The following 16 watercolour views of the Quebec City area were once mounted in an album titled *American Portfolio No. II* and inscribed *J.C. 1827* inside the album cover.

388 Quebec from the Micmac Encampment

w.c. over soft pencil on prepared ground. 11 15/16 x 20 7/16 (303 x 519)
The sources of the Micmac composition are discussed under cat. no. 139.   955.20.1

389 Quebec from the River

w.c. over soft pencil on prepared ground. 12 3/8 x 20 13/16 (314 x 529)   955.20.2

390 Quebec from the River

w.c., pencil, on prepared ground. 12 1/2 x 20 5/8 (317 x 524)   955.20.3

391 Quebec from Cape Diamond Harbour

w.c. over pencil on prepared ground. 12 3/4 x 20 7/8 (324 x 530)   955.20.4

392 Quebec from the Pointe Lévis Side

w.c., pencil on prepared ground. 12 1/2 x 20 1/4 (317 x 514)   955.20.5

393 Quebec from Cliff Cottage, Pointe Lévis

w.c. over pencil on prepared ground. 12 3/4 x 20 3/4 (324 x 527)   955.20.6

394 Cape Diamond from Spencer Wood

w.c. over pencil on prepared ground. 12 3/8 x 20 13/16 (314 x 529)   955.20.7

395 Quebec from Lauzon

w.c. over pencil on prepared ground. 12 9/16 x 20 3/4 (319 x 527)   955.20.8

396 Quebec from Sillery Cove

w.c., touches of gouache, over pencil on prepared ground. 9 x 12 7/8 (229 x 327) 955.20.9

397 The Church of Château Richer

w.c., touches of gouache, pen and ink over soft black pencil on prepared ground. 9 3/8 x 13 (251 x 330)   955.20.10

397

398 Montmorency Falls
w.c., pen and ink over pencil on prepared ground. 12 3/4 x 10 1/2 (324 x 267)
955.20.11

399 Wolfe's Cove
w.c., pencil on prepared ground. 10 3/16 x 12 3/4 (259 x 324)   955.20.12

400 Wolfe's Cove
w.c. over pencil on prepared ground.
10 1/8 x 12 3/4 (257 x 324)   955.20.13

401 The Cone at Montmorency
w.c. over pencil. 10 7/8 x 15 (276 x 381)
955.20.14

401

Cockburn

402 The Cone at Montmorency
w.c., touches of gouache over pencil.
20 5/16 x 14 5/8 (262 x 371)
955.20.15

403 The Cone at Montmorency
w.c. over pencil on prepared ground. 13 x
20 5/8 (330 x 523)   955.20.16

end of albums

404 Grenville Camp, Ottawa River
brown wash. 5 1/4 x 8 5/16 (133 x 211)
Inscribed verso *Grenville Camp Ottawa 1827*
J P Cockburn
Grenville is situated on the Quebec side of
the Ottawa River, opposite Hawkesbury, at
the head of the Long Sault Rapids. A canal
was built here between 1821 and 1828 to
create a navigable channel.   954.173.2

404

405 Bridge over the Chaudière, Ottawa
w.c. over pencil. 12 x 19 1/2 (305 x 495)
Inscribed verso, title. 942.48.25

406 Falls of the Chaudière, Ottawa
w.c. over pencil. 13 7/16 x 19 13/16 (341 x
503)
Inscribed verso *Falls of the Chaudiere-
Ottawa Jas. Cockburn* 942.48.26

**407 The Little Kettle of the Chaudière,
Ottawa**
brown wash over pencil. 13 1/4 x 20 7/8
(336 x 530)
Inscribed verso *The little kettle of the
Chaudiere, Ottawa, Augt. 1827. Jas Cockburn*
950.224.9

**408 Entrance of the Rideau Canal, Ottawa
River**
brown wash over pencil. 5 1/4 x 8 5/16
(133 x 211)
Inscribed verso *Entrance of Rideau Canal,
Ottawa River, Canada* 956.26.1

408

Cockburn

409 Rideau River from Long Island
w.c. over pencil. 4 7/8 x 9 1/2 (124 x 241)
Inscribed verso *Rideau from Long
Island–18th Augt. 1830. Jas. Cockburn* and
From the dam at Long Island, 18th Aug. 1830
942.48.12

410 Long Island on the Rideau River
w.c., pen and ink. 14 1/4 x 10 5/8 (362 x
270)   942.48.11

**411 Indian Hunters Between Merrickville
and Edmonds Rapids, Rideau River**
w.c. over pencil. 6 1/16 x 9 1/2 (154 x 241)
Inscribed verso *Indian Hunters between
Meyreck Mills and Edmonds Rapids–Rideau.
19th Augt. 1830 Jas. Cockburn.*   942.48.13

412 On the Rideau
w.c. over pencil. 11 3/16 x 9 1/8 (284 x 232)
942.48.14

412

Cockburn

413 Maitland's Rapids, Rideau River
w.c. 6 x 9 9/16 (152 x 243)
Inscribed verso *Maitlands' Rapids, Rideau,*
Jas. Cockburn/19 Augt. 1830.
P. and J. Maitland owned land at the dam
site on the northern curve of the Rideau
river half way between Merrickville and
Smiths Falls.   942.48.10

414 Captain Cole's House, the Isthmus,
Rideau Lakes
w.c. 3 9/16 x 4 3/4 (91 x 121)
Inscribed verso *Captn. Cole's House, the*
Isthmus/Jas. Cockburn
The Isthmus, later called Newboro, was
one of the work centres in the building of
this portion of the Rideau waterway.
Captain Cole, R.E., was a regimental officer
working on the canal at Newboro in 1829.
942.48.8

415 Davies Mills, Lake Opinicon, Rideau
Lakes
w.c. over pencil. 4 x 8 1/4 (101 x 209)
Inscribed verso *Davies Mills-Lake Opinicon.*
Rideau/Jas. Cockburn   942.48.9

416 Brewer's Mills, Cataraqui River
w.c., pen and ink. 9 5/8 x 13 3/8 (244 x
340)
Inscribed verso *Brewer's Mills-Rideau*
1831. J.C.   942.48.7

416

417 Brockville, Upper Canada
w.c. over pencil. 4 7/8 x 8 1/16 (124 x 205)
Inscribed verso *Brockville, U. Canada-Jas.*
Cockburn   942.48.23

417

Cockburn

418 The Thousand Islands
w.c. over pencil. 4 1/2 x 7 1/8 (114 x 181)
Inscribed verso *Thousand Islands. U.*
Canada/Jas. Cockburn   942.48.24

419 Kingston Waterfront
w.c. over pencil. 2 3/4 x 5 (70 x 127)
Inscribed verso *Kingston, Upper Canada–Jas.*
Cockburn   942.48.20

420 Kingston: View from Ontario and
Queen Streets
w.c., pen and ink. 11 1/4 x 18 3/4 (286 x
476)
Inscribed verso *Kingston, July 25th*
1829–J.C.
Counter-impression on verso of mount.
942.48.19

421 Kingston from Cataraqui Bridge
w.c. over pencil. 6 x 9 1/2 (152 x 241)
Inscribed verso *Kingston from the*
bridge–Augt. 1830–J.C.
View to south-west, from Tête de Pont
Barracks to Mississauga Point.   951.82.1

421

Cockburn

422 Artillery Barrack Yard, Kingston
w.c. over pencil. 5 1/8 x 8 1/8 (130 x 206)
Inscribed verso *Artillery Barrack
yard/Kingston, Augt. 31st 1830*   942.48.21

**423 Fort Henry, Kingston, and Barriefield
Village from the North**
w.c., pen and ink over pencil. 10 3/4 x
19 5/16 (273 x 490)
Inscribed verso *Fort Henry, July 1830. J.C.*
942.48.22

424 Steamship Landing, Bay of Quinte
w.c. over pencil. 5 x 9 1/2 (127 x 241)
Inscribed l.l. *Johanasburgh*; verso
Johanasburgh-Bay of Quinte-Jas. Cockburn
942.48.17

425 Bath, Bay of Quinte
w.c. over pencil. 3 15/16 x 5 3/4 (100 x 146)
Inscribed verso *Bay of Quinte-Jas. Cockburn
Bath-31st Augt. 1830*   942.48.18

426 Cramachi, Bay of Quinte
w.c. over pencil. 3 1/8 x 6 7/8 (79 x 174)
Inscribed verso *Cramachi-Bay of
Quinte-Jas. Cockburn*
Site now named Colborne, in Township of
Cramachi; has also been known as Keeler's
Corners after Keeler's Tavern shown in cat.
no. 427.   942.48.15

427 The Inn at Cramachi, Bay of Quinte
w.c. over pencil. 4 x 7 3/8 (101 x 187)
Inscribed verso *Cramachi-Inn Bay of Quinte
Jas. Cockburn Upper Canada*
The inn is Keeler's Tavern; see cat. no. 426.
942.48.16

427

428 The Corduroy Road Between York and Burlington

w.c., pen and ink. 10 3/4 x 15 5/8 (273 x 397)

Inscribed lower recto *Corderoy road;* verso *Hemlock swamps between Yorke and Burlington* 1830   949.39.9

428

Cockburn

429 The Court House at Hamilton
w.c. over pencil. 3 1/2 x 7 1/4 (89 x 184)
Inscribed verso *Court House at*
Hamilton–Burlington–Upper Canada–Jas.
Cockburn   942.48.6

429

430 Near Forty Mile Creek, Ontario
w.c. over pencil. 3 x 4 1/2 (76 x 114)
Inscribed verso *Near the Forty Mile Creek,
Ontario 1830*   960x276.202

431 Brown's and Forsyth's Hotels, Niagara
w.c. over pencil. 4 3/8 x 6 (111 x 152)
Inscribed verso *Brown's & Forsyth's Hotels,
J.C. July 17th, 1827/Niagara–Jas. Cockburn*
Pencil sketch of a shoreline on verso.
942.48.1

432 Brown's and Forsyth's Hotels, Niagara
w.c. over pencil. 4 3/8 x 6 (111 x 152)
Inscribed verso *Brown's & Forsyth's. Niagara
J.C./Jas. Cockburn July 1827*   942.48.2

433 American Falls from the English Side
w.c. over pencil. 13 7/16 x 20 1/16 (341 x
509)
Inscribed verso *American Fall, Niagara–from
the English side–Jas. Cockburn*; old mount,
title and *1827*   949.39.5

434 Horseshoe Fall from Goat Island
w.c. over pencil. 22 5/16 x 32 9/16 (566 x
827)
Inscribed l.r. *J. Cockburn 1831*; l.l. *JC 1831*;
verso *The Horseshoe or English Fall of Niagara
from Goat Island–Octr. 27th 1831 Jas:
Cockburn*
This composition, which includes a
picnicking group on Goat Island, was
engraved in aquatint and published by
Ackermann & Co., London, 1833 and 1857.
954.107.1

434

435 Niagara Falls from the Canadian Shore

w.c., touches of gouache. 21 1/2 x 31 7/8 (546 x 809) (sight)   953.131.8

436 American Falls from the Old Ferry

w.c. over pencil. 10 9/16 x 18 1/8 (268 x 460)

Inscribed verso *American Fall–Niagara from the old Ferry Jas. Cockburn*   949.39.1

437 Horseshoe Falls from the English Side

brown wash over pencil. 13 9/16 x 20 1/2 (344 x 521)

Inscribed on old label *General view of the Falls of Niagara from the English side.*
950.224.6

438 Niagara Falls

brown wash over pencil. 13 3/4 x 21 1/2 (349 x 546)

Printed label of *J.H. Chance, Carver, Gilder & Print Seller, Fitzroy Square* on verso of mount.   951.41.15

439 Niagara Falls

brown wash over pencil. 13 7/8 x 21 1/4 (352 x 539)

Printed label of *J.H. Chance* (see cat. no. 438) on verso of mount.   951.41.16

440 From Niagara Falls Looking up the River

w.c. over pencil, gum arabic. 22 1/4 x 32 3/16 (565 x 817)

Inscribed verso of mount *The Falls looking up the River. Jas. Cockburn   No. 1*   951.188.2

441 American Fall, Niagara, from the Old Ferry

w.c. over pencil. 13 5/16 x 20 1/16 (338 x 509)

Inscribed verso *American Fall–Niagara– from the old Ferry. Jas Cockburn*   949.39.4

442 The Stairway and Path to the Foot of the Gorge Near Table Rock, Niagara

w.c. over pencil. 21 1/4 x 31 7/16 (539 x 798)   953.131.7

442

Detail of 442

Cockburn

443 Horseshoe Falls from Below Table Rock
w.c. over pencil. 13 1/2 x 18 15/16 (343 x 481)   949.39.7

444 Niagara Falls from Below Table Rock
brown wash over pencil. 15 1/4 x 20 15/16 (387 x 531)   950.224.5

445 Below the Old Ferry, Canada Side
w.c. over pencil. 11 11/16 x 17 5/8 (297 x 448)
Inscribed verso *Below the old Ferry, Niagara-Jas. Cockburn*   949.39.3

446 Stairway to the Old Ferry
w.c. over pencil. 13 3/8 x 20 1/16 (339 x 509)
Inscribed verso *Steps of the Old Ferry Niagara/Jas. Cockburn*   949.39.2

447 Niagara from the Upper Bank of the Canadian Side
w.c. over pencil. 13 7/16 x 20 (341 x 508)
Inscribed verso *Niagara from the Upper Bank-Jas. Cockburn*   949.39.8

448 Pavilion Hotel at Niagara
w.c. over pencil. 6 x 9 1/2 (152 x 241)
Inscribed verso *The Pavillion at the Falls-Niagara Sept. 9th. 1830 J.C.*   942.48.3

449 Bridge over the American Rapids, Niagara
w.c. over pencil. 5 7/8 x 9 1/2 (149 x 241)
Inscribed verso *Bridge over the American Rapids/Niagara. Sept 5th, 1830-J.C.*
942.48.5

450 The Island Between Bridges over the American Rapids, Niagara
w.c. 3 7/8 x 9 1/2 (98 x 241)
Inscribed verso *The Island between the Bridges that are over the American Rapids-Niagara. Sept. 5th, 1830 Jas. Cockburn*   942.48.4

451 Horseshoe Falls from the English Side
w.c. 12 x 19 (305 x 482)
Inscribed verso *Niagara Horse Shoe from the English Side. Jas. Cockburn*   957.106.24

452 The Artist Sketching Niagara from Goat Island
w.c. over pencil, scraping. 32 1/2 x 22 (825 x 559)   953.131.1

453 Trenton Falls, New York
brown wash over pencil. 13 1/4 x 19 1/8 (336 x 485)
Inscribed l.l. *Trenton Falls, U.S.-J.C.*
950.224.8

454 Trenton Falls, New York
brown wash over pencil. 15 1/16 x 21 5/8 (382 x 549)   950.224.3

455 Trenton Falls, New York
brown wash over pencil. 13 7/16 x 19 1/4 (341 x 489)
Inscribed l.l. *Trenton Falls, U.S.*; l.r. *J.C.*
950.224.10

456 The Rapids, Trenton, N.Y.
brown wash over pencil. 17 1/4 x 22 (438 x 558)   950.224.2

457 Waterfall and River
brown wash over pencil. 15 1/16 x 21 1/2 (382 x 546)
Site probably also Trenton Falls, N.Y.
950.224.4

458 Dover from the Deal Road, Kent, England
w.c. over pencil. 8 5/8 x 14 1/2 (219 x 368)
962.58.8

459 Dover Castle and Town from Archcliff Fort, Kent, England
w.c., touches of gouache over pencil. 9 3/4 x 23 5/8 (248 x 600)
Inscribed recto *J.P.C./35*; verso, title.
962.106.3

460 Dover Castle, Keep and Constable's Tower, Kent, England
w.c. over pencil. 12 13/16 x 19 3/4 (325 x 502)
Inscribed l.l. *J.P.C./36*; verso *Dover Castle, Keep and the Constable's Tower. Jas. Cockburn*
962.106.4

461 Lympne Castle, Kent, England
w.c., touches of gouache over pencil. 13 x 20 (330 x 508)
Inscribed l.r. *J.P.C./36*; verso *Lympne Castle near Hythe*   962.106.5

462 Saltwood Castle Near Hythe, Kent, England
w.c. over pencil. 13 x 20 (330 x 508)
Inscribed l.r. *J.P.C./36* and *Saltwood Castle near Hythe*   962.106.6

463 Mountain Waterfall and Lake
w.c. over soft black pencil. 18 7/8 x 25 5/16 (479 x 650)
Site probably in Swiss or Italian alps; man's costume indicates a date late in the artist's life.   953.131.3

Cockburn, H.

Possibly Lieutenant Henry Cockburn, 60th Regiment, King's Royal Rifle Corps, 1848-57.

464 Fort White, St. Kitts, B.W.I.
w.c. over pencil. 6 1/8 x 9 1/16 (155 x 230)
Inscribed l.l. *H. Cockburn, 60 rifles*; verso, title.   955.290.1

465 Iron Mountain from Mount Misery, St. Kitts, B.W.I.
w.c. over pencil. 7 3/16 x 10 (182 x 254)
Inscribed l.l. *H.C. 60*; verso, title.
955.190.2

Coleman, Arthur Philemon
(1852-1939)

Born at Lachute, P.Q. Studied at Victoria University, Cobourg (M.A. 1880) and University of Breslau, Germany (Ph.D. 1882). Professor of geology and natural history, Victoria University, Cobourg, 1882-91. Professor of assaying and metallurgy, School of Practical Science, Toronto 1891-1901. Professor of geology, University of Toronto until his retirement in 1922; Dean of Faculty of Arts 1914-22. First director of Museum of Geology, one of the five museums which joined together to form Royal Ontario Museum in 1912. Author of numerous articles and books on geology. Painted in watercolour from his youth; later took some lessons from Otto Jacobi (q.v.). Member OSA 1880-1905; ARCA 1903. Exhibited OSA 1880-1904; RCA 1881-8; TIE 1881-1901.

Note: The titles on the following catalogue entries are taken from Coleman's lists and/or labels on old mounts. Also belonging to this collection, but not included in the present catalogue, are 153 watercolours of non-Canadian landscapes.

466 Fogo, Newfoundland 1925
w.c. over pencil. 5 1/2 x 8 7/8 (139 x 225)
Inscribed l.r. *Coleman/Small harbor near Fogo*
932.39.114

467 A Northeaster, Fogo, Newfoundland 1925
w.c. over pencil, touches of gouache. 8 7/8 x 5 1/2 (225 x 139)
Inscribed l.r. *Coleman*   932.39.115

468 Cliffs Near Twillingate, Newfoundland 1925
w.c. over pencil. 8 7/8 x 5 1/2 (225 x 139)
Inscribed l.c. *Coleman*   932.39.116

469 Mount Gaff, Topsail, Newfoundland 1924
w.c. over pencil. 6 x 9 (152 x 228)
Inscribed l.l. *Coleman*   932.39.117

470 Part of the Long Range, Newfoundland 1925
w.c. over pencil. 10 x 6 5/8 (254 x 168)
Inscribed l.c. *Coleman*   932.39.118

471 Bay of Islands, Newfoundland, Snow on Mountains, End of June 1924
w.c. over pencil. 9 x 5 1/2 (228 x 139)
Inscribed l.r. *Coleman/From Humbermouth*
932.39.119

472 South Arm of Bonne Bay, Newfoundland 1925
w.c. over pencil. 9 5/8 x 6 1/2 (244 x 165)
Inscribed l.r. *Coleman*   932.39.120

473 Battle Island, Labrador 1924
w.c. over pencil. 5 1/2 x 8 7/8 (139 x 225)
Inscribed l.l. *Coleman*   932.39.121

474 Head of Komaktorvik Bay, Labrador
w.c. over pencil. 5 x 6 7/8 (127 x 174)
Inscribed l.r. *Komaktorvik*   932.39.122

475 Six Miles South of Komaktorvik Bay, Labrador, a Cirque, 1915
w.c. over pencil. 5 x 6 7/8 (127 x 174)
932.39.123

476 Glacier Near Komaktorvik Bay, Labrador 1915
w.c. over pencil. 5 x 6 7/8 (127 x 174)
932.39.124

477 Mugford Tickle, Labrador
w.c. over pencil. 5 x 7 (127 x 178)
Inscribed l.r. *Mugford Tickle*   932.39.125

478 In Mugford Tickle, Labrador
w.c. over pencil. 7 x 5 (178 x 127)
932.39.126

479 Nachvak Fiord, Labrador, 1916
w.c. over pencil. 5 1/4 x 8 3/4 (132 x 222)
Inscribed l.l. *Coleman*   932.39.127

480 Nachvak Bay, Early August
w.c. over pencil. 6 1/8 x 9 7/8 (155 x 251)
932.39.128

481 Nachvak Bay
w.c. over pencil. 5 x 6 7/8 (127 x 174)
Inscribed l.r. *Navak*   932.39.129

482 Tallek Cliffs, Nachvak, Labrador
w.c. over pencil. 6 7/8 x 5 (174 x 127)
Inscribed l.l. *Nakvak*   932.39.130

483 Tallek, Looking South from Nachvak Bay, Labrador, U Shape of a Fiord
w.c. over pencil. 5 1/2 x 8 3/4 (139 x 222)
Inscribed l.r. *Coleman*; l.c. *S. Bay Nakvak*
932.39.131

484 Mountains, South of Nachvak, Labrador
w.c. over pencil. 7 x 4 7/8 (178 x 124)
932.39.132

485 Valley South of Third Cove, Nachvak
w.c. over pencil, touches of gouache. 4 3/4 x 6 7/8 (121 x 174)
Inscribed l.c. *Morning 3rd Cove*   932.39.133

486 Cape Naksarsktok, South of Nachvak Bay, Labrador
w.c. over pencil. 6 1/4 x 9 1/2 (159 x 241)
932.39.134

487 The Mitre, Labrador
w.c. over pencil. 5 x 7 (127 x 178)
Inscribed l.l. *Bishopic Mitre*   932.39.135

488 Cape Blomidon, Nova Scotia, 1927
w.c. over pencil. 6 x 9 (152 x 228)
Inscribed l.c. *Coleman*   932.39.136

489 Sable River, Nova Scotia
w.c. over pencil. 5 x 6 7/8 (127 x 174)
932.39.137

490 On the Restigouche, Looking South from Matapedia, New Brunswick, 1918
w.c. over pencil. 4 7/8 x 6 7/8 (124 x 175)
Inscribed l.l. *Coleman*   932.39.138

491 Dam on St. Croix River, New Brunswick, 1927
w.c. over pencil. 5 1/2 x 8 (139 x 203)
Inscribed l.l. *Coleman/Dam on St. Croix R.*
932.39.139

492 Fishermen's Landing, Percé, Quebec
w.c. over pencil. 3 3/8 x 9 3/4 (86 x 247)
Inscribed l.l. *Coleman/Perce*   932.39.97

493 Near Percé
w.c. over pencil. 6 7/8 x 4 3/4 (124 x 121)
Inscribed l.r. *Coleman*   932.39.98

494 Unloading Fishing Boats, Grand River, Gaspé, 1918
w.c. over pencil. 5 x 6 7/8 (127 x 174)
Inscribed l.l. *Coleman*   932.39.102

495 Gaspé Basin
w.c. over pencil. 3 3/4 x 5 1/2 (222 x 139)
Inscribed l.r. *Coleman*   932.39.100

496 Cape Rosier, Gaspé
w.c. over pencil. 4 3/4 x 6 3/4 (124 x 171)
Inscribed l.l. *Coleman*   932.39.99

497 Near Marcil, Gaspé
w.c. over pencil. 4 7/8 x 6 3/4 (124 x 171)
Inscribed l.c. *Coleman*   932.39.101

498 On Ste Anne River Among the Shickshock Mountains
w.c. over pencil. 8 3/4 x 5 1/2 (222 x 139)
Inscribed l.r. *Coleman*   932.39.105

499 From the Edge of Tabletop, Shickshock Mountains, 1918
w.c. over pencil. 5 3/8 x 8 3/4 (136 x 222)
Inscribed l.r. *Coleman*   932.39.104

500 Mount Nicol Albert from 2500 Feet, Gaspé, 1918
w.c. over pencil. 6 3/4 x 9 3/4 (171 x 247)
Inscribed l.l. *Coleman*   932.39.111

501 Mount Nicol Albert from Cap Chat River, Gaspé, 1918
w.c. over pencil. 8 3/4 x 5 1/2 (222 x 139)
Inscribed l.l. *Coleman*   932.39.110

502 Clearing in the Hills South of Cap Chat, Quebec
w.c. over pencil. 6 1/8 x 9 3/4 (156 x 247)
Inscribed l.r. *Coleman*   932.39.109

503 Cap Chat Harbour, Quebec, 1918
w.c. over pencil. 8 1/4 x 5 1/4 (209 x 133)
Inscribed l.l. *Coleman*   932.39.108

504 Falls of Ste Anne River, Gaspé, 1918
w.c. over pencil. 8 5/8 x 6 1/2 (219 x 165)
Inscribed l.l. *Coleman*   932.39.106

505 Tourelle, a Monument to Wave Work, Ste Anne des Monts
w.c. over pencil. 5 1/4 x 8 3/4 (133 x 222)
Inscribed l.r. *Coleman*   932.39.107

506 Near Cap au Renard
w.c. over pencil. 6 3/4 x 4 3/4 (172 x 121)
Inscribed l.l. *Coleman*   932.39.103

507 Near Ruisseau à la Martre, Gaspé
w.c. over pencil. 4 7/8 x 6 3/4 (124 x 172)
Inscribed l.l. *Coleman*   932.39.140

508 Near Ruisseau à la Martre, Gaspé
w.c. over pencil. 5 x 6 5/8 (127 x 169)
Inscribed l.l. *Coleman*   932.39.141

509 Mount Orford, Eastern Townships, Quebec, Late September
w.c. over pencil. 4 3/4 x 7 (121 x 178)
Inscribed l.r. *Coleman*   932.39.113

510 Foggy Day, Lower St. Lawrence, 1878
w.c. over pencil. 6 x 11 1/8 (152 x 283)
Inscribed l.r. *Coleman*   932.39.112

511 Mount Elephantus, Eastern Townships, Quebec, Late September
w.c. over pencil. 4 3/4 x 7 (121 x 178)
Inscribed l.r. *Coleman*   932.39.142

512 Ottawa River from the Laurentian Hills, 1927
w.c. over pencil. 5 1/2 x 8 3/4 (139 x 222)
Inscribed l.l. *Coleman*   932.39.143

513 Parliament Hill, Ottawa
w.c. over pencil. 6 3/4 x 9 3/4 (172 x 247)
932.39.39

514 Mill Near Kingston, Ontario
w.c. over pencil. 5 3/4 x 8 3/4 (146 x 222)
Inscribed l.r. *Coleman*   932.39.40

515 Farm House, Ormsby, Eastern Ontario: Mild Morainic Landscape
w.c. over pencil. 5 7/8 x 9 (149 x 228)
Inscribed l.r. *Ormsby*   932.39.41

516 Frenchman's Bay, 1927
w.c. over pencil. 5 1/2 x 8 3/4 (139 x 222)
Inscribed l.c. *Coleman*   932.39.42

517 Near Highland Creek, 1919
w.c. over pencil. 5 1/2 x 8 3/4 (139 x 222)
Inscribed l.l. *Coleman / Near Highland Cr.*
932.39.43

518 Highland Creek in October, 1927
w.c. over pencil. 5 1/2 x 8 3/4 (139 x 222)
Inscribed l.l. *Coleman*   932.39.44

519 Scarborough
w.c. over pencil. 6 3/4 x 9 7/8 (172 x 251)
Inscribed l.r. *Coleman*   932.39.45

520 A Ravine, Scarborough, 1924
w.c. over pencil. 5 1/2 x 9 (139 x 228)
Inscribed l.l. *Coleman*   932.39.46

521 Creek Near Scarborough
w.c. over pencil. 10 x 6 3/4 (254 x 172)
Inscribed l.r. *Coleman*   932.39.47

522 Scarborough Heights, 1926
w.c. over pencil. 5 1/2 x 8 7/8 (139 x 225)
Inscribed l.r. *Coleman*   932.39.48

523 Scarborough, December 2nd, 1916
w.c. over pencil. 8 3/4 x 5 1/2 (222 x 139)
932.39.49

524 A Peak at Scarborough, 1926
w.c. over pencil. 7 3/4 x 5 1/2 (197 x 139)
Inscribed l.r. *Coleman*   932.39.50

525 October in the Don Valley, 1921
w.c. over pencil. 9 3/4 x 6 1/8 (248 x 156)
Inscribed l.l. *Coleman*   932.39.51

526 On the Don River
w.c. over pencil. 8 3/4 x 5 1/4 (222 x 133)
Inscribed l.r. *Coleman*   932.39.52

527 The Lower Don, 1919
w.c. over pencil. 5 1/4 x 8 3/4 (133 xe222)
Inscribed l.r. *Coleman*   932.39.53

528 A Corner Near Convocation Hall, University of Toronto
w.c. over pencil. 6 5/8 x 5 (168 x 127)
Inscribed l.l. *Coleman*   932.39.54

529 Biological Building, University of Toronto
w.c. over pencil. 6 3/4 x 9 3/4 (172 x 247)
Inscribed l.r. *Coleman*   932.39.55

530 Government House, Toronto, 1919
w.c. over pencil, touches of gouache. 8 7/8 x 5 1/2 (225 x 140)
Inscribed l.r. *Coleman*
"Chorley Park," Rosedale, official residence of Lieutenant Governor of Ontario 1915-1937; demolished 1961.
932.39.56

530

531 After the Snowstorm, Toronto
w.c. over pencil. 7 1/8 x 10 1/8 (181 x 157)
Inscribed l.r. *Coleman*   932.39.57

532 Golden Rod and Asters Near Toronto, 1924
w.c. over pencil. 5 1/2 x 8 7/8 (140 x 225)
Inscribed l.r. *Coleman*   932.39.58

533 Humber River, End of April
w.c. over pencil. 9 3/4 x 6 3/4 (247 x 171)
Inscribed l.r. *Coleman*   932.39.59

534 Suburbs of Hamilton
w.c. over pencil. 5 1/2 x 8 7/8 (140 x 225)
Inscribed l.l. *Coleman*   932.39.60

535 The Toronto Boat at Queenston, 1919
w.c. over pencil. 7 x 4 7/8 (177 x 123)
932.39.61

536 Queenston
w.c. over pencil. 8 1/2 x 5 3/4 (216 x 146)
Inscribed l.r. *Coleman*   932.39.62

537 Niagara Falls
w.c. over pencil. 4 7/8 x 8 (123 x 203)
932.39.63

538 Lake Panache, South of Sudbury
w.c. over pencil. 5 x 7 (127 x 177)
932.39.64

539 Near Windy Lake, Ontario
w.c. over pencil. 6 5/8 x 9 3/4 (168 x 247)
Inscribed l.l. *Coleman*   932.39.65

540 Montreal River, North Shore of Lake Superior, 1899
w.c. over pencil. 6 7/8 x 9 3/4 (174 x 247)
Inscribed l.r. *Coleman*   932.39.66

541 From Long Portage, Nipigon River, Ontario
w.c. over pencil. 6 x 9 (152 x 228)
Inscribed l.r. *Up Nipigon R. from Long Portage*
932.39.144

542 Split Rock Rapids, Nipigon River
w.c. over pencil. 6 x 9 (152 x 228)
Inscribed l.c. *Split Rock, Nipigon*
932.39.145

543 Up Nipigon River from Split Rock Rapids
w.c. over pencil. 6 x 9 (152 x 228)
Inscribed l.c. *Looking up from Split Rock*
932.39.146

544 Lifting Nets, Poplar Lodge, Lake Nipigon
w.c. over pencil. 5 7/8 x 9 (149 x 228)
Inscribed l.r. *Coleman*   932.39.147

545 Poplar Lodge, Lake Nipigon
w.c. over pencil. 6 x 9 (152 x 228)
Inscribed l.r. *Coleman*   932.39.148

546 Atikokan River, 1900
w.c. 6 3/4 x 9 3/4 (171 x 247)
Inscribed l.r. *Coleman*   932.39.67

547 A Backwood Farm, Northern Ontario
w.c. over pencil. 6 1/8 x 9 3/4 (155 x 247)
Inscribed l.l. *Coleman*   932.39.68

548 A Ruin, Old Ontario
w.c. over pencil. 5 1/2 x 9 (140 x 228)
Inscribed l.r. *Coleman*   932.39.69

549 Ontario After the Snowstorm, February, 1924
w.c. over pencil. 6 x 9 (152 x 228)
Inscribed l.c. *Coleman*   932.39.70

550 A River, Ontario
w.c. over pencil. 8 1/4 x 5 3/4 (209 x 146)
Inscribed l.l. *Coleman*   932.39.71

551 Autumn Colours, 1923
w.c. over pencil. 6 x 8 3/4 (152 x 222)
Inscribed l.l. *Coleman*   932.39.72

552 Country, Ontario, Mid-October
w.c. over pencil. 9 x 6 1/4 (228 x 159)
932.39.73

553 Farm in Winter, Ontario
w.c. over pencil. 6 1/2 x 10 (165 x 254)
Inscribed l.l. *Coleman*   932.39.74

554 Ontario Hills in Winter, 1919
w.c. over pencil. 6 7/8 x 10 (174 x 254)
Inscribed l.r. *Coleman*   932.39.75

555 Forks of the Saskatchewan
w.c. over pencil. 7 x 10 (178 x 254)
Inscribed l.l. *A P Coleman*   932.39.95

556 Near Head of Main Fork, Saskatchewan River
w.c. over pencil. 10 x 6 7/8 (254 x 174)
Inscribed l.l. *A P Coleman*   932.39.96

557 Hudson Bay Post, Lac Ste Anne, Alberta, 1907
w.c. over pencil. 4 7/8 x 6 7/8 (124 x 174)
932.39.79

557

Coleman

558 Tepee on Edmonton Trail
w.c. 6 x 9 (152 x 228)
932.39.76

559 Autumn Colour, West of Edmonton
w.c. over pencil. 6 7/8 x 5 1/8 (174 x 130)
Inscribed l.r. *Coleman*   932.39.77

560 Fernie Mountain, Crow's Nest Pass, Alberta
w.c. over pencil. 5 5/8 x 9 (142 x 228)
Inscribed l.l. *Coleman*   932.39.80

561 The Rockies from Kootenay Plains, Alberta
w.c. over pencil. 6 1/4 x 9 3/4 (159 x 247)
Inscribed l.r. *Coleman/Kootenay Plains*
932.39.78

562 Mount Assiniboine, Morning, 1920
w.c. over pencil. 6 7/8 x 5 (174 x 127)
Inscribed l.l. *Coleman*   932.39.87

563 Tepee, Assiniboine Camp, 1920
w.c. 6 7/8 x 5 (174 x 127)
Inscribed l.r. *Coleman*   932.39.86

564 Tower Mountain Near Assiniboine, Evening, 1920
w.c. 6 7/8 x 5 (174 x 127)
Inscribed l.r. *Coleman*   932.39.88

565 Tower Mountain Near Assiniboine, Morning, 1920
w.c. over pencil. 5 x 6 7/8 (127 x 174)
Inscribed l.l. *Coleman*   932.39.89

566 Bow Pass, Alberta
w.c. over pencil. 5 x 7 (127 x 178)
Inscribed l.r. *Bow Pass*   932.39.158

567 Near Head of Atikosipi, Alberta
w.c. over pencil. 6 3/8 x 9 3/4 (162 x 247)
Inscribed l.r. *Coleman*   932.39.159

568 Shack in Bow Pass, Alberta: Firewood in Bloom
w.c. over pencil. 6 1/2 x 9 1/2 (165 x 241)
Inscribed l.r. *Coleman*   932.39.157

569 Mount Temple, Laggan
w.c. 7 x 10 (178 x 254)
Inscribed l.l. *Mt. Temple, Laggan*   932.39.85

570 Saskatchewan River, Rocky Mountains, Alberta
w.c. over pencil. 26 x 18 3/4 (660 x 476)
Inscribed l.l. *Coleman*   932.39.83

571 Up the Saskatchewan
w.c. 6 7/8 x 9 7/8 (174 x 251)
Inscribed l.r. *A P Coleman*   932.39.84

572 Gregg's House, Foothills, Alberta, 1907
w.c. over pencil. 7 x 10 (178 x 254)
932.39.92

573 Roche Miette from Gregg's, 1917
w.c. over pencil. 7 x 10 (178 x 254)
932.39.91

574 Glacier, Cataract Pass, 1893
w.c. over pencil. 6 1/2 x 9 3/4 (165 x 247)
Inscribed l.l. *Coleman*   932.39.156

575 Near Head of Brazeau River, Alberta
w.c. over pencil. 6 3/4 x 9 1/2 (171 x 241)
Inscribed l.l. *Coleman*   932.39.81

576 Seracs, Brazeau Glacier, Alberta
w.c. over pencil. 5 1/4 x 8/ 3/4 (133 x 222)
Inscribed l.l. *Coleman*   932.39.82

577 Mountain of the Cross
w.c. 6 11/16 x 9 15/16 (170 x 252)
Inscribed l.r. *Coleman*   932.39.160

578 A Valley in Jasper Park, 1936
w.c. over pencil. 5 1/2 x 9 (140 x 228)
Inscribed l.r. *Coleman/F . . . Valley*
932.39.90

579 Fortress Mountain, Alberta, 1892
w.c. over pencil. 4 3/4 x 6 3/4 (121 x 171)
Inscribed l.r. *Coleman*   932.39.162

580 Late Afternoon in the Alberta Rockies, 1930
w.c. over pencil. 6 1/2 x 9 3/4 (165 x 247)
Inscribed l.r. *Coleman*   932.39.94

581 Fog Rising, Alberta, 1930
w.c. over pencil. 5 1/2 x 8 3/4 (140 x 222)
Inscribed l.l. & r. *Coleman*   932.39.93

582 Kootenay Plains, Rocky Mountains
w.c. over pencil. 6 x 9 3/4 (152 x 247)
Inscribed l.r. *Coleman*   932.39.1

583 Kicking Horse Canyon, 1921
w.c. over pencil. 9 x 5 1/2 (228 x 140)
Inscribed l.l. *Coleman*   932.39.4

584 The End of Yoho Glacier, 1928
w.c. over pencil. 6 3/8 x 9 3/4 (162 x 247)
Inscribed l.l. *Coleman*   932.39.5

585 Glacier, Selkirk Mountains, B.C.
w.c. over pencil. 21 1/2 x 31 (546 x 787)
Inscribed l.r. *Coleman*   932.39.2

586 The Selkirks from Golden, 1921
w.c. over pencil, touches of gouache. 5 1/2 x 9 (140 x 228)
Inscribed l.r. *Across the Valley Golden*
932.39.6

587 Glacier in the Selkirks from Surprise Mountain
w.c. over pencil. 6 1/4 x 9 1/4 (158 x 235)
Inscribed l.r. *Coleman*   932.39.3

588 At Reco Mine, Slocan, B.C., 6000 Feet above Sea, June, 1920
w.c. over pencil. 5 1/2 x 9 (140 x 228)
Inscribed l.c. *Coleman*   932.39.155

589 Slocan Silver Region, B.C., June, 1920, 5,500 Feet
w.c. over pencil. 5 1/2 x 8 7/8 (140 x 225)
Inscribed l.r. *Coleman*   932.39.153

590 Slocan Silver Region Near Noble Five Mine, 6000 Feet, June, 1920
w.c. over pencil. 5 1/2 x 9 (140 x 228)
Inscribed l.l. *Coleman*   932.39.154

591 On Fortress Lake, B.C.
w.c. 10 1/16 x 6 15/16 (255 x 176)
Inscribed l.r. *Coleman*   932.39.151

592 Seracs, Main Glacier, Misty Mount, B.C.
w.c. 5 1/4 x 8 3/4 (133 x 222)
Inscribed l.r. *Coleman*   932.39.152

593 Moose Lake, Fraser River, B.C.
w.c. over pencil. 7 x 10 (178 x 254)
932.39.29

594 Near Robson, B.C., 1920
w.c. over pencil. 8 3/4 x 5 1/2 (222 x 140)
Inscribed l.r. *Coleman*   932.39.16

595 Mount Robson from Grand Forks River
w.c. over pencil. 5 7/8 x 8/ 7/8 (149 x 225)
932.39.27

596 Mount Robson
w.c. over pencil. 10 x 7 (254 x 178)
932.39.7

597 Sunrise on Mount Robson, B.C.
w.c. over pencil. 26 3/4 x 39 1/4 (679 x 997)
Inscribed l.r. *Coleman*   932.39.8

598 Berg Lake from Main Glacier, Mount Robson, 1918
w.c. over pencil. 7 x 10 (178 x 254)
Inscribed l.r. *A P Coleman*   932.39.25

599 Mount Robson at Sunrise
w.c. over pencil. 6 5/8 x 9 5/8 (168 x 244)
Inscribed l.r. *Coleman*   932.39.9

600 Where the Glacier Meets the Lake, Mount Robson, B.C.
w.c. over pencil. 8 3/4 x 5 1/2 (222 x 140)
Inscribed l.l. *Coleman*   932.39.10

601 Camp at Foot of Mount Robson
w.c. over pencil. 10 x 7 (254 x 178)
Inscribed l.l. *Coleman*   932.39.11

602 Mount Robson from Moraine at Dawn: Sun from Northeast
w.c. over pencil. 7 x 10 (178 x 254)
932.39.12

603 Camp on Moraine, Mount Robson
w.c. over pencil, touches of gouache. 7 x 10 (178 x 254)   932.39.13

604 Tree Line Camp, Mount Robson
w.c. over pencil. 10 x 6 7/8 (254 x 174)
932.39.14

605 Tree Line Camp, Mount Robson
w.c. over pencil, touches of gouache. 10 x 6 7/8 (254 x 174)   932.39.15

606 Main Glacier, Mount Robson, B.C.
w.c. over pencil. 18 3/4 x 25 3/4 (476 x 654)
Inscribed l.l. *Coleman*   932.39.17

607 On Main Glacier, Mount Robson, B.C.
w.c. over pencil. 6 x 8 7/8 (152 x 225)
Inscribed l.r. *Coleman*   932.39.18

608 East Foot of Glacier, Mount Robson
w.c. over pencil. 10 x 7 (254 x 178)
932.39.19

609 East Foot of Main Glacier, Robson: The River Divides its Waters Between the Pacific and Arctic Oceans
w.c. over pencil. 10 x 7 (254 x 178)
932.39.20

610 Mount Robson from North East
w.c. over pencil. 7 x 9 7/8 (178 x 251)
932.39.21

611 West Foot of Main Glacier, Mount Robson
w.c. over pencil. 7 x 10 (178 x 254)
Inscribed l.r. *A P Coleman*   932.39.22

612 Mount Robson from North West, 1908
w.c. over pencil. 10 x 7 (254 x 178)
Inscribed l.r. *A P Coleman*   932.39.23

613 Mount Robson from Across Berg Lake
w.c. over pencil. 10 3/4 x 7 (273 x 178)
Inscribed l.r. *Coleman*   932.39.24

614 Lake Kinney Near Mount Robson
w.c. over pencil. 6 7/8 x 10 (174 x 254)
932.39.26

615 Falls on Grand Forks River Near Foot of Mount Robson
w.c. over pencil. 10 x 7 (254 x 178)
932.39.28

616 Near Hope, 1920
w.c. over pencil, touches of gouache. 9 x 5 1/2 (228 x 140)
Inscribed l.l. *Hope*; l.r. *Coleman*   932.39.30

617 Mount Cheam from Agassiz, B.C., 1921
w.c. over pencil. 9 3/4 x 6 3/4 (247 x 171)
Inscribed l.l. *Coleman*   932.39.149

618 Gold Range Near D'Arcy, B.C. 1920
w.c. over pencil. 6 1/2 x 10 (165 x 254)
Inscribed l.l. *Coleman*   932.39.31

619 Westkunnist Mount on Skeena River
w.c. over pencil. 10 x 7 (254 x 178)
932.39.33

620 Seven Sisters, Skeena Valley, B.C.
w.c. over pencil. 18 5/8 x 25 5/8 (473 x 651) (sight)
Inscribed l.l. *Coleman*   932.39.34

621 Hazelton Mountain, B.C.
w.c. over pencil. 10 x 7 (254 x 178)
Inscribed l.l. *Hazelton*   932.39.32

622 Lake Agnes, B.C.
w.c. over pencil. 5 x 7 (127 x 178)
932.39.150

623 Near Port Simpson
w.c. over pencil. 4 3/4 x 7 (121 x 178)
Inscribed l.r. *At Port Simpson*   932.39.35

624 Cannery, Mouth of Skeena, B.C.
w.c. over pencil. 6 7/8 x 10 (174 x 254)
Inscribed l.r. *Cannery near Mouth of Skeena*
932.39.36

625 Llewellyn Glacier, Atlin, B.C.
w.c. 26 1/8 x 39 3/4 (663 x 100.9)
932.39.37

626 Fresh Snow on the Mountains, 1928
w.c. over pencil. 6 1/8 x 9 1/2 (155 x 241)
932.39.38

627 Snow Capped Mountains
w.c. over pencil. 20 x 27 (508 x 685)
Inscribed l.l. *Coleman*   932.39.310

628 Iceberg
w.c. over pencil. 5 3/8 x 8 7/8 (136 x 225)
932.39.311

629 A Crevasse, 1928
w.c. over pencil. 5 1/2 x 9 7/8 (140 x 251)
Inscribed l.r. *Coleman/O . . . Glacier*
932.39.312

630 Jasper Folding in the Iron Formation
w.c., touches of gouache. 6 x 9 (152 x 228)
932.39.313

Colville, Charles John
(c. 1820-1903)

Ensign, 85th Regiment and Aide-de-camp to Lieutenant-Governor Sir George Arthur in Toronto 1838-40. Promoted to captain 1844; retired from forces 1847. Visited Canada second time in 1874. Created Viscount of Culross and Knight of the Thistle, 1902.

631 Government House, Toronto
soft black pencil, heightened with brown wash, on blue-grey paper. 6 5/8 x 10 1/16 (168 x 255)

Inscribed l.l. *C.J. Colville 1840*; verso *Govt. House, Toronto, 1840, by Capt. Colville/Ballroom under verandah–Drawingrm. to right–(Sir George's office beyond–the other side of the house)–Ac. [?] Belle & Mothers room 2 windows over Drawingrm.*

This house, built 1828 and burned down 1862, was on King St. at Simcoe St. 956.25.2

632 Bottom of the Garden, Government House, Toronto
soft black pencil, heightened with brown wash, on blue-green paper. 6 5/8 x 10 1/6 (168 x 255)

Inscribed l.c. *C.J. Colville, 22nd August*; verso *Bottom of the Gardens Govt. House, Toronto–by Capt (now Lord) Colville*   956.25.3

631

Cotton, W. Henry
(1817-1877)

Born at St. Petersburg, Russia, son of William Miles Cotton. Came to Canada 1836. Entered Civil Service for Upper Canada until union of provinces in 1841, when he was appointed chief clerk in office of Governor General. Retired after 40 years' service; died in Ottawa.

An amateur artist, Cotton is said to be author of four views of Quebec City which were published as lithographs in 1850 by Sarony & Major, New York. The four pencil sketches in this collection appear to be copies of the lithographs rather than original compositions for them. See cat. nos. 2142-2145.

Cresswell, William Nichol
(1822-1888)

Born in Devonshire, England. Studied art in London under W.E. Cook, R.A., and Clarkson Stanfield. Emigrated to farm at Harperhaye near Seaforth, Ontario in 1855. Painted in oil and watercolour, chiefly landscapes in Ontario and New England. OSA 1874-88; RCA 1880; SCA 1870-72. Died at Seaforth.

633 Lake George with Timber Raft
w.c., touches of gouache. 10 3/8 x 14 3/4 (263 x 374)
Inscribed l.r. *Wm. N. Cresswell 1866.* ; verso *Lake George, Lake Huron.*
The height of the mountains in background suggest Lake George in New York state rather than on Lake Huron.   957.97.4

634 Near the White Horse Ledge, White Mountains
w.c., touches of gouache. 10 5/16 x 14 11/16 (262 x 373)
Inscribed l.r. *Wm. N. Cresswell 1866.*; verso, title.   957.97.5

635 Beaching the Boat, Lake Nipigon
w.c., touches of gouache, over pencil. 15 1/4 x 25 (387 x 635)
Inscribed l.r. *W.N. Cresswell. 1876.*
Bequest of Mrs Frederick W. Cowan, Toronto.   961.229

Detail of 635

635

Cresswell

Cuming, J.B.
(active 1805)

Probably the English artist J.B. Cuming who exhibited at the Royal Academy 1793-1812.

636 Sydney, Norfolk Island, Australia

w.c. over pencil. 7 3/4 x 12 15/16 (197 x 328)

Inscribed l.r. *J.B. Cuming 1805*; verso of mount *Sydney, Norfolk Island*; printed sales catalogue entry pasted to verso of mount *CANADA (NOVA SCOTIA): View of Sydney, Norfolk Island, water-colour, signed and dated 1805, J.B. Cuming.*

Early catalogue entry confuses Sydney, N.S. with Sydney, Norfolk Island, which was a penal settlement 800 miles east of New South Wales, Australia.

Several earlier versions of this composition are known: pen and wash view of 1796 by William Neate Chapman; copy of Chapman view by P.P. King, 1804; undated copy by John Eyre, all in Mitchell Library, New South Wales. Also w.c. copy by Philip Gidley King, State Library of Victoria, Melbourne. The view was published as an etching in David Collins: *An Account of the English Colony in New South Wales*, London 1798.   950.9.25

Cuthbertson, George Adrian
(1900-1969)

Born in Toronto. Studied drawing and painting under William Brymner, P.R.C.A. Attended Royal Military College of Canada. Served in Navy during war of 1914-18. Marine artist and researcher; author and illustrator of *Freshwater: A History and a Narrative of the Great Lakes*, Toronto 1931.

637 The Old Fish Wharf, Toronto

soft black pencil on yellow-brown paper. 16 1/8 x 11 3/4 (409 x 298)

Inscribed l.r. *George A. Cuthbertson* and an anchor.

Copy of a portion of the engraving after W.H. Bartlett *Fish Market, Toronto*. 960x276.3

Dalton, John Joseph
(1856-1935)

Born in Toronto, son of Dr. W.H. Dalton and grandson of Thomas Dalton, editor of *Patriot* newspaper. Commissioned as Dominion Land Surveyor 1879; received title of Dominion Topographical Surveyor 1881. According to federal government records he surveyed for them on the prairies during only one season, spending the summer of 1882 near Carlyle, Saskatchewan.

638 Indian Buffalo Hunters on the Prairies

w.c. 27 x 40 (685 x 1001.6) (sight)

Inscribed l.r. *John J. Dalton, D.T.S.* 970.223.1

639 Indian Hunters Killing a Buffalo

w.c. over pencil. 27 x 40 (685 x 1001.6) (sight)

Inscribed l.r. *John J. Dalton, D.T.S.* 970.223.2

639

Dartnell, George Russell
(1798-1878)

Born in Ireland, son of George Russell Dartnell, cashier to Duke of Devonshire, Lismore Castle. Entered British army medical corps 1820; served with First Royal Regiment of Foot. Posted to Canada 1836-43, serving at Penetanguishene, Montreal, Quebec and London. His account, *A Brief Narrative of The Shipwreck of the Transport Permier near the mouth of the River St. Lawrence, on the 4th November 1843* illustrated with engravings after his sketches, was published in London in 1845. Retired as Inspector General of Hospitals in 1856.

640 Snowshoers Crossing the St. Lawrence Near Montreal
w.c., touches of gouache, over pencil on grey paper. 6 3/16 x 9 1/16 (157 x 230)
Inscribed on mount *Ice Road over the St Lawrence near Montreal. 1839*   952.87.6

641 Broken Ice on the St. Lawrence Opposite Montreal
w.c., touches of gouache, over pencil.
7 1/16 x 10 1/4 (179 x 260)
Inscribed on mount, title and *18 Jany. 1840*; verso *An ice shove on the St. Lawrence–near Montreal, 18 January 1840*   952.87.3

642 Niagara Rapids seen from Goat Island
w.c. over pencil. 6 3/4 x 10 (171 x 254)
Inscribed, mount *Niagara. The Rapids above the great Fall, from Goat Island. G R D–25 Sept. 1843*   952.87.2

643 Horseshoe Falls, Niagara, from the Canadian Side
charcoal. 9 1/16 x 12 5/8 (230 x 320)
Inscribed recto of mount *General view of Niagara from the Canada side. G.R.D. in charcoal. 1843*   952.87.4

644 At Port Talbot, Lake Erie, 1842
w.c. 6 1/4 x 9 1/4 (159 x 235)
Inscribed on mount, title.   952.87.1

645 View from the Summit of the Ridge above Nicholl's Tavern, Penetanguishene Road
w.c., pen and brown ink. 5 7/16 x 8 3/16 (138 x 208)
Inscribed on mount, title and *30 May 1836*
Watermark: *Whatman 1833*   952.87.8

645

646 The Barracks and Penetanguishene Harbour from Matchedash Bay
w.c. over pencil. 8 3/16 x 12 9/16 (208 x 319)
Inscribed verso *No. 8 Entrance to Penetanguishene Bay–Lake Huron Geo. R. Dartnell/25 Sept. 1837*; mount, title and *Geo. R. Dartnell 15 Sept. 1837* 952.87.5

646

Dartnell

647 Head of Penetanguishene Bay, 1838
pen and brown ink. 8 1/2 x 12 1/2 (216 x
317)
Inscribed u.l., title.   952.87.9

648 Catskill Falls, New York
w.c., touches of gouache over pencil. 14 3/4
x 9 3/4 (374 x 247)
Inscribed, mount *Katskill Falls–New York
State–G R D September 1843*   952.87.7

Davanston, Mrs G.N.
(active 1882)
An unidentified amateur artist.

649 Lumber on the Ottawa River
w.c. and gouache. 11 5/8 x 15 1/8 (295 x
384)
Inscribed l.r. *By Mrs. G.N. Davanston 1882*
View taken from the Quebec side above
the Chaudière rapids looking towards the
Parliament Buildings, Ottawa.   970.191.7

Davies, Thomas
(*c.* 1737-1812)
Born at Shooters Hill, England. Educated at
Royal Military Academy, Woolwich, from
1755. Posted to Halifax, 1757; served at
siege of Louisbourg, 1758; Fort Frederick,
1759; Lake Champlain and Montreal with
General Amherst's forces, 1759-60.
Surveyed shores of Lake Ontario, 1761;
Lakes George and Champlain, 1762.
Returned to England 1763. Posted in New
York state 1764-6. In England 1767-73.
Posted to Halifax 1773; probably present at
Bunker Hill in June 1775, returning to
Halifax when British left Boston the
following year. Served in New York state
from late 1776 until 1778. Returned to
England 1779. Posted to Gibraltar 1783-84.
Returned to Canada via the West Indies in
1786; posted at Quebec until 1790 as
lieutenant-colonel in charge of four
companies of artillery. Stationed in
England after 1790. Died at Blackheath.
Known for his brilliant watercolour views
of landscape and natural history subjects.
Six of his paintings of North American
waterfalls were published in London as line
engravings about 1768. Davies exhibited at
Royal Academy 1771; became Fellow of
Royal Society of London, 1781.

**650 The Falls of Otter Creek, Lake
Champlain, with a Saw Mill**
w.c., black ink margins. 14 7/16 x 20 3/16
(366 x 513)
Inscribed lower margin & verso *A View of
the Falls of Otter Creek Lake Champlain, North
America*; l.r. *T Davies delint 1766*   956.19.1

650

651 South View of Passaic Falls, New Jersey

w.c., black ink margins. 11 3/8 x 19 1/8 (289 x 485)

Inscribed lower margin *A South View of the Pisaiack Falls in the Province of New Jersey in North America*; l.r. *Thos. Davies. Pinxit 1766*

Watermark: Lily & letters.   956.19.2

Detail of 651

Davies

651

Davies

652 View of the Hudson River from Fort Knyphausen

w.c. 13 5/8 x 20 3/4 (346 x 527)
Inscribed verso *A View on the Hudson River looking down towards New York from Fort Knyphausen 1779.*
Watermark: *J. Whatman*
The fort (which is not shown in the view) was built in 1776 at the north end of Manhattan Island and named Fort Washington. When captured by the British in 1776, it was re-named Fort Knyphausen until they withdrew in 1783.   958.14.8

652

Davies

653 The Siege of Fort Royal in Martinique
w.c., pen and ink, black ink margins.
14 7/8 x 21 (378 x 533)
Inscribed lower margin *A View of the Seige of Fort Royal on the Island of Martinique*; l.r. *T. Davies Excut. 1763*
Watermark: IHS with Cross
As Davies does not seem to have accompanied the Monckton expedition against Martinique in late 1761, it is assumed that this is a copy of another artist's work. Another version of this subject by Davies, dated 1762, is in the collection of The Mariners Museum, Newport News, Va.   958.14.6

654 Basseterre in St. Christopher
w.c. 13 9/16 x 20 7/8 (344 x 530)
Inscribed verso *A View of the Town of Basseterre and Road in the Isle of St Christophers taken in 1786*
Watermark: *J. Whatman*   958.14.5

655 Kingstown Harbour in St. Vincent
w.c. 13 1/4 x 20 (336 x 508)
Inscribed verso *A View of Kingstown Harbour and part of the Town in St. Vincents, with the Isle of Bechenay, Union &ca. 1786*
Watermark: Lily on Shield surmounted by Crown.   958.14.2

656 Fort George and George Town in Grenada
w.c. 13 15/16 x 20 5/8 (354 x 523)
Inscribed verso *A View of Fort George and part of George Town in Grenada taken from the Bay 1786*
Watermark: Lily on Shield surmounted by Crown, over W.   958.14.3

657 Roseau in Dominica
w.c. over pencil. 13 3/4 x 19 11/16 (349 x 500)
Inscribed verso *A View of the Road and lower part of Roseau in Dominica taken in 1786*
Watermark: *J. Whatman*   958.14.4

658 Government House, Dominica
w.c., black ink margins. 14 3/4 x 21 1/2 (374 x 546)
Inscribed verso *A View of Government House Morn Bruce and Part of Charlot Town in the Isle of Dominica taken in 1786*
Watermark: *J. Whatman*   958.14.7

659 Gibraltar from the North Pavilion
w.c. over pencil, black ink margins. 15 5/16 x 23 5/16 (389 x 592)
Inscribed lower margin *A View of Gibralter with the situation of the Spanish Flotantes in the Morning of 14 of September 1782 taken from the North Pavillion*; l.r. *T. Davies fecit 1783*
Watermark: *J. Whatman*   960.224.1

660 The Navy Hospital, Parson's Lodge and Apes' Hill, Gibraltar
w.c. over pencil, black ink margins. 15 7/8 x 23 3/8 (403 x 593)
Inscribed lower margin *A View of the Navy Hospital Parsons lodg &ca. Gibralter and Apes hill &ca. in Affrica. taken from the South Pavillion*; l.r. *T. Davies fecit 178-*[cut off]; dated on verso in another hand, *1783*
960.224.2

661 The Inside of St. Michael's Cave, Gibraltar
w.c., with black ink margins. 14 15/16 x 21 1/16 (379 x 535)
Inscribed lower margin *A View of part of the inside of St Michaels Cave at Gibralter*; l.r. *T. Davies fecit 1783*
Watermark: *J. Whatman*   960.205.3

662 The Inside of Harding's Cave, Gibraltar
w.c., pen and ink, with black ink margins. 13 5/8 x 19 3/16 (345 x 487)
Inscribed lower margin *A View of the Inside of Hardings Cave under the Sugar loaf, Gibralter*; l.r. *T. Davies fecit 1784*
Watermark: *J. Whatman*   960.205.4

663 View from a Cavern, Gibraltar
w.c. 12 1/8 x 19 1/4 (308 x 489)
Watermark: *I. Taylor*   960.205.2

Detail of 659

Davies

Davis, Henry Samuel
(active 1818-52)

British army officer and topographer.
Served with 52nd Light Infantry 1827-52.
May have visited Canada *c*. 1818; in
Canada 1831 and 1847; in 1847 made
honorary member of Montreal Society of
Artists and exhibited at their first show.
The four following watercolour views of
Niagara Falls were lithographed by
Thomas McLean, London, 1848.

664 Horseshoe Falls from Goat Island
w.c., gum arabic. 22 15/16 x 17 7/8 (582 x
454)
Inscribed l.l. *HSD 1847* in monogram.
960x282.104

664

665 Horseshoe Falls with a Storm
w.c., gum arabic. 18 1/8 x 24 3/4 (460 x
628)   960.282.102

666 Horseshoe Falls at Sunset
w.c., gum arabic, over pencil. 17 3/8 x 23
(441 x 584)
Inscribed l.l. *HSD 1847* in monogram.
960x282.105

667 Horseshoe Falls and Table Rock
w.c., gum arabic. 23 1/4 x 20 1/8 (590 x
522)
Inscribed l.c. *HSD* in monogram.
960x282.103

667

Davis

Dawson, Richard
(active 1748-1758)
Officer in Royal Engineers. Served in
Flanders 1748; in Newfoundland 1755.
Promoted to Captain 1758.

**668 Placentia, Newfoundland, from the
South East**
w.c., pen and black ink with black ink
margins on laid paper. 9 5/8 x 13 1/2 (244
x 343)
Inscribed lower margin *View from the S: E:
of the Town of PLACENTIA from a View taken
by Capt. Richd. Dawson, Ingineer 1758.*
The wording of the inscription suggests
that this may be an early copy of Dawson's
original view.   951.84

View from the S: E: of the Town of PLACENTIA from a View taken by Capt. Richd. Dawson Ingineer 1758.

668

Dawson

Des Barres, Joseph Frederick Wallet
(1722-1824)

British officer and military cartographer. Educated at Basel, Switzerland and at Royal Military College, Woolwich, England. Posted to America from 1756, participating in various actions of Seven Years' War. From 1763 to 1773 surveyed coast of Nova Scotia for British Admiralty, resulting in publication of *The Atlantic Neptune*, 1777. Appointed lieutenant-governor of Cape Breton 1784-87; and of Prince Edward Island 1805-12. Died at Halifax, N.S.

669 Crow Harbour, Chedabucto Bay, Near Canso

w.c., pen and ink. 12 5/8 x 11 3/4 (320 x 299)

This chart, with inset view of coastline, duplicates plate 49, v. II of *The Atlantic Neptune* and is probably a later copy of the engraving rather than the original drawing by Des Barres.   955.102.10

Downman, John
(1750-1824)

Born in Wales. Studied under Benjamin West and at Royal Academy from 1769. Known principally for his watercolour and chalk portraits; also painted watercolour landscapes. Exhibited FSA 1788; RA 1769-1819. Not known to have visited Canada. Died at Wrexham, England.

670 Portrait of a Gentleman

black chalk and stump, touches of red chalk, on wove paper. 9 x 7 3/8 (228 x 187)
Inscribed l.r. *JD 1780*   968x341.3

670

Dudley, Robert
(active 1857-1891)

English painter. Recorded the 1857-58
attempt to lay a trans-Atlantic cable
between Ireland and Newfoundland. Staff
artist aboard cable ship *Great Eastern* during
the successful laying of the Atlantic
Telegraph Cable, 1866. Painted oil and
watercolour views of these events. Three
lithographs after his 1857-8 sketches
published by Day & Son, London 1866.
Many of his 1865-66 views reproduced in
Illustrated London News. Exhibited RA
1865-91.

**671 Heart's Content Bay, Newfoundland:
Arrival of the Transatlantic Cable**
w.c., touches of gouache, over pencil.
14 1/2 x 24 1/4 (368 x 539)
Inscribed l.r. *Robert Dudley 1866*
Heart's Content Bay
Newfoundland 952.72.1

**672 Heart's Content Bay, Newfoundland:
View of the Town**
w.c., touches of gouache, over pencil.
14 1/4 x 20 7/8 (361 x 530)
Inscribed l.r. *Robert Dudley 1866*; l.l. *Heart's*
Content Bay, Newfoundland 952.72.2

671

Dudley

Duncan, James
(1806-1881)

Born in Coleraine, Ireland. Emigrated to Canada 1825; settled in Montreal by 1830. Married Caroline Benedict Power of Sorel, P.Q., 1834. Served as lieutenant in Light Infantry during Rebellion of 1837. Professional artist, painting in oil and watercolour. Best known for watercolour views of Montreal area landscape, street scenes and figure groups. Designed 'Habitant' penny and half-penny tokens for Bank of Montreal 1837. Studies of Montreal buildings reproduced in *Hochelaga Depicta* 1839. Nine general views of Montreal published as lithographs between 1847 and 1878. One Quebec city view published as chromolithograph 1874 (see note preceding cat. no. 727). Illustrator for *Illustrated London News* and *Canadian Illustrated News*. Partner of Young & Duncan, photographic artists and ambrotypists, Montreal 1856. Taught drawing at various Montreal schools. ARCA 1880. Member SCA 1867. Treasurer MSA 1847. Exhibited AAM 1865-79; MSA 1847; QPEM 1863-5; RCA 1881; SCA 1867-71.

673 Baie St. Paul
w.c., touches of gouache, over soft pencil.
12 3/4 x 19 (324 x 482)
Inscribed l.l. *J Duncan*   960x276.85

673

Duncan

674 Montmorency Falls from the Lévis Shore

w.c. over pencil. 4 7/16 x 6 3/16 (113 x 157)
Inscribed l.l. *J. Duncan;* l.r. *Bobin's . . .
P . . . sc*   952.165.1

675 Distant View of Montreal

w.c., touches of gouache, over soft pencil.
6 5/8 x 12 1/8 (168 x 308)
Inscribed l.l. *J Duncan;* verso of old mount
Montreal, a distant View–J. Duncan 1854
950.224.20

676 View of Montreal from Longueuil

w.c., touches of gouache, over pencil. 12 x
20 1/16 (305 x 509)
Inscribed l.l. *J Duncan;* verso *View of
Montreal in distance from Longueuil, June 20,
1883.* Date obviously incorrect.   960.59.2

676

Duncan

677 Montreal from the Mountain
w.c. over pencil. 15 5/8 x 27 1/4 (397 x 692)
Unfinished sketch of same view in
pink-brown wash and pencil on verso.
The watercolour view is a close variant of
the lithograph after Duncan published by
Matthews, Montreal, about 1849. See also
cat. no. 1003.   960x276.21

678 The Quebec Tandem Club, Champ de Mars, Montreal
w.c. and gouache over soft pencil. 12 11/16
x 18 1/2 (322 x 470)
Inscribed l.l. *J. Duncan*; verso *from the collection of General L.G. Phillips, Grenadier Guards, who was stationed in Canada about 1840.*   953.186.1

678

Duncan

679 St. Antoine Hall, Montreal
w.c., touches of gouache, over soft pencil.
19 1/4 x 27 3/16 (489 x 691)
Inscribed l.r. *J. Duncan/Montreal. 1850.*
Watermark: *J. Whatman, Turkey Mill 1848*
The house was the residence of John
Torrance on St. Antoine Street.
957.17.1

679

Duncan

680 Greene Avenue in Westmount, Looking Towards the Mountain
w.c. over pencil. 11 11/16 x 19 (297 x 482)
Inscribed l.l. *J. Duncan*; verso *Green Ave.–Westmount, Que., in 1872. House in left foreground still standing, inhabited by a member of the original family.*   960x276.86

680

Duncan

681 The Ice House at Nun's Island, Montreal
w.c., touches of gouache, over soft pencil. 9 1/8 x 12 3/4 (231 x 324)
Inscribed l.c. *Ice House*
This view was reproduced in the *Illustrated London News*, 16 April 1859. A similar, but not identical, composition by Duncan is in the sketchbook formerly in the Reford collection, described in Sotheby (Canada) catalogue of 28 May 1968.   950.66.2

682 Ice Cutting on the St. Lawrence at Montreal
w.c., touches of gouache, pen and ink over pencil. 9 3/16 x 14 1/8 (233 x 358)
Reproduced in *Illustrated London News*, 16 April 1859, titled *Sawing and Ploughing Ice on the St. Lawrence*. See also cat. no. 692. 950.66.1

683 The American Fall and Town at Niagara
w.c. over pencil. 16 5/16 x 24 5/8 (414 x 625)
Inscribed l.r. *J. Duncan*   951.39.1

684 General View of Niagara Falls from the Canadian Shore
w.c. over pencil, scraping. 16 3/8 x 24 1/2 (415 x 622)
Inscribed l.r. *J. Duncan*   951.39.2

685 View of the Thames at London, Ontario
w.c. over pencil. 3 1/4 x 4 9/16 (82 x 116)
Inscribed l.l. *Duncan*
View includes tower of Methodist Church which stood on North Street, later Queen's Avenue. Duncan is said to have visited London in 1848.   952.165.3

686 Landscape with Buildings
w.c. over pencil. 3 5/16 x 4 1/2 (84 x 114)
Inscribed l.l. *Duncan*
Site probably Montreal.   952.165.2

687 Portage at Waterfall with Lumber Crib
w.c. over soft pencil. 21 5/8 x 25 3/4 (549 x 654) oval composition.
Inscribed, old mount *James Duncan, Artist, Montreal C.E.*   965.205.1

688 A Waterfall
w.c. over soft pencil. 19 5/8 x 25 3/8 (498 x 644) oval composition.
965.205.2

689 Indian Encampment by Moonlight
w.c., touches of gouache. 8 3/16 x 10 (208 x 254)
Inscribed l.l. *J Duncan*   952.179

687

690 A Carrying Place
w.c. over pencil. 4 5/8 x 6 7/8 (117 x 174)
Inscribed u.c., title; l.r. *JD*.   967.50.2

THE DUNCAN SKETCHBOOK

The following 36 studies of life in Montreal
were originally bound into one sketchbook.
Several of the leaves have *Whatman*
watermarks of 1831 and 1834; the costume
(notably cat. no. 706) illustrates a fashion of
c. 1840-45. Duncan painted several versions
of some of the subjects, e.g. those in the
1847 sketchbook (formerly colln. of Robert
W. Reford, Montreal) and at least two of
the themes were reproduced as newspaper
illustrations in 1859.

691 Pig Market
w.c. over pencil. 9 1/8 x 13 (232 x 330)
Inscribed l.c., title.   951.158.1

**692 Cutting Ice on the St. Lawrence at
Montreal**
w.c. over pencil. 9 1/8 x 13 1/8 (232 x 333)
Watermark: *J. Whatman 1834*
Composition similar to the wood engraving
published in the *Illustrated London News*, 16
April 1859; also to this cat. no. 682.
951.158.2

693 Trees on Mount Royal
pencil. 9 1/8 x 13 1/8 (232 x 333)
Watermark: *J. Whatman, Turkey Mill 1834*
951.158.3

694 Sleigh with Load of Hay
w.c. over pencil. 9 3/16 x 13 3/4 (233 x 349)
Same view repeated in the Reford
sketchbook.   951.158.4

695 A Market Group
w.c. over pencil. 9 1/8 x 13 1/8 (232 x 333)
951.158.5

696 Frozen Sheep at Montreal Market
w.c. over pencil. 9 3/16 x 13 3/16 (233 x
335)
Inscribed l.c. *Frozen Sheep Market–Montreal*
Watermark: *J. Whatman, Turkey Mill 1834*
951.158.6

697 Selling Tobacco, Montreal Market
w.c. over pencil. 9 1/8 x 13 1/8 (232 x 333)
Inscribed l.c. *Canadian Selling Rolls of Baccy*
Watermark: *J. Whatman* [Turkey] *Mill 1831*
951.158.7

698 Carrying Timber
w.c. over pencil. 9 1/8 x 13 1/8 (232 x 333)
Inscribed l.c., title.
A similar scene is in the Reford
sketchbook.   951.158.8

698

699 Hay Sleigh Returning Home
w.c. over pencil. 9 1/8 x 13 1/8 (232 x 333)
Inscribed l.c., title over a previous pencil
inscription in same hand which reads *Hay
Sleigh returning from Market.*
Same view repeated in Reford sketchbook.
951.158.9

700 Celebrated Blind Fiddler, Montreal
pencil. 9 1/8 x 13 1/8 (232 x 333)
Inscribed l.c., title; u.r. on sign over door
FRANCIS PIGEON. Rum. Gin.   951.158.10

700

Duncan

701 Selling Canadian Homespun Cloth, Montreal

w.c. over pencil. 9 1/8 x 13 1/8 (232 x 333)
Inscribed l.c., title over previous inscription
reading *Market Scene*.
Same composition, with figure variations,
reproduced in *Illustrated London News*, 19
March 1859.   951.158.11

701

Duncan

702 Old Market, Montreal
w.c. over pencil. 9 1/8 x 13 3/16 (232 x 335)
Inscribed l.c., title; on sign over door
POLICE STATION A.   951.158.12

703 Canadian Woman with Maple Sugar
pencil. 9 1/8 x 13 1/8 (232 x 333)
Inscribed l.c., title.   951.158.13

703

Duncan

704 Canadian Wedding
w.c. over pencil. 9 1/8 x 13 1/8 (232 x 333)
Inscribed l.c., title.   951.158.14

704

Duncan

705 Montreal Swells
w.c. over pencil. 9 1/8 x 13 1/8 (232 x 333)
Inscribed l.c., title.
A variant of this composition is in Reford
sketchbook.   951.158.15

705

Duncan

706 Lady Swells, Officer and Muffin
w.c. over pencil. 9 1/8 x 13 1/8 (232 x 333)
Inscribed l.c., title.   951.158.16

706

Duncan

707 Montreal Market

w.c. over pencil. 9 1/8 x 13 1/8 (232 x 333)
Inscribed l.c., title; on sign, u.l. *WM.*
KELL/Farmers' [?] Hotel.   951.158.17

708 Carting Snow from Streets

w.c. over pencil. 9 1/8 x 13 1/8 (232 x 333)
Inscribed l.c., title.
A more finished version of this scene is in
the Reford sketchbook. A careful but less
accomplished copy of the same
composition, sketched in or after 1845 and
possibly not by Duncan, is listed as cat. no.
731. A fourth version of the subject was
copied by Mrs Dyneley, *c.* 1848-52.
951.158.18

709 Carting Ice from River

w.c. over pencil. 9 1/8 x 13 /8 (232 x 333)
Inscribed l.c., title.   951.158.19

710 Carting Ice for Ice House

w.c. over pencil. 9 1/8 x 13 1/8 (232 x 333)
Inscribed l.c., title.   951.158.20

711 Nelson's Monument and Old Market

w.c. over pencil. 9 1/8 x 13 1/8 (232 x 333)
Inscribed l.c., title.   951.158.21

711

712 Stage Crossing River
w.c. over pencil. 9 1/8 x 13 1/8 (232 x 333)
Inscribed l.c., title; on coach *UPPER
CANADA*. 951.158.22

713 St. Patrick's Society Parade
w.c. over pencil. 9 1/8 x 13 1/8 (232 x 333)
Inscribed l.c. *St. Patrick's Society*
The parade moves along Notre-Dame
Street, Montreal. It has been suggested that
because the church is shown with
completed twin towers, the view was
sketched after 1849 when the towers were
added. However, prints of Notre Dame
with towers were issued as early as 1829.
951.158.23

713

Duncan

714 St. Andrew's Society Parade

w.c., pen and ink over pencil. 9 1/8 x
13 1/8 (232 x 333)
The parade is passing Nelson's Column on
Notre Dame Street, Montreal. The group is
unidentified by inscription, but one of the
banners depicts St. Andrew's cross.
951.158.24

714

Duncan

715 Wood Sawyers Waiting to be Hired at Montreal Wharves

w.c. over pencil. 9 1/8 x 13 1/8 (232 x 333)
Inscribed, l.c. *Wood Sawyers waiting to be hired* 951.158.25

716 The Painter Shows his Work, Montreal Market

pencil. 9 1/8 x 13 1/8 (232 x 333)
Inscribed l.c. *Scene in Market*
The painter is showing a portrait to a market woman, possibly his subject.
951.158.26

716

Duncan

717 A Market Scene
pencil. 9 1/8 x 13 1/8 (232 x 333)
951.158.27

718 Sleigh with Ice Blocks
pencil. 9 1/8 x 13 1/8 (232 x 333)
Watermark: *J. Whatman, Turkey Mill 1831*
951.158.28

719 Wood Sawyer at Work
w.c. over pencil. 9 1/8 x 13 1/8 (232 x 333)
Inscribed l.c., title.   951.158.29

720 Water Carriers
pencil. 9 1/8 x 13 1/8 (232 x 333)
Inscribed l.c., title.   951.158.30

721 Swell and His Object
w.c. over pencil. 9 1/8 x 13 1/8 (232 x 333)
Inscribed l.c., title. Faint pencil sketch of
man pulling loaded sleigh on verso.
951.158.31

722 Indians Going to Cut up a Moose
w.c. over pencil. 9 1/8 x 13 1/8 (232 x 333)
Inscribed l.c., title. Faint pencil sketch of
three figures, one shovelling, on verso.
951.158.32

723 Boys on Coasters
w.c. over pencil. 9 1/8 x 13 1/8 (232 x 333)
Inscribed l.c., title.
Watermark: *J. Whatman, Turkey Mill 1831*
A similar composition is included in the
Reford sketchbook.   951.158.33

724 Indian Baby in Cradleboard
w.c. over pencil. 9 1/8 x 13 1/8 (232 x 333)
Inscribed l.c. *Indian Kid*   951.158.34

725 Indian Encampment Near Montreal
w.c. over pencil. 9 1/8 x 13 1/8 (232 x 333)
Inscribed l.c., title.
Watermark: *J. Whatman, Turkey Mill 1831*
For H.W. Barnard's copy of this
composition, see cat. no. 98.   951.158.35

**726 Hunter Drawing Toboggan in a
Snowstorm**
w.c., touches of gouache, over pencil. 9 1/8
x 13 1/8 (232 x 333)
Inscribed l.c. *Snow Storm–Hunter drawing his
toboggin*
Watermark: *1831*   951.158.36

THE SPROULE QUEBEC VIEWS

In 1832 four sketches of Quebec by Robert
Auchmuty Sproule (1799-1845) were
printed as black-and-white lithographs by
C. Hullmandel of London for publisher
Adolphus Bourne of Montreal. When
Bourne decided to re-print the set as
chromolithographs in 1874, Sproule was
dead and the original sketches were
probably no longer available for the
Montreal lithographer to use as colour
reference. This leads us to assume that the
publisher asked James Duncan to paint the
four following watercolours, which are
copies of Sproule's views with minor figure
variations. When they were issued as
chromolithographs in 1874, a fifth Quebec
view by Duncan was added to the set.

727 View of Quebec from Pointe Lévis
w.c., touches of gouache, over pencil.
10 5/16 x 14 11/16 (262 x 373)
959.128.1

728 View of the Place d'Armes, Quebec
w.c., touches of gouache, over pencil.
10 5/16 x 14 3/4 (262 x 374)
959.128.2

**729 View of the Market Place and
Catholic Church, Uppertown, Quebec**
w.c., touches of gouache, over pencil.
10 3/16 x 14 3/4 (259 x 374)
959.128.3

**730 View of the Esplanade and
Fortifications of Quebec**
w.c., touches of gouache, over pencil.
10 1/4 x 14 3/4 (260 x 374)
959.134

attributed to James Duncan

731 Removing Snow in Montreal
w.c., touches of gouache, over pencil.
9 1/16 x 12 15/16 (230 x 328)
Faint pencil sketch of sleigh on verso.
Watermark: *J. Whatman, Turkey Mill 1845*
See cat. no. 708 for discussion of 4 versions
of this view.   956.51.1

**732 Niagara Falls from the American
Shore**
w.c. over pencil, with scraping. 12 13/16 x
17 3/8 (325 x 441)
Acquired as work of Major Henry Davis
(q.v.), but closer in style to Duncan.
950.65

733 Two Figures Viewing a Waterfall
w.c. and pencil. 7 1/16 x 9 (179 x 229)
951.41.1

Dyneley, Mrs A.F.
(active 1848-52)
Wife of Colonel Thomas Dyneley, C.B.,
Aide-de-camp to Queen Victoria and
senior staff officer with British forces in
Canada, commanding Royal Artillery in
Ottawa, Montreal and Quebec 1848-52.
Mrs Dyneley borrowed numerous
topographical views of Canada, which she
copied and signed.

**734 Ice Road Between Montreal and St.
Helen's Island**
pencil and white gouache on grey-green
paper. 6 15/16 x 10 3/8 (176 x 264)
Inscribed l.r. *From Molson's buildings Island of
St Helens 1848, Febr/& Be L'Oeil Mountain in
distance*; l.l. *M*. [or *W*?] *F. Dy./copied from
Duncan's sketch* [reference is to James
Duncan, q.v.]; verso, *Dyneley*.   951.41.3

**735 Nun's Island seen from Monklands,
Montreal**
blue and brown washes, scraping, over
pencil. 5 3/8 x 9 7/8 (136 x 251)
Inscribed verso *View of Nuns Island & the
river near Montreal from Monklands. F.D.*;
l.c. of mount *Nun's Island, St. Lawrence, from
the Garden at 'Monklands', Montreal*; l.r. of
mount *F.D. July 1850*
Watermark: *What*[man] *Turk*[ey Mill]
'Monklands' (the actual building is not
shown in view), a viceregal residence on
slopes of Mount Royal, had become a hotel
in 1850. It is now the central building of
Villa Maria Convent.   969.299.2

736 Winter Scene with Indians
w.c., touches of gouache. 9 1/8 x 12 1/4
(231 x 311)
Inscribed l.r. Montreal, July 22, 1848 . . . A.
[M?] F. Dy.
Watermark: *J. Whatman, Turkey Mill* [184]6
Copy of the painting *Indians and Squaws of
Lower Canada* by Cornelius Krieghoff which
was published as a colour lithograph by G.
& W. Endicott, New York, in 1848, and
advertised for sale by John McCoy of
Montreal on 15 July 1848.   951.67.6

ED.T.
·,(active 1835)
Possibly Daniel Thomas Egerton, English
landscape artist who exhibited with Royal
Society of British Artists from 1824-29 and
1838-40. Spent his last years travelling in
America. Assassinated in Mexico, 1842.

737 The Cascade, American Side, Niagara
pencil, black and white chalks on buff
paper. 18 7/16 x 11 13/16 (468 x 300)
Inscribed recto with descriptive notes;
verso *The Cascade, American Side, Niagara,
July 1835. D.T.E.*   951.41.17

Eagar, William
(*c.* 1796-1839)
Artist, born in Ireland and thought to have
studied art in Italy. Emigrated to
Newfoundland 1830. His view of St. Johns
published as engraving, London 1831.
Moved to Halifax 1834 and advertised as
landscape and portrait painter, in oil and
watercolour. Nineteen of his views were
published as lithographs, Boston 1839;
sixteen of these were issued in wrappers, in
four parts, titled *Nova Scotia Scenery*. A
number of the views were drawn on stone
by the artist. Eagar died at Saint John, N.B.
while returning from a trip to England.

**738 Celebration on Halifax Common of
the Coronation of Queen Victoria, 28th
June 1838**
w.c. over pencil. 8 3/4 x 13 15/16 (222 x
354)   955.218.1

738

Detail of 738

739 Province House, Hollis Street, Halifax
w.c., touches of gouache, pen and ink over
pencil. 6 3/16 x 9 (157 x 228)
View shows the legislative building and old
St. Matthew's Church. Preparatory sketch,
with minor variations, for the lithograph by
Jenkins & Colburn, Boston, published *c.*
1839.   955.218.2

739

Eagar

740 Pleasant Street, Halifax
w.c., touches of gouache. 6 x 9 1/16 (152 x 230)
View taken from Morris Street looking north along Pleasant Street, showing Stewart and Inglis houses.   955.218.3

740

Eagar

741 Market Wharf and Ferry Landing, Halifax
w.c. over pencil. 5 13/16 x 9 1/8 (147 x 232)
View shows ferry slip at foot of George
Street.   955.218.4

Eagar

741

Eagar

742 Saint Paul's Church, Halifax
w.c., touches of gouache, pen and ink over
pencil. 6 x 9 (152 x 228)
View of St. Paul's Church and Grand
Parade seen from corner of Argyle and
Duke Streets looking south-east, with old
St. Mary's Catholic chapel in distance.
Preparatory sketch, with minor variations,
for lithograph titled *Argyle Street, Halifax*,
published by Jenkins & Colburn, Boston,
c. 1839.   955.218.5

742

Eagar

Fisher, Sir George Bulteel
(1764-1834)
Born at Peterborough, England; member of
the family who were among the first
patrons of the painter John Constable.
Probably studied at Royal Military
Academy, Woolwich. Second Lieutenant,
Royal Artillery, 1782; First Lieutenant,
1790. Well known amateur watercolourist.
Exhibited his views at Royal Academy
1780, 1800 and 1808. Posted to Canada *c.*
1785-95. Six of his Canadian views and one
American view were engraved in aquatint
by J.W. Edy and published in London, 1795
and 1796. Fisher served in the Peninsular
Campaign and later became Commandant,
Royal Military Academy, Woolwich.

743 View of the Potomac Falls, Virginia
w.c., touches of gouache, on grey paper.
16 x 21 (406 x 533)   950.224.33

743

Forbes, John Colin
(1846-1925)

Born in Toronto, son of Duncan Forbes.
Studied art at South Kensington Art
Schools and Royal Academy School,
London, England, and at Union
International des Beaux-Arts, Paris, France.
On return to Canada he lived in Toronto,
Montreal and Ottawa. Known chiefly as a
portrait painter, he also painted marine and
genre subjects early in his career, and
western landscapes for Canadian Pacific
Railway in 1885. Father of painter Kenneth
Forbes. Member OSA 1880-93; RCA 1880.

744 Sailing at Toronto Island
w.c., touches of gouache, over pencil.
13 1/2 x 20 1/2 (343 x 521) (sight)
Inscribed l.l. *J. Colin Forbes*; verso of old
frame (in part) *The Water colour was painted
in Toronto Bay. . . . One of the canoes belonged to
J.C. Forbes, another to Captain Dick, owner of
the Queen's Hotel . . . another to . . . McLaughlin
[?], who was connected with McLean's Magazine.
. . . The custom was to sail to the island, sleep in
the canoes, and sail back. Presented to Mrs.
Warren A. Stevens By Stuart Forbes, McGill
University, 1947.*
The sails bear the insignia of the Toronto
Sailing and Canoe Club.
Gift of Mrs Warren Stevens, Toronto.
970.327

744

Forrest, Charles Ramus
(active 1778-1828)

Infantry officer and artist. Served in West Indies as Lieutenant with 90th Regiment, *c.* 1778-81; his watercolour views of St. Lucia were published as aquatint engravings 1783-86. With 3rd Regiment 1802-14. Promoted to Major 1808. With 34th Regiment 1814. Lieutenant-Colonel 1815 and placed on half-pay 1817.

Aide-de-camp to Earl of Dalhousie at Quebec 1821-23. Painted large watercolour views of Quebec and of French River route from Ottawa to Lake Huron while accompanying Dalhousie on official tours. Returned to England and appointed Assistant Quarter-Master General, 1824. In this capacity signed charts of New Orleans and Florida taken during war of 1812. No longer on army lists in 1828.

745 Cape Diamond and the St. Lawrence River from the Seigniory of Lauzon
w.c. over pencil. 21 1/4 x 39 3/8 (540 x 1000)
Inscribed, old label on stretcher *Cape Diamond, Quebec and the St. Lawrence River, taken from the Seat of the Hon. S. Caldwell, 1823–by Col. C.R. Forrest–Louisa P. Wood.*
'S. Caldwell' refers to Sir John Caldwell (1775-1842), owner of Lauzon Seigniory in 1823.   952.71

745

746 Bridge on the Path from Wolfe's Cove to Spencer Wood

blue wash over pencil. 13 1/8 x 21 (333 x 533)

Inscribed l.l., title.

Spencer Wood was so named by the Hon. Michael Percival after he acquired this historic house (not shown in view) in 1815. Originally known as 'Bois de Coulonge', it became 'Powell Place' from 1780 until 1815, then 'Spencer Wood' until it was given back its original name by the Canadian government in 1950.   955.189.1

747 On the French River

blue wash over pencil. 12 9/16 x 20 11/16 (319 x 525)

Inscribed l.l. *No. 3 & 57. On French River*

Same view (colln. NGC) was painted in w.c. by Forrest in 1822.   955.189.2

747

Forrest

748 Above the Grand Récollet

blue and grey washes over pencil. 12 5/8 x
20 3/4 (320 x 527)
Inscribed l.r. *No. 6 & 62. Above the Grand
Recollet. 18th Sheet of Journal.* D
955.189.3

749 Cascade of the Grand Récollet, French River

blue wash over pencil. 13 1/2 x 21 1/16
(343 x 535)
Inscribed verso *Grand Recollet*
Same view (colln. NGC) was painted in
w.c. by Forrest in 1822.   955.189.4

749

Forrest

750 Petite Faucille Portage on the French River

blue wash over pencil. 12 11/16 x 20 15/16
(322 x 532)

Inscribed l.r. *No. 12. Portage de la Petite
Faucille on the Rivière des François*

Watermark: *1814*   955.189.6

750

751 Rapide de la Montagne below the Grand Calumet, Ottawa River

blue wash over pencil. 12 15/16 x 20 15/16 (328 x 532)
Inscribed l.l. *No. 10.* and title; in view *White marble rocks.*   955.189.7

752 Falls of the Grand Calumet on the Ottawa River

blue wash over pencil. 12 11/16 x 20 7/8 (322 x 530)
Inscribed l.r. *No. 9.* and title.   955.189.8

753 Looking up the Niagara River at Queenston

blue wash over pencil. 12 1/2 x 21 (317 x 533)
Inscribed l.r., title.   955.189.5

Foster, Frederick Lucas
(1842-1899)

Born Toronto, son of Colley Foster, barrister and grandson of Colonel Foster, sometime Commander-in-Chief of forces in Upper Canada. Attended Upper Canada College and the Military School, Toronto. Apprenticed as Land Surveyor 1858-63. Received diploma as Provincial Land Surveyor 1863. Started career as surveyor in Windsor, Ontario, 1865. Made plan of North America for Ontario Government in 1884. Member OSA 1888-99. Exhibited OSA 1890-97; TIE 1891-99. Died in Toronto.

754 North River Depot, Kippawa Lake, Quebec

w.c. over pencil. 4 7/8 x 7 (124 x 178)
Inscribed l.l. *At North River Depot–Kipawa Lake*
View shows lumbering depot north of the Ottawa River in winter. Pencil sketch of tree on verso, inscribed *Beech Tree, Toronto, June 12, 1885*   969.90.4

754

755 Long Sault Rapids, Grenville County, Ontario
w.c. over pencil. 9 7/8 x 13 7/8 (251 x 352)
Inscribed l.r. *Head of the 'Long Sault',
Grenville, Sep. 7/96 F.L.F.*   969.90.1

756 Rock Creek, Ontario
w.c. over pencil, touches of gouache. 7 x
9 7/8 (178 x 251)
Inscribed verso *Rock Creek*
The site is in Nightingale Township,
Haliburton County, near Whitney.
969.90.6

757 Humber River Near Toronto
w.c. over pencil. 4 7/8 x 6 3/4 (124 x 171)
Inscribed l.r. *Humber River, June/85*
969.90.2

758 Humber River and Bridge
w.c. over pencil. 8 7/8 x 11 3/8 (225 x 289)
Inscribed, verso *On Humber River, June/85.
F.L.F. Delt.*   969.90.3

759 Niagara Falls with Staircase Tower
w.c. over pencil. 10 1/4 x 6 1/4 (260 x 159)
Inscribed l.l. *Foster/91*   969.90.5

760 Landscape Near Windsor
w.c. over pencil. 9 3/4 x 13 3/4 (248 x 349)
Unfinished pencil and w.c. sketch of a rural
landscape on verso.   969.90.10

761 Near Windsor, Ontario
w.c. 8 7/8 x 5 7/16 (225 x 138)
Inscribed l.r. *F.L.F. Del*; l.l. *Poplars &c/Near
Windsor, Ont. July 77*; u.l. *30*
Unfinished w.c. of sunset with boats on
verso.   969.90.7

**762 From Strabane, Detroit River, looking
east** *(recto)*; **Rocks on East Sister Island,
Lake Erie** *(verso)*
w.c. over pencil. 5 1/2 x 8 3/4 (140 x 222)
Inscribed l.l. *from Strabane, Detroit River,
looking east* [view taken from foot of
Strabane Avenue in East Windsor]; verso
*Unfinished study of Rocks on East Sister Isd.,
Lake Erie 1877*   969.90.8

763 Waterfront Scene on the Detroit River
w.c. over pencil. 5 1/2 x 14 1/2 (240 x 368)
969.90.9

763

764 On Shoal Lake
w.c., touches of gouache, over pencil.
9 11/16 x 13 1/4 (246 x 336)
Inscribed l.r. *F.L. Foster/99*; on mount, title.
There are several Shoal lakes in Ontario.
957.197.2

765 West Territory, Saskatchewan
brown wash over pencil. 4 7/8 x 11 3/8
(124 x 289)
Inscribed on mount *West Territory,*
Saskatchewan, by F.L. Foster   955.157.5

766 Sunset on the Elbow of the South
Saskatchewan River
brown wash. 4 3/8 x 11 3/8 (111 x 289)
Inscribed verso *Sunset on the Elbow of the*
South Saskatchewan River–Assiniboia
Territory, Canada–Sketched from Nature by
F.L. Foster   955.157.4

767 The North Saskatchewan River
brown wash over pencil. 4 5/16 x 11 5/16
(110 x 287)
Inscribed verso *Sketch on the North*
Saskatchewan River–N.W. Territory of
'Saskatchewan' Canada–20 miles south of Fort
Carlton–(looking North Easterly)–by F.L.
Foster, Dominion Lands Surveyor, 176 Argyle
St. Toronto   955.157.6

767

Fothergill, Charles
(1782-1840)

Born at York, England of a Quaker family. Emigrated to Canada in 1817, settling at Smith's Creek, Port Hope, where he opened a general store. Also owned a hunting lodge on Rice Lake from 1817, and operated a mill there during winter of 1821-22. King's Printer of Upper Canada 1822-26, with headquarters at York. Represented Durham County in Legislative Assembly of Upper Canada 1825-31. Lived at Pickering Mills 1831-37, but his project of establishing a village there failed. Made many efforts to found a provincial museum at York which would include departments of natural and civil history, botanical and zoological gardens, an observatory and an art gallery. His own natural history collection was on display at York from about 1835 until 1840, when the building in which it was housed burned. Known as a naturalist, journalist and author of *A Sketch of the Present State of Canada*, York 1822. Member SAAT 1834. Died in Toronto.

768 The Bridge over Smith's Creek, Port Hope

w.c. over pencil with black ink border.
7 1/4 x 10 3/8 (184 x 263)
Inscribed l.c. margin *The Bridge over Smith's Creek, Port Hope—from the bottom of C. Fothergill's grounds* [ink] *12/11-1819* [pencil].
Watermark: *Wha*[tman] *18 . . .*
Gift of Miss Mary Fothergill Reid, Ottawa.
956.74.1

768

Fothergill

769 The Log House on Rice Lake
w.c. with black ink border. 7 1/4 x 10 3/8
(184 x 263)
Inscribed l.c. margin *Log House on the Rice
Lake./Where we, C.F. & J.H. dined, 12 mo.
10.19–Here I got some Rice grown in the lake, &
Capn. Mohawk's belt. The view of the Rice Lake
is taken from this House.* [ink]
Gift of Miss Mary Fothergill Reid, Ottawa.
956.74.2

769

770 Rice Lake
w.c. over pencil with black ink border.
7 1/2 x 21 5/8 (190 x 549) two sheets
joined at centre.
Inscribed l.l. in ink *Rice Lake, Upper Canada,*
15 miles from Lake Ontario; l.c. in pencil
12/12–1819; l.r. in ink *1. C. Fothergill's*
House stands round this Point. 2. Capn.
Anderson. 3. Wm. Sowden from Leeds.
Numbers correspond to pencil numbers in
view.
Watermark: [Wha]*tman [18]19*
Gift of Miss Mary Fothergill Reid, Ottawa.
956.74.3

Fothergill

770

Fothergill

Fowler, Daniel
(1810-1894)

Born at Downe, Kent, England. Abandoned
study of law for painting. Apprenticed to
J.D. Harding, watercolourist and
draughtsman; also studied briefly in
continental Europe. Associated with
engraver Hullmandel. Worked as artist in
London 1834-42, when ill health caused
him to emigrate to Canada. Farmed on
Amherst Island near Kingston; took up
painting again after 1857-8 visit to England.
Began to exhibit in 1863. Painted
landscape, still life and self-portraits in
watercolour. Won medals at Philadelphia
Sesqui-Centennial Exhibition 1876,
Colonial and Indian Exhibition in London
1886, and World's Columbian Exposition
at Chicago, 1893. Member OSA 1872; RCA
1880. Died at Amherst Island.

771 Passenger Pigeons
w.c. 13 3/4 x 9 3/4 (349 x 248)
Inscribed l.l. *D. Fowler, 1866*; lower recto of
mount *To Edwd. Leigh Esqre. from D.F., with
his very best regards.*
Gift of Mr E.R. Cameron, Toronto.
968.216

771

Fraser, A.M.

Possibly A. McLeod Fraser, lithographer for Hamilton *Spectator* in 1856.

772 View of Niagara Falls from the American Side

w.c. over pencil. 13 x 20 1/16 (330 x 509)
Inscribed l.r. *A.M. Fraser*; verso *Niagara Falls, U.S.A./A.M. Fraser*   951.41.19

Friend, Washington F.
(active 1845-1886)

Artist and entrepreneur. Born about 1820, possibly in England. Taught music and drawing in Boston, where he suffered financial losses in a theatre fire of 1847. Created a 'Floating Museum' on the Wabash River which failed. Travelled extensively in United States and Canada 1849-51, making sketches for a panoramic display of Canadian and American scenery. Gave world premiere of Panorama at Quebec, toured with display to other Canadian and American cities and gave command showing to Queen Victoria at Buckingham Palace. Friend sang American and Canadian folk songs in conjunction with the display. Published guide book to his Grand Tour in 1858. Exhibited series of 5 views of Niagara Falls in Montreal, 1867. Exhibited at Colonial and Indian Exhibition, London 1886, at which time he was living at Littlehampton, Sussex, England.

773 Tadoussac

w.c., touches of gouache. 9 13/16 x 14 1/2 (249 x 368)
Inscribed l.r. *W F Friend*   962.64.1

774 Landscape on the Lower St. Lawrence

w.c. 9 3/4 x 14 7/16 (247 x 367)
Inscribed l.l. *W F Friend*   962.64.2

775 The Falls of Montmorency

w.c., touches of gouache. 14 5/16 x 20 9/16 (363 x 522)
Inscribed l.l. *W.F. Friend*   960x276.4

776 The Quebec Citadel by Moonlight

w.c. and gouache on buff paper. 10 5/8 x 14 7/16 (270 x 366)
Inscribed l.r. *W.F. Friend*; verso *The Citadel, Quebec, Moonlight.*   963.39.1

776

777 The Falls of Lorette Near Quebec
w.c., touches of gouache. 14 7/8 x 10 5/16
(378 x 262)
Inscribed l.r. in ink *W F Friend*; verso of
mount in pencil *N 115/upper view*.
View shows artist sketching bridge from
below.   954.174.1

778 Sherbrooke, Quebec
w.c., touches of gouache. 10 1/2 x 15 1/8
(267 x 384)
Inscribed l.r. *W F Friend*; verso of mount
150 View from Sherbrook   951.67.9

778

779 A General View of Niagara Falls

w.c., touches of gouache. 13 3/8 x 31 7/8
(339 x 809)
Inscribed l.l. *W.F. Friend*
Composition same as cat. no. 780.
960x276.1

780 Niagara Seen from Above the Canadian Falls

w.c. 21 x 49 1/2 (533 x 1257) (sight)
Inscribed l.l. *W.F. Friend*
Composition same as cat. no. 779.
968x341.14

780

781 Kempenfelt Bay, Lake Simcoe
w.c., touches of gouache. 10 3/8 x 15 (263 x 381)
Inscribed l.l. *W F Friend*; verso *Kempenfelt bay, Lake Simco, Canada.* 955.157.7

781

Friend

782 Lumber Mill, Lake of the Woods
w.c., touches of gouache on grey paper.
9 7/8 x 14 13/16 (251 x 376)
Inscribed l.l. *WF Friend*; verso *W.F. Friend.*
Lumber Mill, Lake of the Woods, North Mill.
963.39.2

783 Grand Chasm, Tucson River, Arizona
w.c. 14 9/16 x 10 1/8 (370 x 257)
Inscribed l.l. [W.]F. Friend; verso of mount N
71 Grand Chasm, Tuscon River, North Georg
. . . [cut off]
The river is known as the Santa Cruz.
960.250.19

782

Friend

Garrison, Benjamin
(active 1757)

Possibly the same person as B. Garrison, listed as teacher of 'landskip' and marine painting in watercolour, New York City, 1782.

784 View of Halifax Taken in July 1757
black and grey washes, black ink margins.
14 5/16 x 25 3/8 (363 x 644)
Inscribed u.c., title; l.r. *Taken in 1757/Benjamin Garrison fecit* 950.66.5

784

Gordon, Adam
(see Kenmure)

Gore, Ralph
(active 1821)

Possibly same person as Ralph Gore, 33rd
Regiment 1809-21; listed as Lieutenant-
Colonel on half-pay and Storekeeper,
Ordnance Establishment, Quebec 1824.

785 Niagara Falls from the American Side
w.c. 14 11/16 x 22 (373 x 558)
Inscribed l.r. *R.G. Octr. 1821*; l.c. margin
*The Falls of Niagara from the American side,
with a view of Brown's Hotel & the old Indian
ladder now improved into a cover'd staircase*
951.67.10

786 Niagara Falls with a Rainbow
w.c., touches of gouache. 13 1/2 x 21 1/8
(343 x 536)
Watermark *J. Whatman 1819*   951.67.11

787 Niagara Falls
w.c. 14 7/8 x 21 1/4 (377 x 540)
951.67.12

785

Hall, Basil
(1788-1844)

British naval officer, author and artist of Scottish school. Son of scientist Sir James Hall and brother of painter James Hall. Travelled in North America 1827-8, and published an account as *Forty Etchings from Sketches made with the Camera Lucida in North America*, London & Edinburgh 1830. Exhibited NAD 1829-30.

788 Canadian Voyageurs of Captain Franklin's Canoe

w.c. and pencil. 7 3/8 x 8 3/8 (187 x 212)
Variant of plate 13 in Hall's *Forty Etchings* and possibly a copy after Hall. The subjects of the composition are described as follows:

"We had the good fortune to fall in with Captain Franklin, in Canada, just as he returned from his perilous expedition. He had crossed the Upper Lakes, and finally descended the beautiful Ottawa, in a canoe paddled by 14 voyageurs, of whom this Sketch represents three. The first, François Forcier, we were told, was a highly characteristic figure. The center one, called Enfant La Vallée, was a very cheerful old fellow. The third, named Malouin, was the steersman of the canoe, and of course a very important personage. He accompanied Captain Franklin during the whole of his journey, while the others were his companions only a small part of the way—about fourteen hundred miles—from Fort William, on Lake Superior, to Montreal."   967.308.2

788

Hall

Hall, Mary G.
(active 1833-35)

Topographical artist. Sketched views of Hudson River and Niagara Falls, 1833. Operated Mrs Hall's Drawing Academy, Saint John, N.B., 1834. One of earliest lithographic artists in Canada, she drew six views of Nova Scotia and New Brunswick on stone, which were published as *Views of British America* by Pendleton Lithography, Boston 1835, and issued in a booklet with covers and title page printed in Saint John, N.B.

789 Niagara Falls from the Bank Near the Pavilion Hotel

brown wash, pen and ink, coloured chalks, over pencil. 7 x 9 1/4 (178 x 235)
Inscribed l.c. of mount *Niagara Falls, from the bank near the Pavilion–M.G. Hall–1833*
960x282.135

790 Niagara River below Queenston

w.c., chalks, pen and ink, on grey paper. 6 1/4 x 9 1/4 (159 x 235)
Inscribed l.c. of mount *Niagara River–below Queenston/M.G. Hall–1833*   960x282.136

791 Approach to West Point from New York

w.c., touches of gouache and chalk over pencil. 7 x 9 1/2 (178 x 241)
Inscribed, l.c. of mount *Hudson River–Approach to West Point from New York 1833. M.G. Hall*   960x282.133

792 Hudson River from West Point Hotel

w.c, chalks, pen and ink. 7 x 9 3/4 (178 x 247)
Inscribed l.c. of mount *Hudson River, North, from the basement story of the hotel at West Point, 1833, M.G. Hall*   960x282.134

789

Hallen, Mary E.
(1819-1907)

Born at Haileybury, Worcestershire, oldest daughter of Reverend George Hallen. Family emigrated to Canada in 1835. The Rev. Mr. Hallen was rector of St. George's Church, Purbrook (now Fairvalley) and later chaplain to forces at Penetanguishene, Ontario. Daughters Mary and Eleonora both painted. Mary known for watercolour portraits, marines and landscapes of Penetanguishene area in 1850s. Married one Mr. Gilmour after 1868. Exhibited, OPE 1868; TIE 1879; UCPE 1866.

793 Penetanguishene from the Island
w.c. over pencil. 13 7/8 x 17 1/8 (352 x 435)
Inscribed l.l. *Mary Hallen 1851*; l.r. of mount, title.   964.96

793

Hallen

Hallewell, Edmund Gilling
(active 1839-1866)

Officer with 20th Regiment of Foot, which arrived in Quebec 1847, was posted in Kingston, London and Montreal, and left Canada 1853. Known for landscapes and marines in oil and watercolour. His name appears on army lists 1839-66.

794 Quebec Seen from Lévis
w.c. over pencil. 10 1/2 x 25 7/8 (261 x 657)
Inscribed l.l. *Hallewell XX Regt.*   954.107.2

794

Hay, J.
(active 1813)
Unknown amateur painter, presumably from Edinburgh, Scotland.

795 A Perspective View of Quebec City
w.c., pen and ink. 10 7/8 x 17 (276 x 431)
Inscribed l.c. *Quebec*; l.r. *A perspective view of Quebec, Capital of Canada. J. Hay f. Edin. 24 Sept. 1813*; verso, same title and *J.H. f. Sept. 24, 1813*
Copy of composition by Hervey Smyth as engraved by B. Benazech and published London 1760.   950.224.30

Hayward, Gerald Sinclair
(1845—1926)
Born at Port Hope, Ontario, son of Captain Alfred Hayward and Caroline Hayward, brother of painter Alfred Hayward. The whole family painted; they decorated the walls of their house 'Ravenscourt,' near Port Hope, with mural landscapes. Gerald farmed in youth; served with 10th Royals in 1866; went to England to study painting, 1870. Spent most of professional life in England and later in New York and Boston, but maintained summer home at Gore's Landing, Rice Lake. Known principally as painter of miniature portraits on ivory. Exhibited OSA 1882; RA; RCA 1915. Died at Gore's Landing.

796 Gore's Landing, Rice Lake
w.c., touches of gouache, over pencil.
4 7/16 x 14 1/4 (113 x 362)
Inscribed l.r. *G.S.H.*: verso *From Your old Friend G.S.H. Taken from Hill behind 'The Willows', Rice Lake*
In foreground of view, left to right, are the tower of the Anglican church, the 'white house,' the Harris hotel, store and house, and artist's house. In background are Grape, Sugar, Sheep and Black islands and mouth of Ottonabee River on far shore.
Gift of Estate of Dr Clara C. Benson, Port Hope, through V.B. Blake, Executor.
967.181.5

Henn, Edmund
(active 1789-1800)
Captain, 24th Warwickshire Regiment of Foot, which served in Canada 1789-1800. Stationed in Detroit and Michilimackinac areas in 1795-6.

797 A View of Niagara Falls in 1799
w.c., pen and ink, over pencil. 23 15/16 x 33 5/8 (608 x 854)
Inscribed l.r. *E. Henn Delt. 1799*
Watermark: *1794*   961.129

797

Henn

Heriot, George
(1766-1844)

Born at Haddington, Scotland, son of Sheriff of County of East Lothian. Studied at Royal Military Academy, Woolwich, England. Arrived in Quebec 1791, attached to army treasury department. Served as Deputy Post-Master General of British North America 1800-16. Returned to England 1816.

Known in England as an accomplished amateur watercolourist, Heriot exhibited Canadian views at Royal Academy 1797. Author of *A History of Canada* (1804) and *Travels Through the Canadas* (1807), the latter illustrated with aquatint engravings after his sketches. Also painted a few oil canvases about 1810.

798 View in the Basin of Minas Near Windsor, N.S.

w.c. over pencil. 5 3/8 x 7 1/4 (136 x 184)
Inscribed verso *View in the Basin of Mines near Windsor, N. Scotia./Drawn on the spot by Geo Heriot. 22d June, 1807*   953.132.17

799 View in the Basin of Minas Near Windsor

w.c. over pencil. 9 3/8 x 12 1/2 (238 x 317)
Inscribed l.l. *G. Heriot*   954.102.5

800 View on Partridge Island, Bay of Fundy

w.c. and pencil. 5 x 7 1/4 (127 x 184)
Inscribed verso *View on Partridge Island–Bay of Fundy. Drawn on the spot by Geo Heriot, 24th June 1807*   953.132.20

801 View from Partridge Island in the Bay of Fundy

w.c. over pencil. 4 7/8 x 7 1/4 (124 x 184)
Inscribed verso *View from Partridge island in the Bay of Fundy. Drawn on the spot by Geo Heriot, 24th June 1807.*   953.132.21

802 West View of Partridge Island from Parrsboro

w.c. over pencil. 5 5/16 x 7 5/16 (135 x 186)
Inscribed verso *West view of Partridge island from Parsborough, Bay of Fundy. Drawn on the spot by Geo. Heriot, 24th June 1807*
953.132.19

802

803 Fall of the Pokiok, St. John's River
brown wash. 9 1/2 x 13 1/2 (241 x 342)
Inscribed verso *Fall of the Poquioc, St John's River, New Brunswick*   953.132.29

803

Heriot

804 View on the River St. John near the Pokiok

brown wash over pencil. 5 1/4 x 7 1/4 (133 x 184)
Inscribed verso *View on the river Saint John near the Poquioq. Drawn on the Spot by Geo. Heriot, 23d July 1807* 953.132.2

805 Belle Isle Bay, St. John River

grey-brown wash over pencil. 5 1/4 x 7 1/4 (133 x 184)
Inscribed verso *Belle Isle Bay, St. John's River. Drawn on the spot by Geo. Heriot, 29th June 1807* 953.132.9

806 Narrows of the St. John River

grey-brown wash over pencil on light-pink paper. 4 15/16 x 7 3/8 (125 x 187)
Inscribed verso *Narrows of St. John's River, N Brunswick 1807* 953.132.5

807 Chief Justice Ludlow's House on the River St. John

w.c. over pencil. 13 1/4 x 19 1/4 (336 x 489)
Inscribed l.r. *1807*; verso *Chief Justice Ludlow's on the river St. John New Brunswick.*
Watermark: *J. Whatman*
George Duncan Ludlow (1734-1808), first chief justice of New Brunswick 1784-1808, lived at 'Springhill' 5 miles above Fredericton. 950.31

807

808 Grande Isle, St. John River
black and grey washes. 4 3/8 x 7 1/8 (111
x 181)
Inscribed verso *Grand Isle. Settlement of
Madawaska. River St John. America*
953.132.14

809 Baie St. Paul, River St. Lawrence
w.c. over pencil. 5 1/4 x 7 1/4 (133 x 184)
Inscribed verso *View of St. Paul's Bay, River
St. Lawrence*
Watermark: Seated woman with Spear,
Shield and Flower in Medallion
surmounted by Crown.
Similar view reproduced in aquatint in
Heriot's *Travels*.   953.132.8

**810 Island of Orleans with Quebec in the
Distance**
w.c. over pencil. 8 3/8 x 12 1/16 (213 x 306)
Inscribed l.c. of mount *Isle of Orleans, &c.*
(or Lc?); l.r. of mount *G H*.   954.102.3

**811 Ruins of the Monastery at Château
Richer**
w.c. over pencil. 5 5/16 x 7-313/8 (135 x
187)
Inscribed verso *Ruins of the Monastery at
Chateau Richer, 15 miles N.E. of Quebec. Geo.
Heriot, 1805*
Same view engraved in aquatint to
illustrate Heriot's *Travels*.   953.132.4

**812 Rapids at the Pitch of the Fall of
Montmorency**
w.c. and pencil. 5 1/8 x 7 3/16 (130 x 182)
Inscribed verso *Rapids at the Pitch of the Fall
of Montmorenci Geo. Heriot, 1805*
953.132.11

813 Falls of Montmorency
w.c. over pencil. 5 1/4 x 7 1/4 (133 x 184)
Inscribed l.c. of mount *Falls of*

Montmorenci–1806–Geo: Heriot–
The view shows General Haldimand's
small summer house.   954.102.1

814 Les Trois Saults de Montmorency
grey-brown wash over pencil. 5 1/8 x 7 1/2
(130 x 190)
Inscribed verso *Les Trois Saults de
Montmorenci. 12 miles from Quebec [Geo.]
Heriot, 12th Augt. 1808*   953.132.15

815 West View of Montmorency Falls
w.c. over pencil. 4 7/8 x 7 1/8 (124 x 181)
Inscribed verso *West View of Falls of
Montmorenci. Geo. Heriot*   953.132.3

**816 Side View of Montmorency Falls from
the West**
brown, grey and green washes, scraping.
7 3/8 x 5 3/8 (187 x 136)
Inscribed verso *Side View of the Falls of
Montmorenci from the West./Geo Heriot*
953.132.12

**817 Falls of Montmorency from Pointe
Lévis**
w.c. over pencil. 4 1/2 x 6 1/2 (114 x 165)
Inscribed verso *Falls of Montmorenci from
Point Levy near Quebec. Geo. Heriot*
953.132.10

818 Falls of Montmorency
w.c. over pencil. 5 1/8 x 7 3/8 (130 x 187)
Inscribed l.c. of mount *Falls of Montmorenci*;
l.l. of mount *G. Heriot delin*   955.157.1

819 Distillery at Beauport Near Quebec
w.c. over pencil. 4 3/4 x 6 7/8 (121 x 174)
Inscribed l.l. *G. Heriot*; verso *Distillery at
Beauport near Quebec. Geo. Heriot, March 1812*
View shows distillery and stream in
foreground, Beauport church and town in
background.   954.102.2

819

820 Ruins of the Intendant's Palace, Quebec

w.c. over pencil. 10 7/16 x 14 3/4 (265 x 374)
Inscribed on old mount *Ruins of the Intendant's Palace-Quebec. 1798*   953.132.25

821 Ruins of the Intendant's Palace

w.c., pen and ink over pencil. 10 1/2 x 14 7/8 (261 x 377)
Inscribed on old mount *Ruins of the Intendant's Palace, 1799*   953.132.24

822 Ruins of the Intendant's Palace

w.c., pen and ink over pencil. 10 1/2 x 14 11/16 (261 x 373)
Inscribed on old mount *Ruins of the Intendant's Palace 1799*   953.132.27

822

Heriot

823 Ruins of the Intendant's Palace
w.c., pen and ink over pencil. 10 1/4 x
14 3/8 (260 x 365)
Inscribed on old mount *Ruins of the
Intendant's Palace 1798*   953.132.26

**824 The Citadel, Quebec, seen from the
Plains of Abraham**
w.c. over pencil. 5 3/8 x 7 3/8 (136 x 187)
953.132.1

**825 Quebec seen from Outside the Walls
Near St. Louis Gate**
w.c. over pencil. 9 3/4 x 14 1/4 (247 x 362)
Inscribed verso *Quebec*   953.132.31

825

Heriot

826 Quebec from Cape Diamond
w.c., pen and ink over pencil. 11 7/8 x
18 11/16 (301 x 474)
Inscribed l.r., title; verso *Quebec*   953.163.1

826

Heriot

827 Quebec from Lévis
w.c. over pencil. 6 5/16 x 15 5/8 (160 x 396)
Inscribed verso *Quebec*
Watermark: *J. Whatman 1801*
953.132.30

828 Dorchester Bridge and General Hospital
w.c. 6 5/8 x 10 1/2 (168 x 266)
Inscribed l.c. *Dorchester Bridge near Quebec with a View of the General Hospital.*
Sketched on reverse of cat. no. 829.
953.132.32A

828

Heriot

829 View of the General Hospital, River St. Charles and Beauport Mountains
w.c. 6 5/8 x 21 1/8 (168 x 536)
Inscribed l.l. to r. *View from the North Bank which extends from Quebec to Cape Rouge, showing the General Hospital, River St. Charles & Mountains of Beauport.*
Sketch on centre-fold of two sketchbook leaves; cat. no. 828 is on reverse of one sheet.   953.132.32B

830 The St. Lawrence below Cap Rouge
w.c. over pencil. 5 1/4 x 7 1/4 (133 x 184)
Inscribed verso *Geo. Heriot 1805 / View of the banks of the St. Lawrence below Cape Rouge*
953.132.18

831 View under Cap Rouge
w.c. over pencil. 5 3/16 x 7 5/16 (131 x 185)
Inscribed verso *Geo. Heriot 1805 / View under Cape Rouge.*   953.132.34

832 Falls of the Chaudière, Quebec
w.c. over pencil. 5 3/8 x 8 3/16 (136 x 208)
Inscribed l.c. of mount *Falls of the Chaudiere, Quebec.*; l.r. of mount *Geo Heriot*
955.157.10

833 Falls of La Puce Near Quebec
w.c., touches of gouache, on grey paper.
4 5/8 x 7 1/8 (117 x 181)
Faint pencil sketch on verso.   953.132.6

834 L'Assomption
w.c. over pencil. 7 3/4 x 11 1/8 (196 x 282)
Inscribed verso *L'Assomption. / Geo. Heriot 26 Octob 1810*   953.132.13

834

835 Ferry on the Jacques Cartier River
dark brown wash over pencil. 5 x 7 5/16
(127 x 185)
Inscribed verso *Ferry on the Jacques Quartier*
Sept. 12th, 1807   953.132.7

835

Heriot

**836 Indian Village and Catholic Mission,
Lake of Two Mountains**

brown wash over pencil. 5 x 7 1/4 (127 x
184)
Inscribed verso *Lake of the Two Mountains,
1st October, 1807*
Heriot describes this settlement as the
village called Canasadago (*Travels*, p. 236).
953.132.16

836

Heriot

837 Initiating Voyageurs at Pointe au Baptême, Ottawa River
w.c. over pencil. 7 1/4 x 11 1/8 (184 x 282)
Inscribed l.r. *Pointe au Baptheme, Pictaonaic River*.
Watermark: Lily on shield with finial.
On page 239 of his *Travels* Heriot describes "point au Baptheme . . . so denominated, because the rude ceremony is here performed of plunging into the waters of the Outaouais, such persons as have never before travelled thus far."
953.132.28

838 The Niagara River
pencil and w.c. 5 1/2 x 7 3/8 (139 x 187)
Inscribed verso *Niagara River 1801/June 6th*.
953.132.22

839 The Whirlpool, Niagara River
w.c. over pencil. 5 5/8 x 7 3/8 (143 x 187)
Inscribed verso *Whirlpool Niagara River/1801*   953.132.23

840 Falls of Niagara
w.c. 5 3/8 x 7 1/4 (136 x 184)
Inscribed l.c. of mount *Falls of Niagara–1804–Geo: Heriot*   951.67.1

841 Niagara Falls from Canadian Shore
w.c. over pencil. 7 x 9 7/8 (177 x 250)
Inscribed l.l. *Geo Heriot*
The view includes 'costumed' figures, and varies in colouring and brushwork from Heriot's usual style. Possibly painted late in his life or the work of another hand.
951.67.3

842 View of a Ruin
w.c. over pencil on blue-grey paper. 12 1/8 x 16 5/8 (308 x 422)
Inscribed l.r. of mount *G.H.*; l. c. of mount *Cataract of the Chaudiere*.
The view shows a large ruined building beside a calm expanse of water.   951.41.23

843 Encampment of Domiciliated Indians
w.c. over pencil. 10 x 14 3/4 (254 x 374)
Inscribed verso, title.
This composition was engraved in aquatint and published as one of the illustrations in Heriot's *Travels*, 1807.   950.224.27

843

844 Landscape with Figures and River
w.c. over pencil. 9 3/8 x 13 (238 x 330)
Inscribed l.l. *G. Heriot*;
Watermark: *E & P 1804* (Edmunds & Pine)
951.67.2

845 River Landscape
w.c. over pencil. 9 1/4 x 13 1/4 (235 x 336)
Inscribed l.l. *G. Heriot*
Watermark: *E & P 1804* (Edmunds & Pine)
954.102.4

846 Waterfalls in a Canyon
w.c. over pencil. 6 1/2 x 9 1/2 (165 x 241)
955.157.2

847 Landscape with Mountains
brown wash over pencil. 3 5/8 x 4 11/16
(92 x 119)   951.41.4

848 View on the Hudson River
grey-brown wash over pencil. 5 1/2 x
8 9/16 (140 x 217)
Inscribed verso *View on the Hudson*
953.132.33

849 Plymouth, England
w.c. and pencil. 4 9/16 x 7 3/16 (116 x 182)
Said to have been sketched in 1826.
962.58.7

**850 View Near Crumpford Bridge,
Matlock, England**
w.c. over pencil. 4 3/4 x 7 1/4 (120 x 184)
Inscribed on mount *View near Crumpford
Bridge, Matlock, 29 Sept. 1819*   962.58.6

851 English House and Road
w.c. over pencil. 10 x 13 3/4 (254 x 349)
Watermark: *J. Whatman 1801*   956.54

**852 Upper Lake of Killarney from Turk
Mountain, Ireland**

grey-brown wash over pencil. 5 x 7 1/8
(127 x 181)
Inscribed verso, title.
Originally attributed to Heriot, but
possibly by another watercolourist of his
period.   960.147.1

853 Cascades of the St. Lawrence
w.c. 10 1/2 x 15 1/2 (266 x 393)
Inscribed l.r., title.
Copy by an unknown naive painter of the
aquatint after Heriot which appeared in his
Travels, 1807.   955.130.3

Hind, William George Richardson
(1833-1889)

Born in England. Thought to have studied
art in London and on the Continent.
Emigrated to Canada 1852. Taught drawing
in Toronto; teaching at Toronto Normal
School in 1856. Visited England, returning
in spring of 1861 to join his geologist
brother Henry Youle Hind on expedition to
the Labrador Peninsula. Named official
artist to expedition and his views were
reproduced in H.Y. Hind's report,
*Explorations in the Interior of the Labrador
Peninsula*, London 1863. Travelled to the
Cariboo with the 'Overlanders' of 1862.
Worked as artist in Victoria 1863-65. Spent
his later years working as draughtsman for
railways in Nova Scotia and New
Brunswick. Died at Sussex, N.B.

854 Pierre, The Abenaki
w.c. and gouache over pencil. 7 1/4 x 9 1/2
(184 x 241)
Inscribed l.c. of mount *Pierre the Abenaquis*;
u.r. of mount *65*.
The skill of the guide, Pierre, is described
in *Explorations*, I, 289.   967.227.2

854

855 The First Camp on the Moisie
w.c. over pencil on prepared ground. 5 1/8
x 8 1/4 (130 x 210)
Inscribed l.c., title; u.r. 5; l.r., embossed
blind-stamp of *G. Rowney & Co. London.*
The site of the camp is described by H.Y.
Hind in *Explorations*, I, 23.   967.227.1

856 Portage on the Moisie River
w.c., touches of gouache. 1 5/8 x 3 1/8 (41
x 79)
Inscribed l.c. of mount *"Can we manage
it–Pierre"? Rapids*   968.147.6

**857 Canoe Party Descending the Rapids,
Moisie River**
w.c. 2 x 3 5/8 (51 x 92)
968.147.7

856

857

Hind

Hine, Henry George
(1811-1895)

English landscape painter and engraver.
On the staff of *Punch* 1841-44 and
subsequently contributed illustrations to
Illustrated London News and other
publications. Exhibited landscapes at Royal
Academy and the Suffolk Street Gallery,
London. Member, Institute of Painters in
Watercolours, 1864.

858 Buffalo Hunt on the Prairies

w.c., touches of gouache. 8 1/4 x 22 3/8
(210 x 568)
Inscribed l.l. *H.G. Hine 1847*
Watermark on original mount: *Turkey Mill,
Kent* [Whatman]   957.188

858

Hine

Holdstock, Alfred Worsley
(1820-1901)

Born at Bath, England and educated at Oxford University. Emigrated to Montreal 1850. Taught drawing at National School, Bonsecours Street and gave private lessons. Later gave up teaching. Known for landscape views in oil, watercolour and pastel.

859 Gatineau River

pastel, touches of gouache. 13 7/8 x 20 3/4 (352 x 527)
Inscribed l.l. *Gatineau River, C.W.* [presumably in error for C.E]; l.r. *A.W. Holdstock.*   968x341.4

860 Mékinac River and Lake, C.E.

pastel, touches of gouache. 13 7/8 x 20 9/16 (352 x 522)
Inscribed l.l., title; l.r. *A.W. Holdstock*
The Mékinac drains into the St. Maurice River, P.Q.   968x341.5

860

Holloway, Frederick H.
(active 1840-53)

Artist, probably of English origin. Known for Quebec and Ontario landscape views in pencil, w.c. and oil. A series of his Niagara views were reproduced in lithograph by Sarony & Major (active 1846-57) and by Hall & Mooney (active 1839-50).

861 Kingston seen from Fort Henry
pencil. 6 3/4 x 10 3/4 (171 x 273)
Inscribed l.c. of mount *View of Kingston*
The city hall dome, sketchily indicated in this view, was added to the building in 1843.   970.293

Holmes, James
(1777-1860)

Miniaturist and watercolour painter of the English School. Born at Burslem, Staffordshire. Exhibited at Water-Colour Society 1813-22; Royal Academy from 1819; Society of British Artists from 1850. One of favourite painters of George IV.

862 Portrait of Sir John Young, Baron Lisgar, Governor General of Canada 1868-72

w.c., touches of gouache, pencil. 20 x 14 13/16 (508 x 376)
Inscribed l.r. *J. Holmes, 1850*; on volumes in foreground of portrait *Council of St. John (1835), Committee of the Baronetage for Privileges 1835, (Nova Scotia Question 1840)*; on map in foreground of portrait *(Nova Scotia-Halifax & Quebec Railway 1845)*; on framed painting in background of portrait *London Necropolis, Woking, 1849*. A view of city of Edinburgh, Scotland is seen from window at left.
The bracketed inscriptions are later additions.   951.86

862

Hope-Wallace, James
(1807-1854)
Born James Hope, son of Earl of Hopetoun. Officer with Coldstream Guards 1821-44. Married Lady Mary Francis Nugent, daughter of Earl of Westmeath, 1837. Posted to Quebec 1838, and organized the 'Queen's Volunteers' in November 1838 on the order of Lord Seaton. Left Canada about 1844, the year he succeeded to the estate of his uncle, Lord Wallace, and took on the name. Died at his seat, Featherstone Castle.

THE HOPE ALBUM

The following 69 watercolour views were mounted in an album with marbled covers, leather corners and spine.
Inscribed in ink inside front cover *Mary Frances Hope, Quebec, January 1841.* Label on inside front cover, *T. Cary & Co., Booksellers & Stationers, Freemasons Hall, Buade St., Quebec.*

863 Falls of Rivière La Puce
w.c., scraping. 13 x 8 15/16 (330 x 227)
Inscribed l.r. *R. La Puce/13 Septr 1839*
951.45.41

864 Falls of Ste Anne du Nord River
w.c. over soft pencil. 13 x 9 (330 x 228)
Inscribed l.l. *St. Anne's, 13 Sept. 1839*
951.45.42

865 Falls of River Ste Anne du Nord
w.c. 9 x 13 (330 x 228))
Inscribed l.r. *St. Anne's 13 Sept 1839*
951.45.50

866 Falls of St. Féréol
w.c. over pencil. 13 x 9 (330 x 228)
Inscribed l.l. *St. Feriol/14 Sept. 1839*
951.45.43

867 Montmorency Falls
w.c. over pencil. 8 15/16 x 13 (227 x 330)
Inscribed l.l. *Quebec 27 Augt 1838*
Unfinished pencil sketch of landscape with waterfall on verso. 951.45.10

868 Montmorency Falls seen from Lévis
w.c. 8 15/16 x 13 (227 x 330)
Inscribed l.l. *Quebec/9 Oct 1838*
951.45.8

869 View of the St. Lawrence River from Pointe Lévis, Looking East
w.c. over pencil. 10 5/16 x 14 1/2 (262 x 368)
Inscribed l.r. *Point Levy 12 Sepr 1839*
951.45.60

870 View from Pointe Lévis Looking East
w.c. 10 5/16 x 14 1/2 (262 x 368)
Inscribed l.r. *Point Levy 12 Sept 1839*
951.45.40

871 View of Cape Diamond and the Citadel from Lévis
w.c. 5 3/16 x 7 1/4 (132 x 184)
Inscribed l.l. *3d Sept 1839* 951.45.38

872 View of the Lévis Shore from Quebec
w.c. over pencil. 5 1/16 x 7 1/4 (128 x 184)
Inscribed l.r. *Quebec Sepr 15 1838*
951.45.26

873 View of the St. Lawrence from the Citadel, Looking East
w.c., touches of gouache, over pencil. 9 3/8 x 14 7/16 (238 x 366)
Inscribed l.r. *Quebec/6th Augt/1838*
For similar view of Citadel, see Barnard, cat. no. 73. 951.45.11

874 View of Lower Town from the Citadel
w.c. over pencil. 5 1/16 x 7 3/16 (128 x 187)
Inscribed l.l. *Quebec/25 July 1838*
Faint pencil sketch on verso. 951.45.13

875 View of the St. Lawrence from the Citadel
w.c. over pencil. 9 5/8 x 14 1/2 (244 x 368)
Inscribed l.r. *Aug 6 1838* 951.45.16

876 View from the Citadel Looking East
w.c. over pencil. 10 5/16 x 14 1/2 (262 x 368)
Inscribed l.r. *Quebec/Sept. 15;* l.l. *Sep' 15/1838* 951.45.27

877 Part of Lower Town seen from the Ramparts
w.c. 8 15/16 x 13 (227 x 330)
Inscribed l.l. *Quebec/3 Augt 1838*
951.45.15

878 River St. Charles seen from the Ramparts
w.c. over pencil. 8 7/8 x 12 15/16 (225 x 328)
Inscribed l.l. *Quebec/23 July 1838*
Slight pencil sketch of tree on verso.
951.45.12

879 View from Government House Garden towards the Citadel
w.c. over pencil. 9 x 13 (228 x 330)
Inscribed l.l. *Govn. Garden/Quebec 25th July 1840*
951.45.48

880 Birch Tree in Government House Garden, Quebec
w.c. over pencil. 9 x 13 (228 x 330).
Inscribed l.l. *Govs Garden/Quebec 16 July 1840* 951.45.47

881 View over Quebec Rooftops towards Beauport
w.c. 7 1/4 x 9 7/8 (184 x 251)
Inscribed l.l. *Quebec./10 Augt/40./from back windows.*
The view is taken from the vicinity of St. Louis Street. 951.45.4

882 Mont Carmel Street, Quebec, Looking Towards the River
w.c. over pencil. 10 3/16 x 12 3/16 (259 x 309) 951.45.5

883 View of the St. Lawrence River from Quebec Rooftops
w.c. over pencil. 5 1/16 x 7 3/16 (128 x 187)
Inscribed l.l. *Quebec 25 Sept. 1838*
951.45.28

884 St. Roch Suburb seen from Quebec Rooftops
w.c. over pencil. 8 15/16 x 12 5.8 (227 x 320)
Inscribed l.l. *Quebec, 11th July 1838*
Pencil sketch of Citadel fortifications on verso; a preliminary drawing for cat. no. 876.   951.45.17

885 Part of St. Roch and Martello Tower
w.c. over pencil. 8 15/16 x 13 (227 x 330)
Inscribed l.l. *Quebec/18th Aug 1838*; verso *from the Martello Tower/M. Chaplin.* Millicent Mary Chaplin (q.v.) copied this view in 1841; her signed version is in the PAC collection.   951.45.7

886 Quebec seen from North East Bank of St. Charles River
w.c. over pencil. 8 15/16 x 13 (227 x 330)
951.45.33

887 Timber Cove, Quebec, seen from Above
w.c. over pencil. 8 15/16 x 13 (227 x 330)
Inscribed l.c. *Quebec 22 Augt. 1838*
951.45.9

888 Timber Cove and Pier, Quebec
w.c. over pencil. 9 x 13 (228 x 330)
951.45.49

889 Timber Cove with Houses, Quebec
w.c. over pencil. 8 5/16 x 13 (227 x 330)
Inscribed l.l. *Quebec 8 Oct*   951.45.31

890 Raft on the St. Lawrence at Cap Rouge
w.c. over pencil. 5 1/16 x 7 3/16 (128 x 187)
Inscribed l.l. *Carouge/8 Sept 1838*
951.45.23

891 St. Lawrence River at Cap Rouge
w.c. over pencil. 5 1/6 x 7 3/16 (128 x 187)
Inscribed l.l. *Carouge 8 Sept 1838*
951.45.22

892 St. Lawrence River Seen from the Plains of Abraham
w.c. over pencil. 5 1/16 x 7 3/16 (128 x 182)
Inscribed l.l. *7 Augt 1839*   951.45.3

893 Beached Sailing Ships
w.c. 5 3/16 x 7 1/4 (132 x 184)
Inscribed l.l. *4 Sept 1839*   951.45.39

894 Studies of Sailing Ships and a Sunset
w.c. over pencil. 5 1/6 x 7 3/16 (128 x 187)
Inscribed l.r. *Quebec 4th Sept. 1838*
951.45.18

895 Landscape Near Quebec
w.c. over pencil. 5 1/16 x 7 3/16 (128 x 187)
Inscribed l.c. *Quebec 5 Sept. 1838*
951.45.19

896 St. Lawrence Landscape Near Quebec
w.c. over pencil. 5 1/16 x 7 3/16 (128 x 187)
Inscribed l.l. *Quebec 6th Sept. 1838*
951.45.20

897 Figures by a Roadside Cross Near Quebec
w.c. over pencil. 5 1/16 x 7 3/16 (128 x 187)
Inscribed l.l. *Quebec 7 Sept 1838*   951.45.21

897

898 Chapel of Notre Dame de Sainte Foy
w.c. over pencil. 8 15/16 x 13 (227 x 330)
Inscribed l.r. *St. Foy 17 Sept. 1838.*
951.45.30

898

Hope

899 Landscape with House Near Quebec
w.c. over pencil. 5 1/16 x 7 1/4 (128 x 184)
Inscribed l.l. *Quebec 14 Sepr 1838*
951.45.25

900 River Landscape Near Quebec
w.c. over pencil. 8 15/16 x 13 (227 x 330)
Inscribed l.l. *Quebec, 16 Sept/1838*
951.45.24

901 St. Lawrence River Landscape Near Quebec
w.c. over pencil. 5 1/16 x 7 3/16 (128 x 187)
Inscribed l.r. *Quebec 17 Sept 1838*
951.45.29

902 Landscape with River and Bridge Near Quebec
w.c. over pencil. 5 1/16 x 7 3/16 (128 x 187)
951.45.14

903 Landscape with River and Bridge Near Quebec
w.c. over pencil. 10 3/8 x 14 9/16 (263 x 370)
Inscribed l.l. *Quebec, 15 Augt. 1838*
951.45.6

904 Landscape with St. Lawrence River in Distance
w.c. over pencil. 8 15/16 x 13 (227 x 330)
Inscribed l.l. *Quebec, 15 Aug 1839*
951.45.35

905 Valley Landscape Near Quebec
w.c. over pencil. 8 15/16 x 13 (227 x 330)
Inscribed l.l. *14 Augt. 1839*   951.45.34

906 Fishing on Lake St. Charles
w.c. 9 x 13 (228 x 330)
Inscribed l.l. *Lake Charles, 27 Sept. 1839*
951.45.44

907 Boating on Lake St. Charles
w.c. over pencil. 9 x 13 (228 x 330)
Inscribed l.l. *Lake Charles/27 Sept 1839*
951.45.45

908 View of Lake St. Charles
w.c. 9 x 13 (228 x 330)
Inscribed l.l. *Lake Charles/27 Sept 1839*
951.45.46

909 Bridge over the Jacques Cartier River
w.c. over pencil. 9 x 13 (228 x 330)
Inscribed l.r. *15 July 1841*
See similar view by H.W. Barnard, cat. no. 91.   951.45.52

910 The Jacques Cartier River
w.c. over pencil. 9 x 13 (228 x 330)
Inscribed l.l. *23 July 1841*
See similar view by H.W. Barnard, cat. no. 92, which refers to 'Hope fishing.'
951.45.55

911 Jacques Cartier River
w.c. over pencil. 9 x 13 (228 x 330)
Inscribed l.l. *23 July 1841*   951.45.58

912 Jacques Cartier River
w.c. over pencil. 9 x 13 (228 x 330)
Inscribed l.l. *23 July 1841*   951.45.57

913 River with Rocky Banks
w.c. over pencil. 9 x 13 (228 x 330)
Inscribed l.r. *7 July 1841*
Probably the Jacques Cartier River.
951.45.51

914 River with Rocky Banks
w.c. over pencil. 9 x 13 (228 x 330)
Inscribed l.l. *14 July 1841*
Probably the Jacques Cartier River.
951.45.54

915 Building a Shelter in the Quebec Woods in Winter
w.c. over pencil. 3 15/16 x 5 11/16 (100 x 144)
Possibly the same camping trip as cat. no. 933.   951.45.2

916 Tobogganing
w.c. over pencil. 3 15/16 x 5 3/4 (100 x 146)
951.45.1

917 General View of Niagara Falls from the Canadian Side
w.c. over pencil. 9 7/8 x 14 1/4 (251 x 368)
Inscribed l.l. *4 Sept/41*   951.45.62

918 General View of Niagara Falls from the American Side
w.c. over pencil. 9 x 14 5/16 (228 x 363)
951.45.65

919 Rowboat Approaching the Falls below Terrapin Tower
w.c. over pencil. 9 7/8 x 14 13/16 (251 x 376)   951.45.59

920 The Horseshoe Falls and Terrapin Tower seen from Goat Island
w.c. over pencil. 9 7/8 x 14 1/4 (251 x 368)
Inscribed l.l. *6 Sept. 1841*   951.45.63

921 The American Falls and Niagara River seen from TerrapinTower
w.c. over pencil. 9 7/8 x 14 7/16 (251 x 366)
Inscribed l.l. *6 Sep/41*   951.45.64

922 The American Falls and Niagara River seen from Terrapin Tower
w.c. over pencil. 10 1/4 x 14 7/16 (260 x 366)
Inscribed l.l. *8 Sept 41*   951.45.66

923 The Horseshoe Falls seen from Above on the American Side
w.c. over pencil. 9 1/4 x 14 7/16 (235 x 366)
951.45.67

924 Horseshoe Fall and Moss Islands seen from Table Rock
w.c. over pencil. 10 1/4 x 14 7/16 (260 x 366)
Inscribed l.l. *8 Sept. 1841*   951.45.69

925 Horseshoe Fall and Goat Island seen from Table Rock
w.c. 9 7/8 x 14 1/4 (251 x 368)
Inscribed l.l. *6 Sept. 41*   951.45.61

926 Moss Islands, Niagara River, seen from Goat Island
w.c. over pencil. 10 1/16 x 14 1/4 (255 x 368)
Inscribed l.l. *8 Sept. 41*   951.45.68

927 Wildbad, Germany
w.c. over pencil. 9 3/16 x 13 (233 x 330)
Inscribed l.r. *Wildbad, 10 July 1846*
951.45.56

928 Landscape with Lake and Mountains
w.c. over pencil. 9 1/16 x 13 (233 x 330)
Probably a European view.   951.45.53

929 Sailboats on a Mountain Lake
w.c. 9 3/16 x 13 (233 x 330)
Faint pencil sketch of landscape on verso.
Probably a European view.   951.45.36

930 Harbour with Breakwater and Sailboats
w.c. over pencil. 9 x 13 1/16 (228 x 331)
Probably a European view.   951.45.32

931 Village in a Valley
w.c. over pencil. 9 1/8 x 13 (231 x 330)
Probably a European view.   951.45.37

end of album

932 Campsite on the Saguenay River
pencil, pen and ink. 6 1/2 x 9 5/8 (165 x 244)
Inscribed u.r. *On the Saguenay Octr. 1838*
955.145.2

933 Camping Near Quebec
w.c. 7 9/16 x 13 7/16 (243 x 341)
Inscribed l.l. of mount *Night of 22d Feby 1840* (in ink); l.c. of mount *Hon. James Hope, Lady Mary Hope, Hon. Louis Hope & Lt. Col. & Mrs. Codrington. Camping Nr. Quebec* (in pencil); verso, same list of names.
951.188.1

933

934 My First Shot at a Moose

pen and ink over pencil. 8 x 12 1/2 (203 x 317)

Inscribed l.r. *My first shot at a moose 27 Feby 1840.*

Watermark: armoured bust within oval surmounted by crown.   966.2.9

934

935 Officers at a Dance
pen and ink over pencil on grey paper.
7 15/16 x 12 1/4 (201 x 311)
Inscribed l.c. *Ld. F.K. Paulet.* Lord Frederick
Paulet served in the Coldstream Guards
with the artist.
Watermark: *J. Rump, 1837*
Gift of Mrs Edgar J. Stone, Toronto.
965.49.1

936 Indian Woman of the Micmac Tribe
pen and ink. 7 x 4 5/16 (178 x 109)
Inscribed u.r. *Indian woman/Mick
Mack/Tribe;* verso *In order for Mr. Bells
friends to see the Citadel . . .* [in ink]; *The
General cannot sanction the exchange of Haln [?]
with Boyle & Daniell.* [in pencil]
Watermark: *. . . leirs*   966.2.8

935

Hopkins, Frances Anne
(1838-1918)

Born in England, daughter of Rear-Admiral Frederick William Beechey and grand-daughter of painter Sir William Beechey. Married in 1858 to Edward Martin Hopkins, private secretary to Sir George Simpson, director of Hudson's Bay Company. Lived in Lachine, P.Q., 1858-60, and Montreal 1861-70. Accompanied her husband on Canadian voyages, including a canoe trip to Lake Superior in 1869. Returned to England *c.* 1870-1. Painted in oil and watercolour. Exhibited, AAM 1870; OWCS; RA.

937 Timber Raft on the St. Lawrence
w.c., touches of gouache, on pink paper.
16 5/8 x 20 3/8 (422 x 517)
Inscribed l.l. *F.A.H.*   962.37

937

Hopkins

938 Tobogganing

w.c., touches of gouache, over pencil.
9 1/8 x 19 7/8 (232 x 505)
Inscribed l.r. *FAH/1867;* verso *The "Family
Coach" coming to grief/Mr. Swaine/(pair 8
guineas)*   959.126

939 Parliament Buildings, Ottawa

w.c., touches of gouache, over pencil.
11 3/4 x 17 3/4 (298 x 451)
Inscribed l.r. *FAH/1866;* verso of old
mount *Parliament House, Ottawa, Canada, by
Mrs. Hopkins. Bought by H.R.L.N. 1866.*
Initials refer to Major Henry Richard
Legge Newdigate of Prince Consort's Own
Rifle Brigade.   960.59.1

939

940 The Explorers' Camp
w.c. 10 5/16 x 12 1/4 (278 x 311)
Inscribed l.l. *FAH*; verso of old frame *This watercolour and its companion piece* [cat. no. 941] *were done in Canada and presented to Sir William Collier, KCVO-CB. July 1891.*
952.168.1

940

Hopkins

941 Tracking the Rapids
w.c., touches of gouache, over pencil.
10 1/2 x 12 1/2 (267 x 317)
Inscribed l.r. *FAH*; label on old frame *York Boat Ascending the Mackenzie River*. The craft is a fur-trading canoe rather than a York Boat; the river is probably the Mackenzie which flows through northern Ontario.
See also note on cat. no. 940.   952.168.2

941

Hopkins

THE LACHINE SKETCHBOOK

The following views were sketched during the artist's first years in Canada, 1858-60, showing life at Lachine with her husband and three stepsons, Edward Gouverneur, Peter Ogden and Manley Ogden.
36 pages, bound in brown cloth covers with leather corners and spine. 7 x 10 3/16 (178 x 253)
Gift of Mr Edward Manley Hopkins.
961.219

Flyleaf
Inscribed *This book is to be given to Manley/Frances A. Beechey/February 1st 1858/from Mamma.*

942 Lachine from Caughnawaga
pencil.
Inscribed l.l. *Part of Lachine from Caughnawaga 24 May. 1859.*

943 Hopkins House at Lachine
pencil.
Inscribed l.l. *Our House at Lachine 1859. Manley, Ogden.*

943

944 Edward Martin Hopkins on the Verandah
pencil.
Inscribed l.c. *Our Verandah at Lachine 1859;*
l.r. *E.M.H.* Initials refer to artist's husband
seen sitting on verandah.

944

945 Sir George Simpson's House, Ile Dorval

pencil.

Inscribed l.l. *Sir George Simpson's house on Ile d'Orvale–St. Lawrence River 1859*; l.r. *since burnt down*

The house may have suffered a fire, but was reconstructed, remodelled and extended.

945

Hopkins

946 Landscape with a Canoe, Ile Dorval
pencil.
Inscribed l.l. *Ile d'Orvale*

947 Landscape with Sailboat, Ile Dorval
brown wash over pencil.
Inscribed l.r. *Ile d'Orvale*

948 Children with a Swing
blue wash over pencil.
Inscribed l.l. *On L'Ile d'Orvale–August 1859;*
l.r. *Manley-Ogden*

949 The Lachine Pier seen from Hopkins Garden
pen and black ink over pencil.
Inscribed l.c. *Our Garden Lachine;* u.r.
Caughnawaga

949

950 Caughnawaga seen from Lachine
brown wash over pencil.
Inscribed l.l. *St. Lawrence-13 Aug. 59-*
Caughnawaga

951 Lachine Shoreline with Houses
pencil.
Inscribed l.r. *13 Aug. 1859*

952 Lachine Harbour with Boats
pencil and brown wash.
Inscribed l.c. *Ogden, Manley;* l.r. *In front of*
our house-Lachine-19 Aug. 1859

953 Montmorency Falls
pencil.
Inscribed l.r. *Montmorency-Aug 28, 1859*

954 Landscape with River and Woods
Near Three Rivers
pencil.
Inscribed l.l. *Near Three Rivers*

955 Part of Three Rivers
pencil.
Inscribed l.r. *Part of Three Rivers-*
Sept 5. 1859

955

956 Mrs Hopkins with Children at Lachine

brown wash over pencil.
Inscribed l.r. *Going to meet Gouverneur at the train. View close to our house, Lachine, Sept. 18, 1859*

957 Breaking up of the Ice in Spring at Lachine

pencil.
Inscribed l.l. *Breaking up of the ice in spring*

958 The Cricket Ground, Montreal

pencil. Sketch extends on verso of cat. no. 957.
Inscribed l.r. *The Cricket Ground–Montreal–Sept 26. 1859*
The playing field was situated between St. Catherine and Sherbrooke Streets in the area now run through by Mackay, Bishop and Crescent Streets. 'Kildonan,' the house of Joseph Mackay (right background) occupied the north-east corner of Sherbrooke and Redpath Streets.

958

959 House on Banks of St. Lawrence River near Montreal
brown wash over pencil.
Inscribed verso of cat. no. 958 *St. Lawrence River/Sept. 1859*

960 A Wooded Island, St. Lawrence River
pencil.

961 Street Scene, Lachine
pencil.
Inscribed l.r. *Turning to "the Switch"–Lachine. Nov: 1859*

961

Hopkins

962 Wilgress House and Garden, Lachine
pencil and brown wash.
"The Cottage", residence of Colonel E.P. Wilgress at time of sketching, is now the Lachine Museum.

963 Child Watching Ice Jam, Lachine Pier
pencil.
Inscribed l.c. *Wharf*

964 Timber Rafts on the Ottawa River Near Carillon
pencil.
Inscribed l.l. *Looking down the Ottawa from Carillon–May 16, 1860*; below figure of child *M.O.H.* (stepson Manley Ogden Hopkins)

965 Boating at Ile Dorval
pencil.
Inscribed l.l. *L'ile d'Orvale. May 1860*

966 Standing Woman
pencil sketch on stub of cut page.

967 Distant View of Montreal from Caughnawaga
pencil.
Inscribed l.l. *June 12, 1860*; l.r. *Montreal Mountain from Indian side.*

968 Timber Rafts on the St. Lawrence
pencil

969 River Landscape
pencil

970 Cabin in a Clearing by the Shore
pencil.
Inscribed l. to r. in sketch *Cord wood*; *Wharf*; *Water*; *Bushes*; *Loose wood*; *Stones.*

971 View from a Small Wharf
pencil.
Inscribed l.c. *Wharf*; l.r. *Wood/Stony Shore*

972 Man and Woman Climbing a Wooded Hill, Ste Anne de Bellevue
pencil.
Inscribed l.l. *Stones & picturesque creepers*; verso *Sketch taken from the only ruin in Canada, near St. Anne's–July 23, 1860.* Probably a reference to the ruins of Fort Senneville, not shown in the view.

973 Cabin and Ottawa River Landscape
pencil.
Inscribed on verso *Sketch near St. Anne's/Ottawa/July 23. 1860*

974 River Landscape
pencil.

975 Hudson's Bay Company Canoes Waiting for the Prince of Wales at Dorval Island
pencil.
Inscribed l.l. *Canoes waiting for the Prince of Wales*; verso *delicate blue atmosphere on low part of sky/softly edged with white. Trees & reflection quite green.*
On August 29, 1860 ten fur-trade canoes of the first class, each manned by 12 Iroquois Indians in the employ of the Hudson's Bay Company, met the Prince as he crossed to Dorval Island from the Village of Lachine.

975

976 Off Ile Dorval
w.c. over pencil.
Inscribed l.l. *Off Ile d'Orvale*

977 Ile Dorval
pencil.
Inscribed l.l. *Ile d'Orvale*; below sketching
figures *F.A.H./Tot.*

978 Church and Graveyard
pencil.
Inscribed l.l. *April 23*

Hulley, E.
(active 1867)

979 Portrait of a Young Girl
w.c. and coloured pencils. 17 15/16 x
11 5/8 (455 x 295)
Inscribed l.r. *E. Hulley, 1867*   966.69

Hurd, L.P.
(active 1873)
Artist known for his copies of watercolour
views by William Armstrong (*q.v.*).

**980 Hudson's Bay Company Post,
Northwest Shore, Lake Nipigon**
w.c., touches of gouache, over soft pencil.
11 3/8 x 20 (289 x 507)
Inscribed l.r. *L.P. Hurd '73*
Watermark: *J. Whatman*
Variant of the watercolour by William
Armstrong which was reproduced in the
Illustrated London News in 1870.   949.39.12

980

981 Fort William

w.c. over pencil. 8 1/2 x 12 13/16 (216 x 325)

Originally owned by Peter Warren Wentworth Bell (1831-1901), Chief Factor of Hudson's Bay Company; said to have been painted by L.P. Hurd in 1863. Three versions of the same composition, painted by William Armstrong and dated 1865 and 1866, are in the PAC collection.   961.221

Hutchins, Ernest J.
(active 1900-1912)

Artist, living in Winnipeg in 1909.

982 Old Fort Garry, Winnipeg

w.c., touches of gouache, over pencil. 9 3/8 x 12 5/8 (238 x 320)

Inscribed l.l. *"Old Fort Garry"*, Winnipeg, *1870/(Demolished 1882)/E.J. Hutchins. 1912.;* verso *Fort Garry 1870 from an original picture of Maj. Swinford [?] by E.J. Hutchins, Winnipeg.*

Bequest of the Estate of Mary Adelaide Lindsay, Port Perry, Ontario.   970.50.26

983 Old Fort Garry, Winnipeg

w.c., pen and ink over pencil. 6 x 15 1/8 (152 x 384)

Inscribed l.l. *OLD FORT GARRY 1869 DEMOLISHED 1882/E.J. HUTCHINS/10*

Gift of Mrs C.S. Band, Toronto.
971.181.1

984 Main Street, Winnipeg

w.c., pen and ink. 6 x 15 1/4 (152 x 387)

Inscribed l.c. *MAIN ST. WINNIPEG 1871 E.J. HUTCHINS. 10*

Gift of Mrs C.S. Band, Toronto.
971.181.2

984

985 Mounts Lefroy and Victoria, Lake Louise, Alberta
w.c., touches of gouache, over pencil. 9 3/8 x 12 1/2 (238 x 317)
Inscribed l.l. *Mts. Lefroy, and Victoria, on "Lake Louise", Rockies./E.J. Hutchins. 1912*
Bequest of the Estate of Mary Adelaide Lindsay, Port Perry, Ontario. 970.50.8

986 Eagle Peak, Selkirk Mountains, B.C.
w.c. over pencil. 9 3/8 x 12 1/2 (238 x 317)
Inscribed l.l. *Eagle Peak in the Selkirk Mountains B.C./E.J. Hutchins. 1912.*
Bequest of the Estate of Mary Adelaide Lindsay, Port Perry, Ontario. 970.50.9

Irwin, De La Cherois Thomas
(1843-1928)
Born in County Armagh, Ireland. Educated at Royal Military Academy, Woolwich and staff college, Sandwich, England. Studied watercolour painting under Callow and Needham in England and attended Ottawa Art School later in his life. Posted to Canada with Royal Artillery, 1861.
As Inspector of Artillery, supervised construction of gun batteries on Vancouver Island in 1878. Retired from active military service 1882, but held various Canadian military appointments until 1909. Painted in oil and watercolour. Exhibited, RCA 1881.

987 Gilmour's Shipyard and Lumberyard at Wolfe's Cove, Quebec
w.c. over pencil. 8 1/8 x 14 1/2 (206 x 368)
Inscribed l.c. *D. Irwin*; l.r. *D.T. Irwin*
950.61.13

987

988 Fishing on the Banff River
w.c. over pencil. 9 x 13 7/8 (228 x 352)
Inscribed l.r. *D. Irwin*; verso of mount *The Banff River, Canada.* 950.61.14

989 St. Paul's Church, Esquimalt, from Brothers Island
w.c., touches of gouache, over pencil. 4 x 6 (101 x 152) 950.9.13

989

Irwin

990 Entrance to Esquimalt Harbour
w.c. over pencil. 5 3/8 x 8 3/4 (136 x 222)
Inscribed on verso *by Maj. D.T. Irwin* and
title; old label, title.   950.9.15

991 View from the Gun Battery, Macaulay's Point, Victoria, Looking toward Holland Point and the Sooke Hills
w.c., touches of gouache, on buff paper. 4 x
6 1/16 (101 x 154)
Inscribed on verso *Coast Scene, Victoria by Maj. D.T. Irwin*   950.9.14

Jacobi, Otto Reinhold
(1812-1901)
Born in Königsberg, Prussia, where he
received his early art education. Studied at
Berlin and Düsseldorf Academies 1832-5.
Court painter to Duchess of Nassau at
Wiesbaden, *c.* 1841-60. Invited to Canada
in 1860 to paint view of Shawinigan Falls
for presentation to visiting Prince of Wales.
Settled in Canada. Worked as professional
painter in Montreal for a number of years;
in Ardock, U.S.A. 1877; Toronto 1878 and
1891-3; Philadelphia 1882. Retired to his
son's ranch in Dakota shortly before his
death. Painted landscapes in Ontario,
Quebec and Rocky Mountains in oil and
watercolour. Executed some figure groups
and portraits early in his Canadian career.
Founding member, SCA 1867. Charter
member, RCA 1880. PRCA 1890-93.

992 Sunset on the Montmorency River
w.c., touches of gouache. 14 x 21 (355 x
533)
Inscribed l.r. *O R Jacobi. 1886.*; verso of old
frame *Sunset on the Montmorency*.   960.142

993 A Woodland Stream
w.c. 6 1/8 x 10 5/8 (155 x 270)
Inscribed l.r. *O R Jacobi, 1879*

Gift of Brigadier T. Graeme Gibson,
Toronto.   964.211.1

994 Lake at Sunset
w.c., touches of gouache. 10 5/8 x 14 (270 x
355)
Inscribed l.r. *O R Jacobi. 1879.*   954.167

995 Landscape with Lake
w.c. 6 3/8 x 10 13/16 (162 x 274)
Inscribed l.l. *O R Jacobi, 1879*
Gift of Brigadier T. Graeme Gibson,
Toronto.   964.211.2

996 Landscape with Lake by Moonlight
w.c. 11 1/16 x 17 1/8 (281 x 435)
Inscribed l.r. *O R Jacobi.1882*   968x341.6

997 Moonrise in the Backwoods
w.c., touches of gouache. 10 1/4 x 14 1/2
(260 x 368)
Inscribed l.l. *O R Jacobi. 1888*; verso of
mount, title.   968x341.7

998 Houses on Lakeshore at Sunset
w.c. 5 7/8 x 13 (149 x 330)
Inscribed l.l. *O R Jacobi . . . 65*   961.47

Jewell, Harry
(active 1907)
Designer of 'artistic advertisements'.
Conducting business on Victoria Street,
Toronto, 1907.

999 St. Lawrence Hall, Toronto
w.c., pen and ink over pencil. 18 5/8 x
13 5/8 (473 x 346)
Inscribed l.l. *H. Jewell, 1907*
View shows the King Street facade of hall.
Gift in memory of Mrs A.G. Walwyn of
Toronto by her family.   970.159

999

Jones, Arthur James
(active 1838-1849)

Officer, 23rd Regiment of Foot, Royal Welsh Fusiliers, which was posted in Canada 1838-53. Second lieutenant, 1839; Captain, 1845; no longer on army lists, 1850-1.

1000 Quebec from the Indian Encampment at Levis

w.c. 10 1/8 x 14 5/16 (257 x 363)

Inscribed verso *Quebec Canada 1849* [in ink]/*Capt. Arthur Jones, 23rd Regt. Royal Welsh Fusiliers* [pencil, in two hands]
951.93.1

1001 Wharves and Citadel of Quebec from Lower Town

w.c. over pencil. 11 15/16 x 18 1/2 (303 x 470)

Inscribed on sail of boat *57*; verso *Quebec 1848* [in ink]/*Captain Arthur Jones* [in pencil]. Drapery design on verso in pencil.
951.93.2

1001

1002 Champlain Street, Quebec, Showing Landslip of 1848
w.c. over pencil. 11 3/4 x 18 13/16 (298 x 478)
Inscribed verso *Quebec–showing Land Slip 1848* [in ink]/*Capt. Arthur Jones* [in pencil, later hand].   951.93.4

1003 Montreal from the Mountain
brown wash over pencil. 10 5/8 x 14 11/16 (270 x 373)
Inscribed verso *Montreal from the Mountain 1848* [in ink]/*Captain Arthur Jones* [in pencil, later hand].
Probably a copy of the view by James Duncan (q.v.) published by Matthews' Lithography, Montreal, *c.* 1849. For Duncan variant see cat. no. 677.   951.93.3

1002

Julien, Octave Henri
(1851-1908)

Born in Quebec. Apprenticed as printer, 1868-9. Accompanied North-West Mounted Police on six-month expedition to the prairies, 1874, sketching scenes of western life for *Canadian Illustrated News* and other newspapers. Head of art department at *The Star* (Montreal) from 1888. Illustrated French Canadian life for books and magazines, and drew a series of cartoons, 'The By-Town Coons,' on Sir Wilfred Laurier and his cabinet, for *The Star*. Also painted in oil and watercolour. Exhibited, RCA 1899-1907.

1004 Montreal Fishmonger
w.c., touches of gouache, over pencil.
18 1/4 x 13 1/2 (463 x 343)
Inscribed l.l. *H. Julien*
Probably a caricature. Figure wears crest of city of Montreal as outsize watchfob.
965.220

1004

Kane, Paul
(1810-1871)

Born in Mallow, Ireland. Emigrated to Toronto with his parents in 1819 or 1820. Probably attended District Grammar School, York, 1819-26. Studied art with Mr. Drury. Apprenticed as furniture painter at Wilson Conger's factory. Possibly the same person as 'Paul Cane' who advertised as a sign, coach and house painter in 1833-4 Toronto Directory. In Cobourg 1834-36, where he painted furniture for Clench's factory and a few portraits of local citizens. In 1836-37 joined American painters James Bowman and Samuel Wall in Detroit. Spent 1839-41 at Mobile, Alabama and worked as an itinerant painter. Travelled from New Orleans to Marseilles in 1841, spending 15 months on the Continent and a winter in England, where he met George Catlin and saw his exhibition of paintings of American Indians. Returned to United States in 1843 and spent two years painting in New Orleans and Mobile. Returned to Canada in 1845 with the idea of painting a series of pictures illustrating the life of the North American Indians and devoted the rest of his life to this purpose. Made three separate trips westwards, the first as far as Sault Ste Marie between June and November, 1845; the second to Vancouver Island and the Oregon Territory between May 1846 and October 1848; and the third as far as Fort Garry, as a guide to Sir Edward Poore, in 1849. Held an exhibition of 240 watercolour sketches at Toronto's old City Hall on Front Street in November of 1848. Wrote an account of his travels, *Wanderings of An Artist among the Indians of North America*, Toronto 1859, dedicated to his patron, the Honourable George William Allan.

The following 343 watercolour and pencil sketches were given to the Royal Ontario Museum by Raymond A. Willis in memory of his mother 'Chelsea' (Mrs E a C. Wolff), daughter of Allan Cassels and granddaughter of the Hon. G.W. Allan.

Note: Page references made to Paul Kane's *Wanderings of an Artist* in the following entries refer to the 1925 edition published by The Radisson Society of Canada Ltd. The numbers noted as inscribed on many of the sketches refer to either the 1848 exhibition catalogue, to an early listing of the Allan collection, or to Kane's own lists of his sketches. These lists are published in J. Russell Harper: *Paul Kane's Frontier*, Toronto 1971.
TCH: Toronto City Hall 1848 catalogue.
KPL: Kane's Portrait Log.
KLL: Kane's Landscape Log.

ITALIAN AND GREAT LAKES SKETCHBOOK

53 pages, bound in green cloth covers titled *Album*. 8 1/2 x 5 3/8 (216 x 131)
Sketchbook used during Kane's visit to Italy, identifiable views being of Florence (May 27—August 12, 1842), Ferrara, and Venice (August 15—September 28, 1842); and during the artist's first expedition westwards through Georgian Bay, Lakes Huron and Michigan in the summer of 1845.

1005 Eleven Studies of Indian Life
pencil, on inside front cover. 5 3/8 x 8 1/2 (131 x 216)
Preparatory studies of figures and artifacts used in Kane's oil painting *Indian Bivouac*, PAC collection.   946.15.1

1006 Sixteen Studies of Indian Life
pencil. 5 3/8 x 8 1/2 (131 x 216)
Preparatory studies of Indians and canoes which were incorporated into Kane's oil painting *Indian Bivouac*, PAC collection. 946.15.2

1007 A Roman Urn
pencil. 8 1/2 x 5 3/8 (216 x 131)
946.15.3

1008 Sculpture of Saint George by Donatello, Florence (*recto*); **Profile Study of Indian Woman's Head** (*verso*)
pencil. 8 1/2 x 5 3/8 (216 x 131)
946.15.4

1009 Italian Late Renaissance Chair
pencil. 5 3/8 x 8 1/2 (131 x 216)
946.15.5

1010 Sculpture of Saint Philip by Nanni Di Banco, Florence
pencil. 8 1/2 x 5 3/8 (216 x 131)
946.15.6

1011 Dado with Cherub and Sculptured Detail of a Head, Italy
pencil. 8 1/2 x 5 3/8 (216 x 131)
946.15.7

1012 Study of Balcony and Niche with Sculptured Details, Italy
pencil. 8 1/2 x 5 3/8 (216 x 131)
946.15.8

1013 Castello Estense, Ferrara
pencil. 5 3/8 x 8 1/2 (131 x 216)
946.15.9

1014 Sculpture of the Judgment of Solomon, Ducal Palace, Venice
pencil. 8 1/2 x 5 3/8 (216 x 131)
946.15.10

1015 Sculptured Capital, Italy
pencil. 8 1/2 x 5 3/8 (216 x 131)
946.15.11

1016 Balcony with Sculptured Motifs, Italy
pencil. 8 1/2 x 5 3/8 (216 x 131)
946.15.12

1017 Houses and a Church, Probably Venice
pencil on yellow-brown paper. 8 1/2 x 5 3/8 (216 x 131)   946.15.13

1018 Entrance to an Italian Courtyard
pencil on brown paper. 5 3/8 x 8 1/2 (131 x 216)   946.15.14

1019 Canal Scene, Venice
pencil on violet-coloured paper. 5 3/8 x 8 1/2 (131 x 216)   946.15.15

1020 A Gondola, Venice
pencil. 5 3/8 x 8 1/2 (131 x 216)
946.15.16

1021 Venice seen from the Lagoon
pencil. 5 3/8 x 8 1/2 (131 x 216)
946.15.17

1022 Indian Man, Seated
pencil and w.c. 5 3/8 x 8 1/2 (131 x 216)
Sketched on verso of cat. no. 1023.
946.15.18

1023 Two Indian Portrait Heads
w.c. over pencil. 5 3/8 x 8 1/2 (131 x 216)
Left: Indian wearing chief's medal; sketch of catfish totem below this portrait.
Right: Inscribed below portrait *Ceth-a-nish-a-na-bay. Black Indian* and sketch of a totem.   946.15.19

1024 The Natural Bridge at Mackinac
pencil. 8 1/2 x 5 3/8 (216 x 131)
Inscribed l.l. *Natural bridge in Manitoulin* (in pencil, not by Kane).   946.15.20

1025 Indian Camp, Sault Ste Marie
pencil. 8 1/2 x 5 3/8 (216 x 131)
Inscribed u.r. *Sault St Marie* (in pencil, not by Kane).
The two domed lodges are preliminary sketches for the oil *Sault Ste Marie*, ROM collection 912.1.9.   946.15.21

1026 Three Birch Bark Canoes and an Indian Lodge
pencil and w.c. 8 1/2 x 5 3/8 (216 x 131)
Probably Sault Ste Marie area.   946.15.22

1027 Five Indian Heads and a Woman Setting a Snare
pencil. 5 3/8 x 8 1/2 (131 x 216)
946.15.23

1028 Indian Camp Scene with Dome-Shaped Lodges and a Fishnet
pencil. 5 3/8 x 8 1/2 (131 x 216)
Probably at Sault Ste Marie.   946.15.24

1029 Ermatinger's Grist Mill, Canadian Shore, Sault Ste Marie
pencil. 5 3/8 x 8 1/2 (131 x 216)
946.15.25

1030 St. Mary's River seen from the American Shore
pencil. 5 3/8 x 8 1/2 (131 x 216)
View shows two Indians in canoe with dip-net, poling the rapids.   946.15.26

1031 Dome-Shaped Lodge and Cook Fire
pencil. 5 3/8 x 8 1/2 (131 x 216)
Probably in Sault Ste Marie area.
946.15.27

1032 Cartoon Profile of a Man
pencil on blue paper. 5 3/8 x 8 1/2 (131 x 216)   946.15.28

1033 Two Indians in Canoe with Dip-Net, Poling the Rapids of St. Mary's River
pencil on blue-grey paper. 5 3/8 x 8 1/2 (131 x 216)   946.15.29

1034 Indians Assembled at Manitowaning for Treaty Presents
pencil. 5 3/8 x 8 1/2 (131 x 216)
The British government representative is seen standing on the porch of house addressing an assembly of standard-bearing Indians.   946.15.30

1035 Ceremonial Drums
pencil and w.c. 5 3/8 x 8 1/2 (131 x 216)
Drums painted with insignia of figures and animals.   946.15.31

1036 Camp Scene with Bark Wigwams and a Canvas Tent
w.c. over pencil. 5 3/8 x 8 1/2 (131 x 216)
946.15.32

1037 Elbow Club, Pipe and Pipestems
pencil and w.c. 5 3/8 x 8 1/2 (131 x 216)
946.15.33

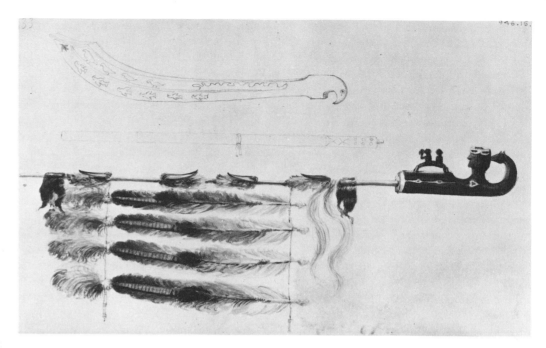

1037

1038 Two Bark Lodges
pencil. 5 3/8 x 8 1/2 (131 x 216)
946.15.34

1039 Two Indian Portraits
pencil and w.c. 5 3/8 x 8 1/2 (131 x 216)
Left: Pencil sketch of young man wearing
Indian chief's medal and inscribed u.r.
E-dah-mak-skaush.
Right: Watercolour and pencil sketch of
young Indian girl. 946.15.35

**1040 Two Pipes and Portrait Head of
Indian**
pencil and w.c. 5 3/8 x 8 1/2 (131 x 216)
Left: Two stone pipes carved with figures of
men and animals, in pencil.
Right: Portrait in pencil and w.c.
The stone pipes are illustrated in Kane's
Travels and described as follows:
"The Sketch No. 3 is that of a pipe carved
by Awbonwaishkum out of a
dark-coloured stone, his only tools being
an old knife and broken file. I leave it to
antiquaries to explain how the bowl of this
pipe happens to bear so striking a
resemblance to the head of the Egyptian
sphynx. I questioned Awbonwaishkum as
to whether he knew of any tradition
connected with the design, but the only
explanation he could offer was that his
forefathers had made similar pipes with the
same shaped head for the bowl, and that he
therefore supposed the model had always
existed among the Indians." 946.15.36

1041 Wigwams and Canoes on Shoreline
pencil. 5 3/8 x 8 1/2 (131 x 216)
Site possibly Georgian Bay area.
946.15.37

**1042 Indians Paddling the Rapids, St.
Mary's River**
pencil, brown wash on brown-green paper.
5 3/8 x 8 1/2 (131 x 216) 946.15.38

1043 Indian Camp on a Shoreline
pencil on grey paper. 5 3/8 x 8 1/2 (131 x
216)
Possibly on Georgian Bay. 946.15.39

1044 Indian Camp with Canoes
pencil on pink paper. 5 3/8 x 8 1/2 (131 x
216)
Possibly on Georgian Bay. 946.15.40

**1045 Portrait of Indian and Landscape
with a High Bluff**
pencil on pink paper. 5 3/8 x 8 1/2 (131 x
216)
The landscape is possibly part of Mackinac
Island. 946.15.41

**1046 Bark Box, Portrait Head and a
Landscape**
pencil on grey-green paper. 5 3/8 x 8 1/2
(131 x 216)
Left: Decorated birch bark box, later used in
Kane's oil portrait of the Saulteaux girl
'The Constant Sky,' ROM collection,
912.1.30, and in an oil portrait of a Chinook
girl in the Stark Collection.
Centre: Portrait head of an Indian wearing
medal.
Right: A high bluff with trees, possibly on
Mackinac Island. 946.15.42

**1047 Indian Encampment with Wigwams
and Campfire**

pencil. 5 3/8 x 8 1/2 (131 x 216)
Possibly Georgian Bay. 946.15.43

1048 Three Indian Portrait Heads
pencil. 5 3/8 x 8 1/2 (131 x 216)
Left: Man's profile inscribed l.l.
Now-qua-ke-zhick/Noon day.
Centre: Boy's bust, inscribed l.c.
Sig-in-nock-ence, that is, son of Sig-innock,
the principal chief at Manetouwaning,
according to Kane, *Wanderings*, p. 7.
Right: Man's profile. 946.15.44

**1049 Manitowaning Village seen from
Across the Bay**
pencil. 5 3/8 x 8 1/2 (131 x 216)
946.15.45

1050 Camp on Spider Island with a Tent
pencil. 5 3/8 x 8 1/2 (131 x 216)
Inscribed u.r. *Spider Islands* (not by Kane).
"Previous to entering the bay of
Manetouawning, we put ashore on one of
the Spider Islands where we found a single
lodge . . . The afternoon being clear . . . I
spent the remainder of the evening in
sketching." (*Wanderings*, p.6)
946.15.46

**1051 Landscape with a Wigwam, Georgian
Bay**
pencil. 5 3/8 x 8 1/2 (131 x 216)
946.15.47

1052 Rocky Shoreline, Georgian Bay
pencil. 5 3/8 x 8 1/2 (131 x 216)
946.15.48

1053 Rocky Islands, Georgian Bay
pencil. 5 3/8 x 8 1/2 (131 x 216)
946.15.49

**1054 Rocky Islands and a Wigwam,
Georgian Bay**
pencil. 5 3/8 x 8 1/2 (131 x 216)
946.15.50

1055 Three Landscapes in Georgian Bay
pencil. 8 1/2 x 5 3/8 (216 x 131)
Upper: Rocky shoreline inscribed u.l. *Rock I.*
Centre: Rocky islands.
Lower: Ojibwa grave shelter in foreground;
Manitowaning village seen across bay.
946.15.51

**1056 Indian with Paddle Standing on
Rocky Headland**
pencil. 5 3/8 x 8 1/2 (131 x 216)
Probably Georgian Bay region. 946.15.52

**1057 Seven Studies of Indian Life,
Georgian Bay**
pencil. 5 3/8 x 8 1/2 (131 x 216)
Top, l. to r.: Indian profile head; white man's
profile head; Indian portrait head inscribed
Oogemah-be-zeo/Chief Young Swan; Indian
portrait head inscribed *Mus-kosh Pike*.
Bottom, l. to r.: Landscape with overturned
canoe; three studies of Indian women
holding children. 946.15.53

1058 Ojibwa Grave Shelter
pencil, on inside back cover. 5 3/8 x 8 1/2
(131 x 216)
Inscribed, u.c., notes in Italian giving street
directions. Sketch of low shelter, l.l.,
similar to Ojibwa grave in cat. no. 1055.
946.15.50a

end of sketchbook

PORTRAITS

1059 Charles Daly Sketching
pencil. 9 1/8 x 5 1/2 (232 x 140)
Inscribed r. *Simco betwene Adalade King Street. Ab. Daley.*
Sketch on verso of cat. no. 1284. Charles Daly was City Clerk of Toronto, 1835-64, and an amateur artist. The profile in this portrait corresponds to the silhouette of Daly, JRR colln., TPL.   946.15.142

1060 Wah-pus, the Rabbit, Indian Chief from Owen Sound
pencil on grey-blue paper. 3 1/4 x 8 1/8 (83 x 206)
Preparatory sketch for Kane's oil portrait of Wah-pus, ROM 912.1.1.
Inscribed recto *85. Etch-a-wich-a-ma-hich, the grisley Bare standing, a calley spell chief/Shew alpey. Se pase. Pe-tic-o-pow-this Eustache Roussone. Su, Sum a-high. Jarves. 30. 315* [not related to portrait of Wah-pus]; verso *Kettuppamoosa or Naumawashkud. He will walk. Sturgeons entrails. Now-a-da-kezick-o-qua the mid day woman.*
Pencil sketch of white woman wearing bonnet on verso.   946.15.311

1061 Two Ojibwa Portrait Heads
pencil and faint wash. 5 1/2 x 9 3/8 (140 x 238)
Inscribed on verso *N. 1., Cash-a-cabut, greedy tuth* [Chief's son from Rat Portage, referred to in Kane's diary as sketched in the Fort Frances region]/*N. 2 Each-a-qunip, one who sits with his fethers on.* A third name, *1. Tipich-la-ga-shick, The Spirit skey,* refers to cat. no. 1062.
Inscribed on recto, two Ojibwa names in a later hand.   946.15.273

1062 Tipich-a-ga-shick, the Spirit Sky, Ojibwa of the Lake Superior Region
pencil. 5 1/2 x 4 1/2 (140 x 114)
Inscribed u.l. *278.* Name of Indian inscribed on verso of cat. no. 1061.
946.15.274

1063 Three Sioux Portraits
pencil. 5 1/4 x 8 5/8 (133 x 219)
Inscribed u.l. *Sioux*
Preparatory sketch for cat. no. 1064. Drawn on verso of cat. no. 1309.   946.15.64

1064 Two Sioux Portraits
pencil and w.c. 5 1/4 x 8 1/2 (133 x 216)
Inscribed u.l. *Sioux*
Head on left is study for Kane's oil portrait, ROM 912.1.29.   946.15.57

1065 She-bah-ke-zuk, Hole in the Sky, Chief of Ojibwas from Lake Superior
pencil. 4 15/16 x 3 1/8 (138 x 79)
Inscribed u.r. *3. She-bah-ke-zuk, Hole in the Sky, Chief of Ojibbeways from L. Superior.*

The number and title refer to the Toronto City Hall exhibition catalogue. However the identification does not coincide with the Stark collection sketch of the same person (Harper III-48). See cat. no. 1066 for another portrait of the same man, who has alternatively been identified as 'Peccothis,' a Saulteaux Indian.   946.15.63

1066 Two Indian Portraits
w.c. and pencil. 5 1/8 x 7 3/16 (130 x 182)
Inscribed l.l. *3. She-vah-ko-whick, Hole in the Sky, an Indian Chief of Ojibbeway tribe from L. Superior.*
See cat. no. 1065 for discussion of this identification.   946.15.62

1067 Indian Portrait (recto); Studies of Cun-ne-wa-bum, a Cree Girl (verso)
w.c. and pencil. 4 3/8 x 3 3/4 (111 x 95)
The Indian portrait is probably a Saulteaux; three of the four pencil studies of heads on the verso are preparatory sketches for the oil portrait of Cun-Ne-Wa-Bum, ROM 912.1.41. The fourth head, in profile, is similar to cat. no. 1068.   946.15.78

1068 Indian Portrait in Profile (recto); Studies of Cun-ne-wa-bum, a Cree Girl (verso)
w.c. and pencil. 4 3/8 x 3 5/8 (111 x 92)
The profile portrait is possibly of a Saulteaux; the four pencil studies of heads on verso are of Cun-ne-wa-bum.
See also cat. no. 1067.   946.15.79

1069 Indian Portrait Head
w.c. over pencil. 4 1/2 x 3 3/4 (114 x 95)
946.15.80

1070 Two Indian Portraits
w.c. and pencil. 5 1/8 x 7 1/4 (130 x 184)
Inscribed c.r. *No. 5;* l.r. *Indians of the same tribe from Lake Superior;* l.l. *Assiniboine . . . 6.*
The Toronto City Hall catalogue describes nos. 5-6 as Indians of same tribe from Lake Superior; Kane's Portrait Log identifies no. 5 as 'The Constant Sky', a Saulteaux girl, but no. 6 on the same listing does not correspond to the Indian shown here.
946.15.61

1071 A Cree from Fort Carlton
w.c. over pencil. 9 x 5 1/2 (229 x 140)
Inscribed u.l. *N. 11;* l.l. *A Cree Indian.*
Kane's Portrait Log described no. 11 as "A Cree taken at Carlton, name not known. This is the man that shot the wolf with an arrow."   946.15.96

1072 Two Cree Portraits
w.c. over pencil. 5 1/2 x 8 7/8 (140 x 225)
Inscribed u.r. *Pe-pa-ka-chas, Cree Indian;* l.l. *Achu-wish-ama-by, The Grisly Bear Standing, Cree Indian.*
Both titles correspond to Toronto City Hall catalogue entries.   946.15.97

Cree Indian

1073 Two Cree Portrait Figures
pencil and w.c. on buff-coloured paper.
6 7/16 x 5 (163 x 127)
Inscribed u.l. *No. 15 The Horn. As.*
U-thay-shun. This refers to the upper sketch
in w.c. The lower sketch, in pencil, is
uninscribed.
Pencil sketch on verso of an Indian.
946.15.151

**1074 Kee-a-kee-ka-sa-coo-way, the Man
Who Gives the War Whoop, Cree from
Fort Pitt**
w.c. over pencil on buff paper, on recto of
cat. no. 1171. 6 3/8 x 5 (162 x 127)
Inscribed u.l. *No. 14* (KPL); l.c. *The man what*
allways speakes. A later inscription, u.r.,
describes the portrait as a Saulteaux Indian.
946.15.59

**1075 Muck-e-too, Cree Chief met at Fort
Pitt**
w.c. and pencil. 4 5/8 x 3 1/2 (117 x 89)
Inscribed u.l. *N. 13* (KPL); verso *Much Boze*
Black Bear, Ottawa Chief, Manitoulin Island.
This title corresponds with no. 13 in the
Toronto City Hall catalogue. However a
portrait of Much Boze in the Stark
collection does not resemble this subject.
946.15.54

1076 A Cree Woman with Fur Skirt
w.c. and pencil. 5 1/2 x 2 3/4 (140 x 70)
Inscribed u.l. *304/N. 18.* (KPL, 'A Cree
Woman')
Pencil sketch of landscape on verso.
946.15.300

**1077 Five Standing Figures of Cree and
Assiniboine Indians**
pencil and w.c. 6 15/16 x 4 7/8 (176 x 124)
Watermark: *Whatman, Turkey Mill.*
Sketches: Bust of a man, in pencil; two
Indians in w.c. and pencil, inscribed *Cr.*
[Cree]; one standing Indian in w.c. and
pencil, inscribed *N. 16. As.* [Assiniboine];
The Man that always runs in the plaines.
Musk-ku-tha-ka-pu-mu-thay; a ceremonial
staff in w.c. and pencil; a seated man in w.c.
and pencil, inscribed *N. 17. Red Shirt. As.*
[Assiniboine].
The numbered inscriptions correspond to
Kane's Portrait Log.   946.15.150

1078 Indian Portait Head *(recto)*; **Detail of
a Sarcee Insignia** *(verso)*
pencil. 5 1/4 x 7 1/4 (133 x 184)
Inscribed u.l. *276*
The ornament sketched on verso is
repeated in the w.c. portrait of
Wah-nis-stow, The White Buffalo, Chief of
the Sarcee in the Stark Collection.
946.15.272

1079 Blackfoot Pipe-stem Bearer
pencil. 7 1/4 x 5 (184 x 127)
Preparatory sketch for Kane's oil portrait,
ROM 912.1.55. Sketch on recto of cat. no.
1177.   946.15.106A

**1080 Wah-he-joe-tass-e-neen, the Half
White Man, Assiniboine Chief**
w.c. and pencil. 5 x 4 1/4 (127 x 108)
Preparatory sketch for the oil portrait, ROM
912.1.59.   946.15.55

1071

1081 Three Indian Women Seated
pencil and w.c. 5 1/2 x 9 1/2 (140 x 241)
Inscribed u.l. *316*
Probably sketched at a prairie
encampment.   946.15.312

1082 Indian Woman Seated
pencil. 5 x 7 1/2 (127 x 190)
Inscribed u.l. *295*
Probably sketched at a prairie
encampment.   946.15.291

1083 Two Standing Figures
pencil. 9 7/8 x 6 7/8 (251 X 175)
Inscribed u.l. *303*
One figure holds a gun, the other shown
with long cape; probably sketched at a
prairie encampment.   946.15.303

1084 Two Indian Portrait Heads
pencil. 5 1/4 x 6 1/2 (133 x 165)
Inscribed u.l. *298*
Pencil sketch of military figure with
tricorne hat and gun, and of a nude boy
holding spear on verso.   946.15.294

**1085 Indian Woman with Papoose in
Cradleboard**
pencil on blue-grey paper. 4 7/8 x 4 (124 x
101)
Inscribed on verso *Bay-je-gi-she-guish-kam,
The Striped Sky. Oh-sah-wah-nah-quoch-ogue,
The Golden Cloud.*
Probably sketched on the prairies.
946.15.154

1086 Seated Indian Woman
pencil and w.c. 5 x 7 1/4 (127 x 184)
Probably sketched at a prairie
encampment.   946.15.81

1086

1087 Elle-a-ma-cum-stuck, a Spokane Chief

w.c. over pencil. 7 x 4 7/8 (178 x 124)
Inscribed u.c. *23* (KPL)
Elle-a-ma-cum-stuck, 'The Chief of the Earth', a Spokane Chief, was painted at Kettle Falls and described as follows by Kane (*Wanderings*, p. 216):
"17 September 1847 . . . These people (The Chualpays near Fort Colville on the Columbia River) are governed by two chiefs, Allam-mak-hum Stole-luch, The Chief of the Earth, and See-pays, the Chief of the Waters. The first exercises great power over the tribe except as regards the fishing, which is under the exclusive control of the latter." 916.15.215

1088 Slo-ce-ac-cum, Chief of the Upputuppets

w.c. and pencil. 7 1/8 x 5 1/16 (181 x 128)
Inscribed on verso *Slo-ce-ac-cum, Chief of the Upputuppets / Haw-e-ago-sun, upet, uppet.*
Kane described the chief as follows (*Wanderings*, p. 191):
"July 14, 1847 . . . Mouth of the Pelouse River, where it empties itself into the Nez-perees. The Chief of this place is named Slo-ce-ac-cum. He wore his hair divided in long masses, stuck together with grease. The tribe do not number more than 70 or 80 warriors, and are called Upputuppets." 946.15.197

1089 Son of the Great Walla Walla Chief, Pe-o-pe-o-maux-maux

w.c. and pencil. 5 1/4 x 4 1/2 (133 x 114)
Inscribed l.c., title; u.r. *80*
The artist mentions meeting this boy near Walla-Walla on July 22, 1847 (*Wanderings*, p. 196). 946.15.196

1090 To-ma-quin, a Cascade Chief, Columbia River

w.c. over pencil. 7 x 4 7/8 (178 x 124)
Inscribed l.l., title; u.l. *24* (KPL).
946.15.195

1090

Kane

1091 Mancemuckt, Chief of the Skeen or Shutes, Columbia River

w.c. and pencil. 7 1/4 x 5 (184 x 127)
Inscribed u.l. *72* (KPL, 'Mani-nucht, the chief of the Skene or Shutes'); l.c. *Kwa-qua-dah-bow-neva-skung, Dawn of Day, Chief of Saugeen Indians, Jany. 24th 1845.* This identification does not correspond to the Stark collection portrait of 'Dawn of Day.'
956.15.56

1092 Old Cox, Sandwich Islander Employed at Fort Vancouver

w.c. and pencil. 7 x 4 7/8 (178 x 124)
Inscribed l.c. *Old Cox, a Sandwich Islander who was present at the death of Capt Cook*; u.l. *39* (KPL).
Watermark: *What*[man] *Turk*[ey Mill] *18 . . .*
946.15.271

1093 Indian with a Parrot

pencil. 5 x 6 1/2 (127 x 165)
Sketched on verso of cat. no. 1216.
946.15.235

1094 Chinook Girl Wearing a Heavy Bandeau

pencil. 7 x 3 3/4 (178 x 95)
Inscribed u.l. *327*
Preparatory sketch for w.c. of Chinook girl from Fort Vancouver in Stark collection. Sketched on verso of cat. no. 1328.
946.15.323

1095 Two Indian Heads

pencil. 7 1/8 x 4 7/8 (181 x 124)
Sketched on verso of cat. no. 1312.
946.15.330

1096 Two Chiefs from the Haro Strait

w.c. and pencil. 5 x 7 1/8 (127 x 181)
Inscribed u.l. *47* (KPL, 'Cloll-uck, chief of the Clallam'); u.r. *48* (KPL, 'E-a-cle, a Cathi chief on the south side of the straits'). Indian implements sketched in pencil on verso.   946.15.98

1097 Sanetech Indian from Haro Strait

pencil and w.c. 7 x 4 7/8 (178 x 124)
Inscribed u.l. *51* (KPL, 'A U-Sanich Indian, Canal de Arrow'); l.l. *U-sa-nich, Indian from the Gulf of Georgia.*   946.15.194

1097

1098 Flat-head Indians
pencil, faint wash on one head. 5 1/2 x
2 3/8 (140 x 60)
Sketches of 5 Indians illustrating head
deformation.
Inscribed verso *Newa-ties* [Nootka?] *at the
North end of Vancouver Island.*
Faint pencil sketch of landscape and one
figure on verso.   946.15.217

1099 Flat-head Indian Child
w.c. over pencil. 7 x 5 (178 x 127)
946.15.216

**1100 Slam-ma-hur-sett, Haida Chief of
Cumshaw, Queen Charlotte Islands**
w.c. over pencil. 7 1/8 x 4 15/16 (181 x 126)
Inscribed u.l. *57* (KPL, "Slam-a-chusset, a
Cum-shaw chief. I could not find out where
his tribe lived. Taken at F. Victoria."); l.l.
Indian at Fort Vancouver; verso
*Slam-ma-hwe-sett, Chief of Camsinnono, taken at
Fort Victoria, Vancouver Island.*   946.15.214

1100

Indian at Fort Vancouver

1101 Head of White Man
Landscape with Indian Spear Fishing from
Platform
pencil. 4 7/8 x 3 1/2 (124 x 89)
Inscribed u.l. *297*   946.15.293

1102 Northwest Coast Indian
w.c. and pencil. 6 7/8 x 4 7/8 (175 x 124)
Inscribed u.l. *41* (KPL, Loch-oh-lett,
Nisqually Chief).
Watermark: *What*[man] *Turk*[ey Mill] *18* . . .
The inscribed number has also been read
as 4, which would correspond to
Na-taw-waugh-cit, The man that was born,
Saulteaux Indian, in Kane's Portrait Log.
946.15.277

1103 A Spurred Rider and his Horse
pencil and w.c. 5 x 7 (127 x 178)
Inscribed verso *Paul Kane* [not in Kane's
hand].
Possibly a self-caricature of the artist, or of
one of his buffalo-hunting companions.
946.15.251

1103

1104 A Voyageur
w.c. and pencil. 6 3/8 x 4 7/8 (162 x 124)
Inscribed l.c. *Sir Geo. Simpson* [not in Kane's hand].
The inscription does not identify the subject, but refers to the general superintendent of the Hudson's Bay Company in North America and an early patron of the artist.   946.15.252

1105 White Woman Seated at a Table
pencil. 5 1/4 x 4 (133 x 102)
Inscribed u.l. *303*   946.15.299

1106 Head of Woman Wearing Kerchief
pencil on ruled paper. 4 1/4 x 4 1/8 (108 x 105)
Inscribed u.l. *296*   946.15.292

1107 Profile Head of Bearded Man
pencil. 5 x 6 3/4 (127 x 171)
Sketched on verso of cat. no. 1203.
946.15.288

1108 Profile of Woman's Head in Classical Pose
pencil. 4 1/2 x 5 1/2 (114 x 140)
Sketched on verso of cat. no. 1230.
946.15.290

1109 Bust of White Woman
pencil. 7 x 5 (178 x 127)
Sketched on verso of cat. no. 1198.
946.25.247

LANDSCAPES; FIGURE STUDIES; ARTIFACTS

1110 Bloor's Brewery, Rosedale Ravine, Toronto
w.c. over pencil. 5 1/4 x 8 7/8 (133 x 225)
For a similar view by Richard Baigent, see cat. no. 56.   946.15.254

1110

1111 Horseshoe Falls, Niagara, from the Canadian Side
pencil. 5 1/2 x 9 1/8 (140 x 232)
Inscribed verso *Niagara. Paul Kane*
946.15.335

1112 American Falls, Niagara, from the Canadian Side
pencil. 5 1/2 x 9 1/8 (140 x 232)
Inscribed verso *Niagara*   946.15.336

1113 Horseshoe Falls and Terrapin Tower from the Canadian Side
pencil. 2 5/8 x 5 1/2 (66 x 140)
Pencil sketch of landscape on verso.
946.15.337

1114 Niagara Falls from Goat Island
pencil. 5 1/2 x 9 1/8 (140 x 232)
Inscribed verso *Niagara*   946.15.338

1115 American Falls, Niagara, from the American Side
pencil. 5 1/2 x 9 1/8 (140 x 232)
Inscribed verso *Niagara, Paul Kane*
946.15.339

1116 Horseshoe Falls, Niagara, from the Canadian Side
pencil. 2 3/4 x 5 1/2 (70 x 140) (picture area)
Lower sketch on same sheet as cat. nos. 1117-8.
Inscribed l.l. *6*   946.15.340

1117 Ruins of Brock's Monument, Queenston
pencil. 5 1/2 x 9 1/8 (140 x 232)
Centre sketch on same sheet as cat. nos. 1116 and 1118.
Inscribed l.l. *7*   946.15.341

1118 Stereoscopic Viewer at Niagara
pencil. 9 1/8 x 5 1/2 (232 x 140)
Upper sketch on same sheet as cat. nos. 1116-7.
Inscribed u.l. *8*   946.15.342

1119 Rocky Landscape
pencil. 9 1/8 x 5 1/2 (232 x 140)
Sketched on verso of cat. nos. 1116-8.
Inscribed u.l. *9*
Probably Ontario.   946.15.343

1120 Ontario Farmhouse with Stream and Bridge
w.c. over pencil. 5 1/2 x 9 (140 x 232)
946.15.310

1121 A Stream in the Woods
w.c., touch of gouache. 3 5/8 x 4 3/8 (92 x 111) oval
Sketched on recto of cat. no. 1122.
Probably Ontario.   946.15.304

1122 Detail Sketches of Church Spire, Man with Broom
pencil. 4 3/8 x 3 5/8 (111 x 92) oval
Sketched on verso of cat. no. 1121.
Probably Ontario.   946.15.305

1123 Paul Kane's Wigwam
w.c. and pencil. 8 x 12 1/2 (203 x 317)
Composition includes sketch of 1 1/2 storey house with verandah, of the type built in Ontario from the 1830s, inscribed by the artist *Paul Kane's Wigwam;* below this is an Indian head *design for knockers* and an ink sketch of man's profile inscribed *P. Kane.*
Other faded notes include the artist's signature (at least 5 times), and *Toronto.*
946.15.253

1124 Fort and Indian Village at Michilimackinac
pencil. 7 x 9 7/8 (178 x 251)
Inscribed u.l. *Michilimacinac*   946.15.255

1125 Sioux Scalp Dance at Fort Snelling
pencil. 5 1/2 x 9 1/8 (140 x 232)
Inscribed verso, title.
Preparatory sketch for Kane's oil, ROM 912.1.15.   946.15.155

1126 Three Figures Dancing
pencil. 7 7/8 x 4 7/8 (200 x 124)
Sketch on recto of cat. no. 1127.
946.15.275

1127 Standing Figure with Robe Falling to Ground
pencil. 7 7/8 x 4 7/8 (200 x 124)
Sketch on verso of cat. no. 1126.
Preparatory study for figure at far right in Kane's oil painting 'Sioux Scalp Dance at Fort Snelling,' ROM 912.1.15.   946.15.276

1128 Sioux Scalp Bearer
pencil. 5 1/4 x 8 1/2 (133 x 216)
946.15.58

1129 Landscape with a Village
pencil. 5 3/8 x 9 3/8 (136 x 238)
Location unidentified.   946.15.317

1130 Kakabeka Falls
pencil. 5 3/8 x 9 5/16 (136 x 237)
Sketch for the oil painting by Kane, ROM 912.1.17.   946.15.66

1131 Slave Falls, Winnipeg River
pencil. 5 x 7 1/4 (127 x 184)
Sketch for Kane's oil, ROM 912.1.20.
946.15.67

1132 Large Smith Rock's Portage
pencil and w.c. 5 1/2 x 9 1/4 (140 x 235)
Inscribed verso, title; not in Kane's hand.
Location unidentified.   946.15.257

1133 Oke Fall
pencil and w.c. 5 1/2 x 9 1/4 (140 x 235)
Inscribed verso, title; not in Kane's hand.
Location unidentified.   946.15.258

1134 Red River Settlement
pencil. 5 1/2 x 9 1/8 (140 x 235)
Inscribed l.l. *Red River.*
View shows St. Boniface Cathedral, blockhouse and Upper Fort Garry.
946.15.68

1135 Three Prairie Landscapes
pencil. 6 1/2 x 4 7/8 (165 x 124)
Sketch on verso of cat. no. 1201.
946.15.118

1136 Red River Cart and Ox
pencil. 4 7/8 x 6 15/16 (124 x 176)
Faint pencil sketch of prairie landscape on verso.   946.15.74

1137 Métis and Red River Carts: Three Sketches
pencil. 4 7/8 x 7 (124 x 178)
Sketches show Métis loading cart with poles (u.l.); cart with ox (l.l.); Indian smoking pipe (r.).   946.15.75

1138 Travois Dog of the Prairies
pencil and w.c. 4 3/4 x 6 1/2 (121 x 165)
w.c. sketch of a sky on verso.   946.15.84

1139 Dog with Travois Carrying Baby
pencil and w.c. 4 7/8 x 6 1/2 (124 x 165)
946.15.85

1140 Two Travois Dogs
pencil. 4 7/8 x 6 1/2 (124 x 165)
Sketch shows one dog with travois, the other with a pack on its back.
Sketch on verso of cat. no. 1195.
946.15.144

1141 Travois Dog
pencil. 4 7/8 x 6 1/2 (124 x 165)
Sketch on verso of cat. no. 1301.
946.15.146

1142 Travois Dog, Bird's Head, Two Figures Carrying Canoe
pencil. 5 1/2 x 9 3/8 (140 x 238)
Pencil sketch of four boats and man with pole on verso, inscribed *Brigade of Boats*; a preparatory sketch for Kane's oil, ROM 912.1.31.
See also cat. no. 1156.   946.15.83

1143 Métis Going to Hunt Buffalo
pencil. 5 3/8 x 9 (136 x 229)
946.15.69

1144 Métis Buffalo Hunting
pencil. 4 7/8 x 7 (124 x 178)
Inscribed l.r. *Half-Breeds Buffalo hunting*.
Upper sketch of a dead buffalo; lower sketch of horsemen in hilly landscape.
Drawn on recto of cat. no. 1148.
946.15.76

1145 Métis Setting up Camp on Prairies
w.c. and pencil. 5 1/4 x 8 7/8 (133 x 225)
Inscribed verso *Half-Breed camp*   946.15.71

1146 Métis Camp
pencil and w.c. 4 7/8 x 7 (124 x 178)
Inscribed u.l. *Half-Breed camp*.
Sketch on recto of cat. no. 1155.
946.15.72

1147 Métis Camp and Hunters on Hilltop
w.c. over pencil. 5 1/4 x 8 7/8 (133 x 225)
Inscribed verso *Half breed camp near Fort Garry*   946.15.70

1147

1148 Métis Travelling

pencil. 4 7/8 x 7 (124 x 178)
Sketch on verso of cat. no. 1144.
946.15.77

1149 Buffalo and Horsemen

pencil and w.c. 4 7/8 x 7 (124 x 178)
946.15.93

1150 A Buffalo Bull

pencil on buff paper. 5 1/2 x 6 1/2 (140 x
165)
Sketch of a buffalo on verso.   946.15.8

1151 Wounded Buffalo Bull

pencil on buff-coloured paper. 5 3/8 x
6 1/2 (136 x 165)
Inscribed with title.   946.15.87

1151

Kane

1152 Landscape with Rocks, Trees and Water
w.c. and pencil. 4 1/4 x 5 1/2 (108 x 140) (picture area)
Sketch on same sheet as cat. no. 1153.
946.15.95

1153 Buffalo Head
pencil. 4 5/8 x 5 1/2 (117 x 140) (picture area)
Sketch on same sheet as cat. no. 1152.
946.15.94

1154 Norway House, Little Playgreen Lake
pencil. 5 1/2 x 9 (140 x 229)
Preparatory sketch for version in oil on paper, Stark coll.   946.15.213

1155 Wesleyan Mission Station, Jack River
pencil. 4 7/8 x 7 (124 x 178)
Sketch on verso of cat. no. 1146.
946.15.73

1156 York Boats and Saskatchewan River Landscape
pencil on blue paper. 8 x 4 7/8 (203 x 124)
The upper sketch of boats may related to Kane's oil subject 'Brigade of Boats,' ROM collection. For another preparatory sketch, see cat. no. 1142. The artist described the drawing, taken between The Pas and Grand Rapids, Manitoba, as follows: "June 12, 1848. I got out my drawing materials and took a sketch of the brigade, as it was coming up with a fair breeze, crowding on all sail to escape a thunder storm rolling fast after them" (*Wanderings*, p. 306).   946.15.334

1157 A Buffalo Pound Near Fort Carlton
pencil. 5 5/8 x 9 1/4 (143 x 235)
Related in subject-matter to Kane's oil, ROM 912.1.33.   946.15.104

1158 Buffalo Hunting Near Fort Carlton
pencil. 5 1/8 x 3 1/8 (130 x 79)
Pencil sketch of Indian and stylized flower on verso.   946.15.103

1159 The Prairie Near Fort Carlton
w.c. over pencil. 4 7/8 x 7 (124 x 178)
Sketch for background in oil 'Buffalo Pound,' ROM 912.1.33.   946.15.107

1160 Cree Indians on the March, Near Fort Carlton
pencil. 4 1/2 x 8 5/8 (114 x 219)
Inscribed verso *Cree Indians on March, Ft. Carlton* [not in Kane's hand].
Preparatory sketch for oil of Crees travelling, ROM 912.1.49.   946.15.102

1161 Cree Tent with Women Gambling, Fort Carlton
pencil. 4 13/16 x 6 1/2 (122 x 165)
Inscribed u.l. *N. 10* (KLL)   946.15.152

1162 Saskatchewan River Near Fort Carlton
w.c. over pencil. 5 1/4 x 8 7/8 (133 x 225)
Inscribed u.l. *N. 13* (KLL); verso
Saskatchewan at Carlton   946.15.119

1163 Saskatchewan River Landscape
w.c. and pencil. 5 1/4 x 8 7/8 (133 x 225)
Inscribed u.l. *N. 14* (KLL)   946.15.125

1164 Saskatchewan River Valley between Fort Carlton and Fort Pitt
w.c. and pencil. 5 1/2 x 9 1/2 (140 x 241)
946.15.126

1165 Saskatchewan River Landscape
pencil. 5 1/2 x 9 (140 x 229)
Inscribed u.l. *N. 15* (KLL); verso
Saskatchewan.   946.15.110

1166 Saskatchewan River Landscape
pencil. 5 5/8 x 9 (143 x 229)
Sketch on recto of cat. nos. 1199, 1200. This view is another version of cat. no. 1165.
946.15.111

1167 Saskatchewan River Landscape
w.c. over pencil. 5 3/8 x 8 7/8 (136 x 225)
Inscribed u.l. *N. 16* (KLL); verso *Belly River* [not in Kane's hand]. 946.15.120

1168 Saskatchewan River Landscape
w.c. and pencil. 4 7/8 x 7 (124 x 178)
Inscribed u.l. *N. 18* (KLL)   946.15.109

1169 Saskatchewan River Landscape
pencil. 4 7/8 x 6 1/2 (124 x 165)
Pencil sketch of horse with travois poles on verso.   946.15.116

1170 The Serpentine Valley, Saskatchewan
w.c. and pencil. 5 1/2 x 9 (114 x 229)
Inscribed u.l. *N. 25* (KLL)   946.15.139

1171 The Golden Valley, Saskatchewan River
w.c. and pencil. 5 1/2 x 9 (114 x 229)
Inscribed u.l. *N. 26* (KLL); verso
Saskatchewan
Preliminary sketch for Kane's oil 'A Valley in the Plains,' ROM 912.1.34.
946.15.108

1172 A Dead Deer
pencil on buff-coloured paper. 5 x 6 3/8 (127 x 162)
Sketch on verso of cat. no. 1074.
946.15.60

1173 Cree Pipestem
w.c. and pencil. 5 3/4 x 9 1/4 (146 x 235)
"May 27th . . . We remained at Fort Pitt two days . . . and I took advantage of the delay to sketch a Cree chief. He was dressed in full costume, with a pipe-stem in his hand" (*Wanderings*, p. 293).
946.15.101

1174 Cree Pipestem and Two Indian Heads
w.c. and pencil. 5 1/2 x 9 1/4 (140 x 235)
Inscribed u.r. *Cree pipe-stem bearer's*.
Preparatory sketch for Kane's oil 'Cree Pipe-Stem Bearer,' ROM 912.1.36.
946.15.99

1175 Two Pipestems

pencil and w.c. 5 5/8 x 9 1/2 (143 x 241)
The upper pipestem is shown with
axe-head bowl; the lower with eagle-head
bowl.   946.15.100

**1176 Two Indians Wearing Lynx
Head-dress**

pencil. 5 1/8 x 7 1/4 (130 x 184)
The cloth animal head-dresses with
pointed ears are similar to those worn by
Cree tribe.   946.15.263

1176

Kane

1177 Landscape with Mountains and River
pencil. 5 x 7 1/4 (127 x 184)
Sketch on verso of cat. no. 1079, Blackfoot portrait.   946.15.106B

1178 Spear Held by Big Snake, Blackfoot Chief
pencil. 7 3/8 x 4 3/8 (187 x 111)
Preparatory sketch for oil portrait of Big Snake, 'Six Blackfoot Chiefs,' ROM 912.1.50.   946.15.105

1179 Ceremonial Jacket Ornamented with Raven, Plains Indians
w.c. over pencil. 7 1/4 x 5 1/8 (184 x 130)
Watermark: [Wha]*tman* [18]*46*
946.15.313

1179

1180 Indian Head-dress Ornamented with Weasel
pencil. 5 3/4 x 9 3/8 (146 x 238)
946.15.314

1181 Two Buffalo
pencil. 5 1/8 x 6 1/2 (130 x 165)
946.15.92

1182 Three Buffalo
pencil. 5 1/4 x 6 1/2 (133 x 165)
946.15.88

1183 Three Buffalo
pencil. 5 x 7 1/4 (127 x 184)
946.15.89

1184 Three Buffalo Bulls in Repose
pencil. 5 1/4 x 6 1/2 (133 x 165)
946.15.91

1185 Buffalo Skull
w.c. and pencil. 2 7/8 x 5 1/2 (73 x 140)
946.15.153

1186 Buffalo Trail
w.c. over pencil. 5 3/8 x 8 7/8 (136 x 226)
946.15.147

1187 Buffalo Grazing
w.c. and pencil. 5 1/2 x 9 (140 x 228)
Inscribed u.l. *N. 28* (KLL); u.r., title.
946.15.148

1188 Nine Buffalo Bulls
pencil and brown wash. 4 3/4 x 6 1/2 (121 x 165)   946.15.90

1189 Landscape Near the Saskatchewan River
pencil. 5 1/2 x 9 (140 x 228)
Inscribed u.l. *N. 22* (KLL describes this entry as 'Salt Lake')   946.15.114

1190 Scene along the Saskatchewan River
pencil. 5 1/2 x 9 1/8 (140 x 232)
Inscribed verso *Saskatchewan.*   946.15.115

1191 A Prairie Slough
w.c. and pencil. 4 7/8 x 6 3/8 (124 x 162)
Inscribed u.l. *N.23* (KLL); verso *Okda* [?] *pond looked.*
"We had passed in our route (prairies, September 1846) daily many *dried-up* lakes, principally small, the basins covered with an incrustation of sub-carbonate of soda. Many of these are bordered with a dense growth of plants resembling in structure the well-known marine production called samphire, but of a rich purple colour. So unbroken is the incrustation of soda, as to give the spots the appearance of being covered with snow" (*Wanderings*, p. 91).
946.15.149

1192 Lake in the Prairies
pencil and w.c. 5 1/8 x 8 7/8 (130 x 225)
Inscribed u.l. *N. 24* (KLL); verso, title.
946.15.138

1193 Prairie Landscape
pencil. 5 1/2 x 9 1/8 (140 x 232)
946.15.121

1194 Rolling Prairie with Trees
w.c. and pencil. 5 1/2 x 9 (140 x 228)
946.15.140

1195 Prairie Landscape
pencil. 4 7/8 x 6 1/2 (124 x 165)
Sketch on recto of cat. no. 1140.
946.15.143

1196 Prairie Fire
w.c. pencil. 7 1/2 x 11 3/4 (190 x 299)
Watermark: *J. Whatman, Turkey Mill, 1838*
946.15.319

1197 Prairie on Fire
w.c. over pencil. 5 1/4 x 8 7/8 (133 x 225)
Inscribed u.r. *N. 21* (KLL).
Preparatory sketch for Kane's oil, ROM 912.1.39.   946.15.124

1198 Fort Edmonton
pencil. 5 3/8 x 9 (136 x 228)
The artist stayed at Fort Edmonton in December 1847, and again in April 1848.
"On the evening of the 5th (Dec.1847) we arrived at Fort Edmonton . . . All the Company's servants, with their wives and children, numbering about 130, live within the palings of the fort in comfortable log-houses, supplied with abundance of firewood" (*Wanderings*, p. 255).
946.15.122

Detail of 1198

1199 Fort Edmonton
pencil. 5 3/4 x 5 5/8 (146 x 143) (picture area)
Sketch on verso of cat. no. 1166.
946.15.113

1200 Saskatchewan River Landscape
pencil. 3 1/4 x 5 5/8 (83 x 143) (picture area)
Sketch on verso of cat. no. 1166.
946.15.112

1201 Saskatchewan River Landscape
pencil and blue wash. 4 7/8 x 6 (124 x 152)
Sketch on recto of cat. no. 1135.
946.15.117

1202 Evergreens Covered with Snow
w.c. and pencil. 5 x 6 7/8 (127 x 175)
Detail sketch for Kane's oil 'Winter Travelling in Dog Sleds,' ROM 912.1.48.
946.15.286

Kane

1203 Evergreens and Rocks in the Snow
w.c. and pencil. 5 x 6 3/4 (127 x 171)
Sketch on verso of cat. no. 1107. Possibly a
preparatory sketch for 'Winter Travelling
in Dog Sleds,' ROM 912.1.48.
946.15.287

1204 Man in a Dog Cariole
w.c. over pencil. 5 5/8 x 9 3/8 (143 x 238)
Detail sketch for Kane's oil 'Winter
Travelling in Dog Sleds,' which showed a
wedding party travelling from Fort
Edmonton to Fort Pitt (ROM 912.1.48).
"The cariole is intended for carrying one
person only; it is a thin flat board, about
eighteen inches wide, bent up in front, with
a straight back behind to lean against; the
sides are made of green buffalo hide, with
the hair scraped completely off and dried,
resembling thick parchment, this entirely
covers the front part, so that a person slips
into it as into a tin bath" (*Wanderings*, p.
271).   946.15.129

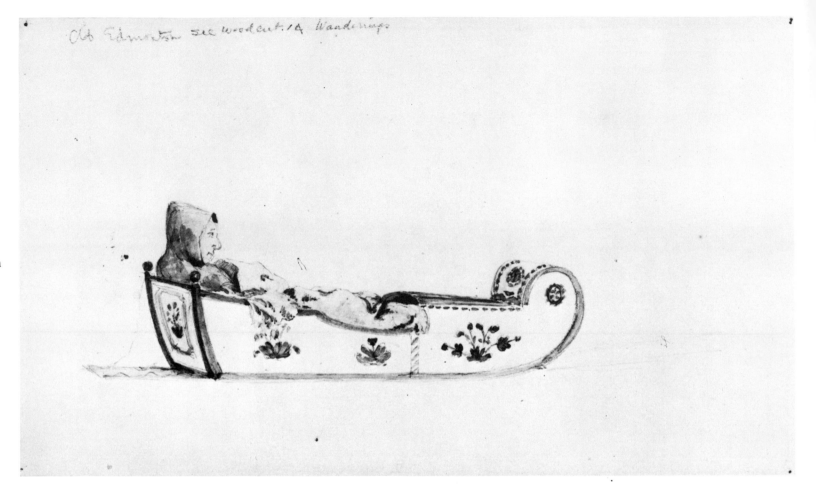

1204

1205 Log Cache for Food Storage
pencil. 5 1/2 x 9 1/8 (140 x 232)
Identified by Harper as a cache between
Rocky Mountain House and Fort
Edmonton.   946.15.302

1206 An Assiniboine Lodge
w.c. and pencil. 5 3/8 x 9 1/4 (136 x 235)
On April 21, 1848 Kane reached Rocky
Mountain House and described the
Assiniboine lodges on the banks of the
Saskatchewan River (*Wanderings*, p. 287).
946.15.127

1207 Indian Camp and a Landscape
pencil. 5 1/2 x 8 1/8 (140 x 206)
Sketches show lake in mountains (left), and
Indian camp scene (right). On recto of cat.
no. 1208.   946.15.219

1208 A Waterfall and a Mountain Lake
pencil. 5 1/2 x 8 1/8 (140 x 206)
On verso of cat. no. 1207.   946.15.220

1209 Plains Indians, Horse and Tepee
pencil on grey paper. 4 3/8 x 6 1/2 (111 x
165)
Inscribed, r. *Nemans*
Watermark: Britannia figure.   946.15.308

1210 Plains Indians, Horse and Tepee
pencil on grey paper. 4 3/8 x 6 1/2 (111 x
165)
Inscribed verso *Paul Kane* and other ink
notations.   946.15.309

1211 Plains Indians Smoking
pencil. 3 3/4 x 5 1/2 (95 x 140)
Inscribed *Currency* and several sums.
Sketch on recto of cat. no. 1212.
946.15.315

1212 Plains Indian Holding Pipe
pencil. 5 1/2 x 3 3/4 (140 x 95)
Sketch of central figure in cat. no. 1211.
946.15.316

1213 Indian Encampment on a Shore
pencil. 3 5/8 x 5 1/16 (92 x 129)
Inscribed verso *Edemonton, March 5th* (in
ink, possibly in Kane's hand).
Watermark: *Whatman . . .* [18]46
946.15.123

**1214 Athabaska River and Rocky
Mountains**
w.c. and pencil. 4 7/8 x 7 (124 x 178)
Inscribed u.l. *31* (KLL); verso *Jasper's Lake*,
and pencil sketch of snow-laden fir trees.
946.15.131

1215 Athabaska River Landscape
pencil. 4 7/8 x 6 1/2 (124 x 165)
Sketch on verso of cat. no. 1217.
946.15.268

1216 Athabaska River Landscape
pencil. 5 x 6 1/2 (127 x 165)
Sketch on recto of cat. no. 1093.
946.15.234

1217 Jasper House and Lake
pencil. 4 7/8 x 6 1/2 (124 x 165)
Sketch on recto of cat. no. 1215.
946.15.267

1218 Jasper's Lake with Miette's Rock
w.c. and pencil. 4 7/8 x 7 (124 x 178)
Inscribed u.l. *32* (KLL). Pencil sketch of
trees on verso.
The site is illustrated by woodcut 7 in
Kane's *Wanderings* and described as follows
(p. 105):
"Jasper's House consists of only three
miserable log huts. The dwelling house is
compased by two rooms . . . One of them is
used by all comers and goers . . . being
huddled together indiscriminately."
946.15.130

1219 Four Pack Horses
pencil. 5 1/8 x 7 1/4 (130 x 184)
Probably the horses used by Kane's party
in crossing the Rocky Mountains.
946.15.133

1220 Two Studies of Pack Horse
pencil. 4 7/8 x 7 1/2 (124 x 190)
Sketch on verso of cat. no. 1338.
946.15.249

1221 A Young Bighorn Mountain Sheep
w.c. and pencil. 5 1/4 x 7 1/4 (133 x 184)
946.15.135

1222 A Mountain Goat
pencil. 5 3/16 x 7 1/4 (132 x 184)
Sketch on recto of cat. no. 1223.
946.15.136

1223 A Mountain Goat
pencil. 5 3/16 x 7 1/4 (132 x 184)
Sketch on verso of cat. no. 1222.
946.15.137

1224 Mountain Sheep's Head
pencil. 5 1/8 x 7 1/4 (130 x 184)
Inscribed *Bad Mountain Goat*.   946.15.134

1225 Rocky Mountain Landscape
w.c. pencil. 5 1/2 x 8 13/16 (140 x 224)
Inscribed u.l. *34* (KLL describes view as
'Prairie with Mountain Sheep,' but actual
view shows mountains without animals);
verso *Mountain scenery in the Rockies*.
946.15.237

**1226 Athabaska River in the Rocky
Mountains**
w.c. and pencil. 5 1/2 x 8 7/8 (140 x 225)
Inscribed u.l. *37* (KLL); verso *in the Rocky
Mountains*.
View shows a dry riverbed.   946.15.238

1227 Crossing the Rockies
pencil, pen and ink. 5 3/8 x 10 1/2 (136 x
267)
Inscribed l. *McKenzie*; r. *Through the Rockies*.
Possibly an imaginary sketch of Sir
Alexander MacKenzie crossing the
Rockies.
Sketch on recto of cat. no. 1250.
946.15.243

1228 Athabaska River in the Rocky Mountains
w.c. and pencil. 5 1/2 x 8 7/8 (140 x 225)
Inscribed u.l. *36* (KLL)   946.15.328

1229 The Rockies in Winter
w.c. over pencil. 4 7/8 x 7 (124 x 178)
Inscribed verso *Rockies in winter*
946.15.132

1230 An Evergreen Covered with Snow
w.c. and pencil. 5 1/2 x 4 1/2 (140 x 114)
Sketch on recto of cat. no. 1108.
946.15.289

1231 The Committee's Punch Bowl, Rocky Mountains
pencil and w.c. 5 1/4 x 8 7/8 (133 x 225)
Inscribed u.l. *39* (KLL)   946.15.239

1232 Waterfall at Headwaters of Columbia River
w.c. and pencil. 5 x 7 (127 x 178)
Inscribed u.l. *40* (KLL)   946.15.278

1233 Mountain Landscape
pencil. 5 3/8 x 8 7/8 (136 x 225)
946.15.241

1234 Mountain Landscape
pencil. 5 1/2 x 8 7/8 (140 x 225)
946.15.240

1235 Mountain Landscape
pencil. 5 1/4 x 8 7/8 (133 x 225)
Sketch on verso of cat. no. 1258.
946.15.160

1236 Camp in the Woods
pencil. 5 x 7 (127 x 178)
Sketch on verso of cat. no. 1302. Similar in theme to Kane's oil 'Boat Encampment,' ROM 912.1.60.
946.15.296

1237 Snow Scene in Mountain Landscape
pencil and w.c. 5 3/8 x 9 1/2 (136 x 241)
Study of mountain peaks as seen from the 'Boat Encampment' (ROM 912.1.60) on the Columbia River.   946.15.236

1238 Three Indians Paddling Birch Bark Canoe
pencil. 5 3/8 x 9 1/2 (136 x 241)
Possibly a preliminary sketch for Kane's oil view of Indians canoeing on mountain lake, ex colln. P. Winkworth.   946.15.301

1239 Sailing on Upper Arrow Lakes
pencil. 5 x 7 (127 x 178)
946.15.82

1240 Shoreline of Upper Arrow Lakes
pencil. 4 7/8 x 6 1/2 (124 x 165)
Faint pencil sketch of fir trees on verso.
946.15.333

1241 Shoreline of Upper Arrow Lakes
pencil. 5 1/2 x 8 7/8 (140 x 225)
946.15.176

1242 Kootenay Canoe on Columbia River Near Grand Rapids
w.c. and pencil. 5 1/2 x 9 (140 x 229)
Inscribed verso *elle a ma cum stiluch.*
Faint pencil sketch of fort and tents on riverbank on verso.   946.15.174

1243 Kootenay Canoes and Lodges, Upper Columbia River
pencil. 5 3/8 x 8 7/8 (136 x 225)
Sketches of Kootenay canoes, sweat house, tepee and mat lodge; studies for Kane's oil 'Falls at Colville,' ROM 912.1.64.
946.15.202

1244 Weir on the Columbia River at Colville
pencil. 5 1/4 x 9 1/2 (133 x 241)
Inscribed l.c., title.
Study for Kane's oil 'Falls at Colville,' ROM 912.1.64.   946.15.161

1245 Fishing Platform at Kettle Falls, Spokane River
w.c. and pencil. 5 x 7 1/4 (127 x 184)
Inscribed c.r. *N. 5* (KLL)
Sketch on verso of cat. no. 1280. Study for Kane's oil 'Falls at Colville,' ROM 912.1.64. Pencil landscape at upper right is identified by Harper as Lost Men's Portage, west of Kakabeka Falls.   946.15.332

1246 Spearing Fish on the Columbia River
pencil. 5 1/2 x 9 3/8 (140 x 238)
Inscribed l.l., title.
Sketch on recto of cat. no. 1252. Study for Kane's oil 'Falls at Colville,' ROM 912.1.64.
946.15.203

1247 Salmon Weir at Kettle Falls, Spokane River
w.c. and pencil. 5 1/2 x 9 1/2 (140 x 241)
Study for Kane's oil 'Falls at Colville,' ROM 912.1.64.
946.15.205

1248 A Fish Drying Camp, Columbia River
w.c. and pencil. 5 1/8 x 8 7/8 (130 x 225)
Inscribed u.l. *81*; verso *Indians Smoking Fish, Lower Columbia.*
Pencil sketch of seated Indian woman on verso.   946.15.206

81.

1248

1249 Three Indians Fishing with Dip-nets
pencil. 5 3/8 x 8 7/8 (136 x 225)
Sketch on recto of cat. no. 1304.
946.15.325

1250 Two Figures Spearing Fish
pencil. 5 3/8 x 10 1/2 (136 x 267)
Sketch on verso of cat. no. 1227.
946.15.244

1251 Fish Drying Camp, Columbia River
pencil. 6 3/4 x 9 7/8 (172 x 251)
946.15.198

1252 Ring and Beads for the Game of Al-kol-lock
pencil. 5 1/2 x 9 3/8 (140 x 238)
Inscribed near each bead (colour notes):
Black, Black, l.g., Blu, Blu, D.Gr
Sketch on verso of cat. no. 1246.
''The principal game played here (Fort Colville) is called Al-kol-lock . . . with a very slight spear . . . and a ring made of bone, or some heavy wood, and wound round with cord; this ring is about three inches in diameter, on the inner circumference of which are fastened six beads of different colours at equal distances, to each of which a separate numerical value is attached'' (*Wanderings*, p. 217).   946.15.204

1253 Material for Hoop and Pin Game of Al-kol-lok

pencil and w.c. 4 3/8 x 6 1/2 (111 x 165)
946.15.210

1254 Playing the Game of Al-kol-lock

pencil. 5 1/2 x 9 3/8 (140 x 238)
Preparatory sketch for Kane's oil, ROM
912.1.65.
Kane watched the game played by the
Chualpay Indians at Fort Colville, and
described it in *Wanderings*, p. 217.
946.15.209

1255 Face Painting and Figure Studies for Scalp Dance

pencil. 5 1/2 x 9 1/2 (140 x 241)
Faces inscribed with colour notations.
Studies for Kane's oil 'Scalp Dance,
Colville,' ROM 912.1.66. Sketch on recto of
cat. no. 1256.
946.15.229

1256 Two Figure Studies for Scalp Dance

pencil. 5 1/2 x 9 1/2 (140 x 241)
Preparatory study for Kane's oil 'Scalp
Dance, Colville,' ROM 912.1.66. Sketch on
verso of cat. no. 1255.
946.15.230

1257 Studies of Figures and Face Painting for Scalp Dance

pencil. 5 3/8 x 9 1/2 (136 x 241)
Preparatory study for Kane's oil 'Scalp
Dance, Colville,' ROM 912.1.66.
946.15.208

1257

1258 Hudson's Bay Company Mill, Fort Colville
pencil. 5 1/4 x 8 7/8 (133 x 225)
Sketch on recto of cat. no. 1235.
946.15.159

1259 Spokane River Landscape
w.c. and pencil. 5 1/2 x 9 1/2 (140 x 241)
Inscribed u.l. *117* (KLL)   946.15.189

1260 Falls of the Spokane River
pencil. 5 3/8 x 9 (136 x 229)
Sketch on recto of cat. no. 1317. Pencil
sketch of a head in u.r. corner.   946.15.190

1261 Rocky Canyon Near the Lower Falls, Pelouse River
w.c. and pencil. 5 7/16 x 9 1/2 (138 x 241)
Inscribed u.l. *101* (KLL)   946.15.180

1262 Rocky Canyon Near the Lower Falls, Pelouse River
w.c. and pencil. 5 1/2 x 9 1/2 (140 x 241)
946.15.181

1263 Looking Down the Pelouse River, with Basaltic Rock
w.c. and pencil. 5 1/2 x 9 1/2 (140 x 241)
Inscribed u.l. *104* (KLL)   946.15.182

1264 Waterfall in Rocky Gorge
pencil. 5 x 7 1/4 (127 x 184)
Inscribed u.r. *Falls of Pelouse* (not Kane's
hand)   946.15.187

1265 Nez Percé River Landscape Near Fort Walla Walla
w.c. and pencil. 5 1/2 x 9 3/8 (140 x 238)
Inscribed u.l. *105* (KLL, 'The Nez Perce
River or south branch of the Columbia
River').
Watermark: *J. Whatman 1845*   946.15.186

1266 River Landscape
w.c. and pencil. 5 1/4 x 8 7/8 (133 x 225)
Inscribed verso *Palouse River*   946.15.188

1267 River Landscape
w.c. and pencil. 5 x 7 1/4 (127 x 184)
Inscribed verso *Columbia River* (possibly the
Pelouse).   946.15.179

1268 Fort Walla Walla
pencil. 5 1/2 x 9 1/2 (140 x 241)
946.15.172

1269 Fort Walla Walla
pencil. 5 3/8 x 8 7/8 (136 x 225)
Sketched in faint pencil on verso of cat. no.
1335.
Inscribed c.r. *Lac-a-num, Se-am*.
Site tentatively identified as Walla Walla
because of similarity to Stark colln. sketch,
Harper, fig. 134.
946.15.233

1270 Beacon Rock, Columbia River
w.c. and pencil. 5 3/8 x 9 1/2 (136 x 241)
946.15.173

1271 Chimney Rocks, Columbia River
pencil. 5 1/4 x 6 1/2 (133 x 165)
946.15.177

1272 Chimney Rocks, Columbia River
pencil. 4 7/8 x 6 1/2 (124 x 165)
946.15.245

1273 The Whitman Mission at Waiilatpu
pencil. 5 1/2 x 9 1/2 (140 x 241)
"Dr. Whitman's duties included those of
superintendent of the American
Presbyterian missions on the west side of
the Rocky Mountains. He had built himself
a house of unburnt clay, for want of timber
. . . on the banks of the Walla-Walla River"
(*Wanderings*, pp. 194-5).   946.15.318
946.15.318

1274 Mrs Whitman's Indian Fan
pencil, w.c., touches of gouache. 5 1/2 x
9 1/2 (140 x 241)
Inscribed u.l. *100*; verso *Sketch of an Indian
fan wh. belonged to Mrs Whitman, murdered by
Tillu-ko-ect, Tama*.
The artist had been a guest of the
Whitmans two months before their
murder, which he described (from hearsay)
in *Wanderings*, chapter 21. He was at Fort
Colville when news of the tragedy arrived
and may well have been given the fan as a
memento of his dead friends.   946.15.207

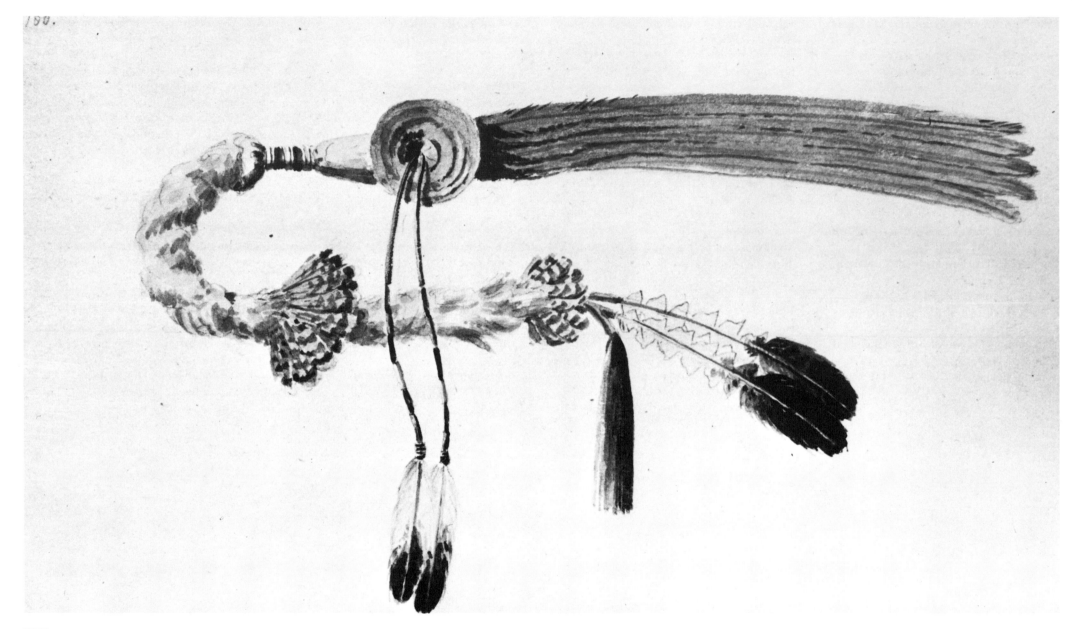

1274

Kane

1275 An Indian Woman and Study of Saddle
pencil and w.c. 5 3/8 x 9 1/2 (136 x 241)
Sketch of woman's saddle at left, and of woman wearing conical hat at right, both of west coast plateau region. 946.15.162

1276 Walla Walla Tribe Lodge of Rush Mats
pencil and w.c. 5 x 7 (127 x 178)
Inscribed u.l. 52 (KLL) 946.15.222

1277 Sand Dunes, Grand Coulee Region
w.c. and pencil. 5 1/2 x 9 3/8 (140 x 238)
Inscribed verso *Alkapowa, a tributary of the Columbia* [not in Kane's hand]. 946.15.192

1278 Landscape with Rocks, Grand Coulee Region
w.c. and pencil. 5 1/2 x 9 1/2 (140 x 241)
Inscribed u.r. *Columbia River* 946.15.178

1279 Landslip Six Miles above the Cascades, Columbia River
pencil. 5 3/8 x 9 1/2 (136 x 241)
Preparatory sketch for w.c. in Stark Colln., Harper, fig. 144.
946.15.297

1280 At the Head of the Cascades, Lower Columbia River
pencil and w.c. 5 x 7 1/4 (127 x 184)
Inscribed u.l. 94 (KLL)
Sketch on recto of cat. no. 1245.
946.15.331

1281 The Cascades, Lower Columbia River
pencil. 5 1/2 x 9 (140 x 229)
Inscribed u.l. 42 (KLL) 946.15.183

1282 Cape Horn, Twenty Miles above Fort Vancouver
pencil. 5 1/2 x 9 1/2 (140 x 241)
Preparatory sketch for w.c. in Stark Colln., Harper IV390. Sketched on verso of cat. no. 1344. 946.15.266

1283 A View of Fort Vancouver, Looking South
pencil. 5 5/8 x 9 1/8 (143 x 232)
A general view, showing the Columbia River, the fort and the village outside the stockade. 946.15.211

1284 A View of Fort Vancouver, Looking Southeast Towards Mount Hood
pencil. 5 1/2 x 9 1/8 (140 x 232)
Sketch on recto of cat. no. 1059.
946.15.141

1285 Fort Vancouver Village, Looking South Towards Mount Hood
pencil. 5 1/2 x 9 (140 x 229)
946.15.169

1286 A Corner of the Stockade at Fort Vancouver
pencil. 4 7/8 x 6 7/8 (124 x 175)
946.15.270

1287 Mount Hood Seen from Near Fort Vancouver
pencil. 5 3/8 x 9 (136 x 229)
Sketch on recto of cat. no. 1288. View with buildings in foreground. 946.15.167

1288 Mount Hood Seen from Near Fort Vancouver
pencil. 5 3/8 x 9 (136 x 229)
Sketch on verso of cat. no. 1287.
946.15.168

1289 Mount Hood Seen from Near Fort Vancouver
pencil. 5 3/8 x 9 (136 x 229)
Sketch on verso of cat. no. 1320. View with trees in foreground. 946.15.200

1290 Mount Hood Seen from Near Fort Vancouver
pencil. 5 1/2 x 9 1/2 (140 x 241)
946.15.185

1291 Studies of Cattle
pencil. 4 5/8 x 7 1/8 (118 x 181)
Watermark: *J. What*[man], *Turkey Mill, 18 . . .*
Possibly the herds kept at Fort Vancouver.
946.15.256

1292 Indian Groups Around Campfire
pencil on blue paper. 9 3/4 x 7 7/8 (248 x 200)
Campfire group possibly at Fort Vancouver. Sketch on verso of an Indian head, and a house similar to cat. no. 1123.
946.15.259

1293 Tree-stump Well Northeast of Fort Vancouver
w.c. and pencil. 7 1/8 x 5 1/8 (181 x 130)
Version of same well in Stark colln., Harper, fig. 115.
946.15.285

1294 Tree-stump Well Northeast of Fort Vancouver, and Child's Head
w.c. and pencil. 5 1/2 x 2 7/8 (140 x 173)
Sketch on verso of cat. no. 1325.
946.15.284

1295 Chinook Fishing Lodge of Woven Rush Mats
pencil. 4 5/8 x 6 5/8 (118 x 168)
Similar lodges are shown in the Kane w.c. in Stark coll., Harper, fig. 160. 946.15.223

1296 Bundle of Rushes Cut for Making Mats
w.c. and pencil. 7 1/2 x 10 1/4 (190 x 260)
Sketch on verso of cat. no. 1331.
946.15.321

1297 Klickitat Lodge
w.c. over pencil. 4 7/8 x 6 15/16 (124 x 176)
Inscribed u.l. 44 (KLL); verso, title.
946.15.221

1298 Gambling Scene in a Lodge
pencil. 5 x 7 (127 x 178)
Sketch on recto of cat. no. 1109.
946.15.246

1299 Group of Indians in a Circle
pencil. 6 1/2 x 8 1/2 (165 x 216)
Watermark: a finial.
Sketch on recto of cat. no. 1300. One of the figures is woman wearing cedar bark string skirt; possibly sketched at Fort Vancouver.
946.15.306

1300 Sketches of Heads
pencil. 6 1/2 x 8 1/2 (165 x 216)
Sketch on verso of cat. no. 1299.
946.15.307

1301 Landscape with Lake
pencil. 4 7/8 x 6 1/2 (124 x 165)
Sketch on recto of cat. no. 1141. Site unidentified, possibly Columbia River valley. 946.15.145

1302 Landscape with Lake and Fir Trees
pencil. 5 x 7 (127 x 178)
Sketch on recto of cat. no. 1236.
946.15.295

1303 Mills in Oregon City
pencil. 5 1/2 x 9 (140 x 232)
View from opposite shore showing upper
end of city with mills and Methodist
church.   946.15.163

**1304 Oregon City, Two Views from the
Shore**
pencil. 5 3/8 x 8 7/8 (136 x 225)
Sketch on verso of cat. no. 1249.
946.15.326

**1305 Oregon City Seen from the Opposite
Shore Beside Waterfall**
pencil. 5 1/2 x 9 (140 x 232)   946.15.164

**1306 Sketches of Buildings, Mount Hood
in Distance**
pencil. 5 1/2 x 8 7/8 (140 x 225)
Possibly Oregon City or Fort Vancouver
area.   946.15.171

**1307 Waterfall Near Oregon City, with
Fallen Tree Trunks**
pencil. 5 3/8 x 9 (136 x 232)   946.15.175

1308 Waterfall Near Oregon City
w.c. and pencil. 5 3/8 x 8 1/2 (136 x 216)
Inscribed u.l. 23
946.15.269

1309 Landscape with a Waterfall
pencil. 5 1/4 x 8 5/8 (133 x 219)
Sketch on verso of cat. no. 1063. Possibly
the falls near Oregon City.   946.15.65

1310 St. Paul's Mission, Willamette Valley
w.c. and pencil. 5 1/2 x 9 3/8 (140 x 238)
"I asencded the Walhamette River, in
company with Father Acolti, a Jesuit
missionary, for about 30 miles. We then
disembarked and proceeded on horseback
about eight miles to the Roman Catholic
mission, where there is a large
establishment of religieuses for the
purposes of education, as well as a good
brick church, situated in a beautiful prairie,
surrounded with woods. It has also a
nunnery occupied by six Sisters of Charity,
who employ themselves in teaching the
children, both white and red, amounting to
forty-two pupils" (*Wanderings*, pp. 133-4).
946.15.264

1310

1311 View of the Willamette Valley and Champoeg Village
w.c. and pencil. 5 1/4 x 8 7/8 (133 x 225)
Inscribed u.l. *62* (KLL)
Preparatory sketch for Kane's oil
'Willamette River from the Mountain,'
ROM 912.1.81.
946.15.193

1312 Mount St. Helens seen from the Lewis River
w.c. and pencil. 4 7/8 x 7 1/8 (124 x 181)
Inscribed u.l. *63* (KLL)
Sketch on recto of cat. no. 1095.
Preparatory sketch for Kane's oil, ROM 912.1.78.
946.15.329

1313 Mount St. Helens seen from the Cowlitz Farm
w.c. and pencil. 5 5/16 x 8 7/8 (135 x 225)
Inscribed u.l. *69* (KLL)   946.15.184

1314 The Fourth Plain Near Fort Vancouver with Three Horses and Riders Resting
pencil and w.c. 3 3/8 x 4 7/8 (86 x 124)
Inscribed u.l. *51* (KLL)   946.15.165

1315 The Fourth Plain Near Fort Vancouver with Horses and Riders Resting
pencil. 5 x 6 3/4 (127 x 172)
A second version of cat. no. 1314.
946.15.166

1316 Mouth of the Lewis River
pencil. 6 7/8 x 9 7/8 (175 x 251)
Sketch for foreground of cat. no. 1312, without the mountain.   946.15.298

1317 Sketch of Rocks
pencil. 5 3/8 x 9 (136 x 229)
Sketch on verso of cat. no. 1260. Possibly on the Columbia River near Coffin Rock.
946.15.191

1318 Rocky Shoreline and Buildings
w.c. and pencil. 5 1/2 x 8 7/8 (140 x 225)
Possibly Columbia River.   946.15.170

1319 A Cowlitz Canoe and a Paddle
pencil. 3 1/2 x 11 3/4 (89 x 298)
Inscribed l.c. *COWELITZ CANOE*
946.15.201

1320 Two Canoes, Columbia River Region
pencil. 5 3/8 x 9 (136 x 229)
Sketch on verso of cat. no. 1289.
946.15.199

1321 A Mossy Tree, Pacific Coast
w.c. and pencil. 5 1/2 x 9 3/8 (140 x 238)
946.15.279

1322 A Mossy Tree, Pacific Coast
w.c. and pencil. 9 3/8 x 5 1/2 (238 x 140)
946.15.280

1323 A Fallen Tree Covered with Moss, Pacific Coast
w.c. and pencil. 3 3/4 x 7 (95 x 178)
946.15.281

1324 A Mossy Tree, Pacific Coast
w.c. and pencil. 5 1/8 x 7 3/16 (130 x 183)
946.15.282

1325 A Mossy Tree, Pacific Coast
w.c. and pencil. 5 1/2 x 2 7/8 (140 x 173)
Sketch on recto of cat. no. 1294.
946.15.283

1326 Prairie de Bute
pencil. 5 x 7 (127 x 178)
Sketch on recto of cat. no. 1342.
946.15.156

1327 Prairie de Bute
pencil. 5 x 6 1/2 (127 x 165)
946.15.158

1328 Nisqually Indian Lodge
w.c. and pencil. 3 3/4 x 7 (95 x 178)
Inscribed u.l. *71* (KLL)
Sketch on recto of cat. no. 1094.
946.15.322

1329 Lodge of Lach-oh-lett, Head Chief of the Nisqually
w.c. and pencil. 5 x 7 (127 x 178)
Inscribed u.l. *72* (KLL)   946.15.324

1330 Kneeling Woman, Bowl and Fire-making Stick, Haro Strait
pencil. 5 x 7 (127 x 178)
Inscribed l.l. *A fire stick made of sedar;* l.r. *cath. i./on the south side of the Straits.*
Sketch on recto of cat. no. 1343.
946.15.224

1331 Landscape with Bundle of Stakes for Salmon Trap Construction
w.c. over pencil. 7 1/2 x 10 1/4 (190 x 260)
Inscribed *Bundled stakes, 4 feet long.*
Site identified by Harper as Clallam village of Such on south shore of Juan de Fuca.
Sketch on recto of cat. no. 1296.
946.15.320

1332 Mountain Landscape with River
pencil. 5 x 6 3/4 (127 x 171)
Inscribed verso *Olympics ex Sooke (W.A.H.) or Beecher Bay.* [not in Kane's hand].
946.15.242

1333 Northwest Coast Canoes
pencil. 5 x 7 (127 x 178)
Inscribed r. *Ciss-Cox* (possibly a reference
to Kis-cox, chief of Cowlitz, whom Kane
sketched on March 30, 1847; sketch in
Stark colln.).
The canoes are a detail sketch for Kane's
w.c. 'War Party, Juan de Fuca,' Stark colln.,
Harper, fig. 185.
946.15.250

1334 Northwest Coast Canoes
w.c. over pencil. 5 3/8 x 9 7/16 (136 x 240)
Watermark: *Whatman, Turkey Mill, 1844*
946.15.231

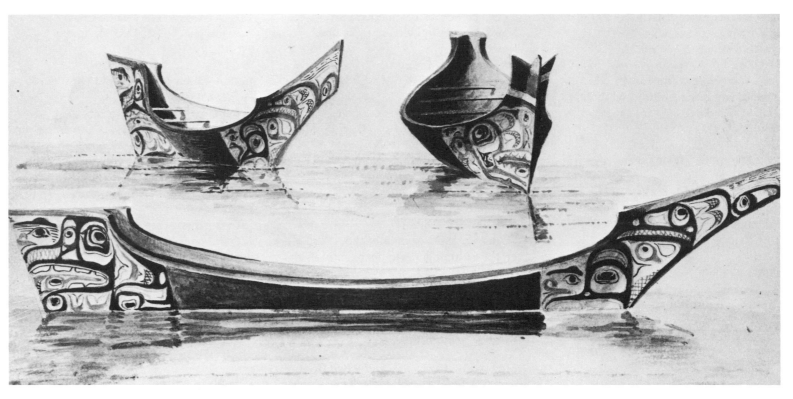

1334

1335 Northwest Coast Canoes
pencil and w.c. 5 3/8 x 8 7/8 (136 x 225)
Sketch on recto of cat. no. 1269.
946.15.232

1336 Fort Victoria and Indian Village
w.c. and pencil. 5 1/2 x 9 1/4 (140 x 235)
Inscribed u.l. *82* (KLL)
Preparatory sketch for Kane's oil 'Return of
a War Party,' ROM 912.1.91.
946.15.212

**1337 Northwest Coast Mask and Plains
War Club**
pencil. 5 5/8 x 9 1/2 (143 x 241)
946.15.128

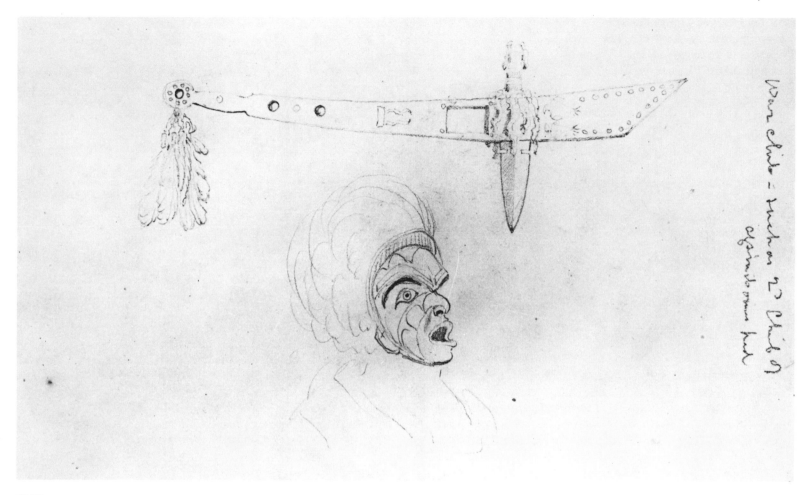

1337

1338 Two Carved House Posts
w.c. and pencil. 4 7/8 x 7 1/2 (124 x 190)
Sketch on recto of cat. no. 1220. Possibly
sketched at Fort Victoria. 946.15.248

1338

Kane

1339 Girl Twisting Yarn in a Clallum Lodge
pencil and w.c. 7 1/8 x 5 1/8 (181 x 130)
Inscribed u.l. *45* (KPL 'A Sangeys girl spinning')
Preparatory sketch for Kane's oil 'Clallum Women Weaving a Blanket,' ROM 912.1.93.
946.15.226

1340 Studies of Figures inside a Lodge
w.c. and pencil. 5 3/8 x 9 3/8 (136 x 238)
Sketches of seven figures in various activities, a cradle, box and woven hat.
946.15.227

1340

Kane

1341 Studies of Five Figures

w.c. over pencil. 5 9/16 x 9 3/8 (141 x 238)
Sketch showing two standing and three reclining Indians; possibly study of lodge interior.   946.15.218

1342 Study of Dog and of West Coast Canoe

pencil. 5 x 7 (127 x 178)
Sketch of canoe being launched, and of a dog.
Inscribed *Sha-tel-san, Samas tillacum.*
Sketch on verso of cat. no. 1326.
946.15.257

1343 Two Dogs and Bed Shelf in Lodge Interior

pencil. 5 x 7 (127 x 178)
Sketch on verso of cat. no. 1330.
946.15.225

1344 Pacific Giant Salamander

w.c. and pencil. 5 1/2 x 9 1/2 (140 x 241)
Inscribed verso *No. 1/Mud puppy?.* (More probably a Pacific giant salamander, since the mud puppy's external red gills are not shown in sketch.)
Sketch on recto of cat. no. 1282.
946.15.265

1345 Tsimshian Ceremonial Blanket

w.c. over pencil. 5 1/2 x 9 1/8 (140 x 232)
Watermark: *J W*[hatman]
Blankets of painted cedar bark and woven wool of mountain goat were made by tribes on the northwest coast from Alaska to as far south as Vancouver. Kane shows this blanket in his oil portait 'A Babbine Chief' (ROM 912.1.87) and in 'Medicine Mask Dance' (ROM 912.1.92).   946.15.228

1345

1346 Three Studies of Northwest Coast Indian Cremation Rites

pencil. 5 3/8 x 8 7/8 (136 x 225)

Inscribed u.l. *N. 11* (KLL)

Kane describes these rites in *Wanderings*, chapter 15. The sketches show a seated woman (left); figures around a smoking pyre (centre); figure with fish, figure touching head of another, seated men with drums and a tall pole with bundle at top (right).   946.15.327

1347 Three Indians Gambling

pencil. 4 7/8 x 7 (124 x 178)

946.15.260

1348 Group of Seven Indians Gambling

pencil. 4 7/8 x 7 (124 x 178)

946.15.261

1349 Five Indians Gambling

pencil. 4 7/8 x 7 (124 x 178)

946.15.262

1347

1349

Kane